Jennifer Foor

I0686937

ISABELLA

A Mitchell-Healy Series

Check out the other books by Jennifer Foor

(Contemporary Romance)

A Mitchell Family Series

Letting Go -Folding Hearts - Raging Love -Risking Fate

Wrapping Up - Wanting More - Saving Us - Blinding Trust

Losing Him - Loving Her

A Mitchell Healy Series

Noah

Isabella

Love's Suicide

The Kin Series

Repair Me - Replace Me - Restore Me

Remember Me – Reject Me

Hustle Me (A Bank Shot Romance)

Hustle Him (A Bank Shot Romance)

Diary of a Male Maid

Twinsequences

Lustly

A Hope and a Chance (Coming Winter 2014)

Beta Readers

Kayla Kennedy, Emma Clifton, Kristy Davidson,
Catherine Roberts, Lara Petterson , Jennifer Harried,
Mechelle Lovell Jackson, Kasey Craig, Teresa Coleman

Web Design and Marketing by: Amy Haigler

Acknowledgements:
This book is for the readers.
I love you!
Thanks to Inkslinger for taking me on as a client.
Danielle, you rock!!
Thank you Ashley Green for the 1000 pictures I
took for this shoot.
Thanks to my kick-ass street team, Foor Players.
FOORWHORES – my super secret society

Thanks to all of my new friends on my FB, Twitter and Goodreads. Thank you for spreading the word and all of the support you give.Thanks to all of my other Independent Author Friends. (you know who you are) Thank you to all the book bloggers out there spreading the word for me and others who write.

This list below are several of the blogs that were involved in promoting the original series.

Rockstars of Romance (Milasy and Lisa), iloveindiebooks, Book Bitches, Maryse Book Blog, Shh Mom's reading, Into the night Reviews, Word, Kindlehooked, , Totally Booked, Word, Reading is my time out, Stick Girl Book Reviews, Wolfels World of Books, Dirty Books and Dirty Boys, Book Broads, Book Studs, Books Books Books, Reality Bites Books, Naughty Mafia, Smutty Book Whores Obsession, Schmexy Girl Book Blog, Just Booked Blog, Book Crazy, BookFri-ends,

Submit and Devour, Three Girls and a Book Obsession, The Whispering Pages Book Blog, All Is Read With Lexipat, Lit Slave, Six Chicks and Their Love For Books, Zee Books Blog, Evette Ashby Sexy Girl Reads, Risque Romance Reads, Nicely Phrased, Books Coffee and Wine, What to read after fifty shades – Summer Daniels

And all of the other bloggers out there working your butts off for us authors.

Special Thanks to: The Mullet Ninjas – Lisa & Milasy

the Mitchell Family
Series
Reference Guide

Please use this guide to follow along with the characters from the original Mitchell Family Series

Each character is listed with a detailed background from the whole 10 book series

Notable Characters and Villains have also been listed as well as a list of Parents and Children

Main Characters

Colt Mitchell – The oldest Mitchell cousin who lives in Kentucky, and is the only son to the eldest of the original Mitchell Brothers. His father owned and operated the largest cattle ranching facility in the state. Introduced in book one when he came to North Carolina to help his uncle (father's brother) run his farm while his cousin Tyler was in a coma, after a near fatal car crash.

He fell in love with his cousin's long-term girlfriend and that became the whole plot of the first book. He battled with right and wrong, finally giving into temptation and straining his relationship with his cousin, Tyler.

Colt and Savanna were eventually married in book three. After Savanna miscarried their first child, Colt discovered he had a son (Noah). They had two daughters after that (Christian and Addison). Colt is an old-fashioned and serious man, who thrives on his love for family and religion to get him through any part of life's journey.

Even in the latter books he struggled with jealousy over his wife's friendship with Tyler. The two friends never crossed any lines, but Colt still worried. It wasn't until book seven where Colt finally understood that Savanna and Ty's love for one another was part of their bond from being first childhood friends and then cousins by marriage, instead of something else.

Colt tells the story in books One, three, four and a half, and seven.

Letting Go

Raging Love

Wrapping Up

Blinding Trust

Relationship to characters

Miranda & Conner Healy are his cousins. (Their mothers are sisters.)

Tyler Mitchell – cousin (Their fathers are brothers.)

Savanna (Van) Mitchell – Introduced in book one as the love interest to both Tyler and Colt, Savanna struggles with right and wrong and which man she's destined to love. After falling head over heels for her boyfriend's cousin in book one, she leaves North Carolina behind to start a future with Colt.

In the second book her friendship with her ex is tested, especially when he falls for someone close to her.

She's kidnapped by Colt's cousin Miranda's lunatic ex-boyfriend in book three and held for ransom-tied up in a basement. At the time she's pregnant and during an escape attempt she miscarries and kills her capturer, who happens to be her niece's (Isabella) biological father (Tucker Chase).

Jennifer Foor

In Book eight she discovers that she has breast cancer, while struggling with the relationship with her step-son Noah.

Throughout every book Savanna grows as a strong woman. She's a major key to the family and the bond that they all share together. Not only does she continue to be close to her ex Tyler, but she's also a best friend to his wife, Miranda and even her sister-in-law Amy.

Savanna tells the story in books One, Three, Four and a half, and Seven.

Letting Go
Raging Love
Wrapping Up
Blinding Trust
Savanna has no blood relation to any of the original characters. She is the wife of Colt Mitchell.

Tyler Mitchell – As a main character in book one, Tyler Mitchell was known as the cheating boyfriend that everyone loved to hate. His family owns and operates a farm in North Carolina. After waking from his coma, he was left without a girlfriend, job or future. It wasn't until book two where he found love, starting with the birth of a young child (Isabella), and later turning into a relationship with Miranda Healy. Miranda, who is Colt's cousin on his mother's side, was no relation to Ty. It still didn't keep their family from forbidding them to be together. When Miranda's ex threatened her and the baby, she goes to stay with Ty to be safe. Their love was undeniable and to stay together they eloped. By the end of book two the family accepts them. New and old friendships are rekindled and the family feels complete in every aspect. This character tells the story in books two, four, four and a half, and nine.

> **Folding Hearts**
> **Risking Fate**
> **Wrapping Up**
> **Loving Her**

Relationship to characters
Colt Mitchell – Cousin (fathers are brothers)
He is not related to his wife, Miranda by

blood. They only share a similar cousin, Colt, by both being related to him on different sides of his family. Growing up he and his wife considered each other cousins because the Healy's lived on the ranch with Colt. This was also a huge reason for their relationship being forbidden.

Miranda Healy (Mitchell) – This character is introduced at the very end of book one. Along side of Tyler, she tells the story in book two. It starts out explaining her failing relationship with her then boyfriend Tucker Chase. He's a criminal that wants nothing to do with her or their child. After threats are made, she flees, falling right into the arms of her new best friend, Ty. By book four the couple is happy. Tucker Chase has died and they thought that their fears have ended. She's found the perfect man that not only loves her, but also adores her daughter as if she were his own flesh and blood. After giving her his name they vow to take the secret to the grave. New threats come into play and to protect their child, they do something unthinkable. Miranda thinks that Ty has cheated on her and she leaves town, very pregnant. An accident on the road sends her into labor and she almost dies, along with her unborn twin boys. By book eight the couple has gotten away from the drama and trust issues. Instead it's their daughter that has all of the problems. It starts out with her being sick and then finally the discovery of Ty not being her biological father. At the end of the day it's the family that helps make everything right with the world. Miranda tells the story in books two, four, four and a half, and nine.

Folding Hearts
Risking Fate
Wrapping Up

Jennifer Foor

Loving Her

Relationship to characters
Colt Mitchell – Cousin (Mothers sisters)
Conner Healy - Brother

Conner Healy – The brother of Miranda and first cousin to Colt, this character was once secondary, only being mentioned in book one at the end of the book. He's a bigger character in the beginning of book two when he interferes with his sister's (Miranda) love life.

He's mentioned in book three because he works alongside of Colt on the ranch.

After being a huge part of book four and four and a half, where he risks his own happiness for his family, Conner gets the next two books, five and six. It follows the story of a drug abusing cowboy with no structure in his life, as he recovers and finds love with a married woman. Conner would do just about anything for his family, but even more for Amy. It takes them a while to admit it, but when they finally do there's no denying it. They end up having four children together, three girls and one boy.

Conner tells the story for books five and six.
Wanting More
Saving Us

Relationship to characters
Miranda (Healy) Mitchell – Sister
Colt Mitchell – Cousin (Mothers side)

Amy Healy– While introduced in the second book as Miranda's boss at the hair salon, she's later a main character playing the role of Miranda's best friend. Amy has lots of secrets, including a husband who drinks too much and takes out his anger on her body. Amy's story begins in the background of the other books, but is front and center in the fifth and sixth edition. Her struggles to get away from her husband (Rick) and finally be with Conner cause them to have two full books back to back. In their second edition Amy is pregnant and the family will do anything in their power to keep her safe, including sending them to Kentucky to stay. It didn't stop her ex from hunting her down and holding her at gunpoint. He meets his demise on the Mitchell ranch when Heather (his mistress and Ty's ex) shoots him to save Amy.

Amy is best friends with Savanna and Miranda.

When the series ends she and Conner are married with four children, Cassie, Cammie, Callie, and Joshua.

She tells the story in two books.

Wanting More

Saving Us

Relationship to characters

None

Villains in the series

Heather – Was introduced in the first book as one of the college girls that Ty was sleeping around with. In book two she's still attempting to win the affections of a newly single Tyler. Obviously he goes on to wed Miranda and they try to forget all about her. She runs into Ty a while after that in book four. He's married and in awe of his wife and adopted daughter. To protect them from Isabella's biological father's family they turn to Heather's brother for a forged paternity test. Heather forces Ty's hand, and she uses extreme measures to break them up, causing Miranda to leave town, distraught and nine months pregnant with his twins. She gets into an accident and not only almost dies herself, but also the twins.

This character continues to cause problems for the Mitchell Family throughout the series, until she is punished and taught a lesson by Conner Healy, Miranda Mitchell's brother, in book six. She ends up becoming the hero in that book when she saves Amy's life by shooting and killing Rick. In book seven she runs into Savanna and through a common medical diagnosis they share a heartfelt moment.

After that Heather gets her own book (Eight) and readers finally find out why she did all of those terrible things to torture the family. In her book we learn that while she was trying to change her life around she fell in love with Rick's (Amy's Ex) son, Jesse. Together they had a son named Jacob. In book eight they finally stop fighting about the past and move forward with a future together, as a family. Heather gets her own book to tell her side of the story.

Losing Him

Tucker Chase – This guy was Miranda's boyfriend in book 2. He was a thug, who didn't ever want to be a father to Miranda's baby (Isabella). It was a good thing that Ty stepped in and became the father that she deserved. In book three Savanna is kidnapped and held for ransom. She loses her baby in a struggle and ends up killing Tucker while trying to get free.

Tucker's mother- This woman shows her face in book three and four, after losing her son in the kidnapping episode with Savanna. She's sets out to gain visitation of her granddaughter, causing Miranda and Ty to go to extreme measures to keep their daughter, including forging a paternity test and almost getting a divorce.

Rick – Was once married to Amy. His verbal and physical abuse was derived from his addiction to alcohol. We later learned that his past secrets included murder and betrayal. Rick dies in book six of the series, after holding Amy and Heather at gunpoint. He is survived by two children, one being Heather's love interest Jesse.

Zeke – The brother of Noah's (Colt's oldest son) biological mother, Krista, is a rock star that comes back to town to get to know his nephew. He's always known that Savanna was his step-mother, but this book destroys his love for the only woman who has raised him. While struggling with breast cancer, Savanna is faced with the fear of losing Noah. We later find out that Zeke only wanted to use Noah for publicity and never cared about the kid at all. Once his secret was exposed, he left town and Noah never tried to contact him again.

Notable Characters

Lucy - This character is known as the housekeeper at the Ranch mansion, and best friend of Colt's mother. She is featured in almost all of the books at least once.

Karen – Miranda and Conner's mother, a widow who eventually marries the sheriff, John. Known as mom-mom to her grandchildren.

John – The town sheriff in Kentucky, who marries Karen. Known as Pop-pop John to the grandkids.

Krista – Noah's biological mother

Jesse - Rick's estranged son. The two characters are never in contact with each other. Jesse never even knew Rick was around.

Shelby – Rick's daughter.

Brina – The once best friend of Savanna in the earlier books. She dated Conner for a time when he moved into North Carolina, but enabled his addiction.

Toby – Heather's brother who falsified the paternity test for Ty and Miranda. He went to jail later on for similar charges.

Savanna's parents. – Known as Mr. and Mrs. Tate or mom-mom and pop-pop to the three children.

Colt's mother – Grandma to the three children.

Ty's parents – Mimi and Poppy to their three

children. His dad is referred to as Uncle Mitch.

Harvey – The ranch hand at the North Carolina Mitchell Farm and Ranch. He was once mentioned to have a connection to Lucy.

Parents/Children

COLT AND SAVANNA (Mitchell)

1. Noah (Savanna is his step-mother)
2. Christian
3. Addison

TYLER AND MIRANDA (Mitchell)

1. Isabella, (Izzy or Bella or Bells) Tyler is listed as her birth father on certificate, but he is really her step-father
2. Jacob (Jake)
3. Jaxson (Jax)

CONNER AND AMY (Healy)

1. Cassie
2. Callie
3. Cammie
4. Joshua

The kids are all related to each other as first cousins.

Isabella Mitchell

Chapter 1
Isabella

I rushed out of the room, trying to get away from his constant badgering. "You don't know what it's like, Noah." Arguing with my cousin was getting me nowhere fast. He couldn't fathom that my heart was broken, and that sometimes I felt like moving to Kentucky had been a huge mistake, because it had forced me to walk away from Tate. There was a time when he was my everything, my reason for existing, and my future husband. Sure, I missed my immediate family, but it didn't compare to the constant ache that I experienced from losing my ex. Yes, he'd cheated on me, several times in fact, but I still loved him. That's why it hurt so much to hear my cousin constantly degrading him. Didn't we all make mistakes? Shouldn't we be able to change without judgment? He of all people had no room to talk.

Noah got up in my face, shouting like he always did. "The hell I don't. You sit there sulkin' about that prick every damn night. I know you're still talkin' to him, Bells. What I don't get is why you can't see that he's a piece of shit. He treated you like dirt, and you refuse to admit it." He turned away, backing up and shaking his head in disappointment.

I took two steps toward him, so that I could jab him in the chest with my finger as I replied. "Stop actin' like you know what's best for me. I'm a grown damn woman. If I tell you that I'm fine, then leave it be. God, you can be so annoyin'. You ain't my daddy, and you sure as shit ain't my keeper."

He lifted his hands to sit on my shoulders, looked down and peered into my eyes. I could already see the worry in his stare. Noah wasn't trying to make me hate him. His determination was built on months of doing everything in his power to make me see that Tate was no good for me. "Bells, look at me. Have I ever given you bad advice? Have I ever steered you in the wrong direction?"

"No." I turned away so that he couldn't see the agony on my face. He was right and I was wrong. What else was new?

"Look, cuz, I love you. Shalan and I like you livin' here in Kentucky at the ranch, but I'll be damned if I sit around watchin' you make this kind of mistake again. The last time this shit happened I was rescuin' you in some flea-bag motel. Please, for the sake of your livelihood, sever ties with that fool for good. I promise you that there's someone out there that's better for you. There's someone that will appreciate you."

I darted for my room in an attempt to end the conversation, huffing and puffing with no means to otherwise defend myself. He didn't know what I was going through. How could he, when all Noah had ever known was to control his own relationships? He'd never been on my side of the situation, or experienced heartache. Hell, he was engaged to a famous country singer that practically worshipped the ground he walked on. Not all of us could be that lucky.

After it slammed in his face, Noah beat on my door, trying to get me to talk as if we were still teenagers arguing over some immature object. I buried my head in my pillow and put my ear buds in, so that I couldn't hear him any longer. The vibration against my leg let me know that I had a new text message. My heartbeat became rapid as I pulled out my phone eagerly hoping it was Tate.

I opened the message to see that it was from my dad. My trip home was only a day away, and for the first time in a long time, I wanted to be there.

One more day until you get to smell your mother's farts. I bet you can't wait. Love: Best Dad

on Earth

I laugh at his humor. My dad was a silly man. While everyone in my life called me Isabella, Bella, or Bells, he'd called me Izzy. He always had and he always would. It was just something that made our bond so special. **I can't wait, Dad. Love you too. – Iz**

Don't forget to pack underwear and deodorant, as we've stopped using both here on account of saving the environment. – Dad

I refuse to come home if you're free-balling. That's where I draw the line, Dad. - Iz

Honey, I've been free-balling since before you were born. It's your mom that's made the change. She loves letting it all air out. – Dad

My father's sick sense of humor actually made me feel better. Believe it or not, after being raised by the constant jokester, it was comforting hearing his banter. My dad had this thing about making me smile. Even in my darkest of times, he would find ways to make it happen. I loved him for it, too. Throughout my life, he'd been my constant rock.

I thought back to the day I discovered that he wasn't my biological father. I'd never felt such heartache as I had in that moment. He'd been my everything, since the day I was born. In fact, he'd helped deliver me in the back of my aunt Van's car. Of course, I was too young to remember that day, but I've been told that from the moment I came out of the womb I'd been wrapped around my daddy's finger. I didn't care what a blood test showed, even though he'd adopted me, he was my one and only father, and I was a Mitchell in every way that counted.

I may have just thrown up in my mouth. – Iz

Better eat light before you come then. – Dad

Having a comedian for a dad wasn't the only perk to being the daughter of Tyler Mitchell. He was my biggest fan, aside from my mother, and because of the way they raised my brothers and me, we'd learned the real meaning of family and love. They'd instilled us with morals, and I knew that one day I'd pass them on to my own children, if I ever had any.

After arguing with my cousin, and very best friend, it was nice to be able to smile at something. For the past couple of weeks I'd been talking to my ex, Tate, again. I'd tried to keep it a secret, but Noah had seen his name appear on my phone one night and hadn't let it go since. He was determined to make sure I had no contact with him. Little did he know that I had my own plans for my visit home, which included a secret rendezvous with the man that I couldn't fall out of love with.

I wasn't a fool. I knew about all of his faults. I also knew that he'd been going through hell since I'd moved to Kentucky. After months of not seeing me, he'd been begging for me to just spend some time with him. As much as I wanted to end up in his arms afterwards, I was determined to be strong. My new life was in Kentucky, and I was going to have to keep reminding myself of that.

My next message came through right as I was getting up to finish packing. I thought it was my dad again, so I ignored it and kept placing things in my suitcase. Once I had it zippered up, and double-checked my list to make sure I hadn't forgotten anything, I peeked at my phone.

You thinking about me, sexy? – Tate

A rush of heat overwhelmed me. He'd been my first real love, and every time I heard from him I would get enthusiastic. **Always – Bella**

I'm craving your pussy. – Tate

Admittedly, reading that made me even hotter. Tate had been my high school boyfriend. We'd experienced so much together, good and bad. My time away had only made my love for him stronger, and it scared the shit out of me, since I'd moved to get as far from him as possible.

Tate said he missed me. He'd been messaging more this week than the whole time I'd been gone. I had to believe that maybe moving away from him had taught him a lesson. I wanted him to know that I wasn't going to stick around and let him walk all over me. He could either change his ways, or lose me forever. I wouldn't allow him to cheat on me and get away with it anymore.

I'll see you tomorrow night. We can meet once my parents go to bed. I'll message you as soon as I'm able to sneak away.– Bella

So we're sneaking around like high school? – Tate

For now. You know why, Tate. They don't trust you. – Bella
I'm going to rectify that, baby doll. I promise. – Tate

I hope so. I love you so much. I can't wait to see you. – Bella
Love you too. See you tomorrow. – Tate

Sneaking around did feel a lot like high school, but it was necessary. If my dad or brothers found out that I was slipping away to see Tate, they would string him up and feed him to the pigs.

A knock on my bedroom door startled me. I put my hand to my heart, even knowing who it was the whole time. "What do you want, Noah?"

I glanced in my mirror as I awaited his reply.

My blonde hair was up in a messy ponytail, and my green eyes had red around the white parts. I was tired, and lonely, and it was affecting my appearance.

I walked over and opened the door seeing him standing there with his bottom lip out, as if he was pouting. "You still mad at me?"

I looked at the door, sighed, and then peered back at him. "Maybe. It's my life, you know?"

"Yeah, but you're a part of mine. Bells, I just want what's best for you. Can't you see that?" I could, except admitting it was only going to make him think he had an advantage over me. I couldn't let that happen, especially when I was lying to the whole family about Tate. If Noah knew the truth he'd tell. When we were kids we would have covered for each other. Times had changed. Sure, we still had each other's backs, but Noah hated Tate just the same as the devil himself. Knowledge of me sneaking to see him wouldn't sit well in his eyes. He'd tell on me to prevent it, causing an uproar with my parents on purpose. I couldn't ever let that happen, at least until I knew for sure that he'd changed his ways. "I get why you're tryin' to protect me. I do. Sometimes it feels like I'm not allowed to make my own choices."

"Bells, promise me one thing."

"What?"

"Promise me that you won't see him while you're in North Carolina. I know you've been talking to him again, but don't see him. You may have gotten over everything that guy's done to you, but I haven't. It wasn't so long ago when I was drivin' to save your ass, after that whole fiasco with that other chick. That girl beat the shit out of you, and he let her. I don't care about nothin' else. He's a bastard, and I don't want him near you."

I bit down on my lip and tried to keep a straight face, avoiding the whole fact that he'd brought up that awful experience again. In Tate's defense, he thought I was an intruder. I'd snuck into the house knowing that it was illegal. Why couldn't Noah see that?

Still, I had to lie to my cousin, and he was good at reading me. I kept my face the same, remaining as calm as possible. "Fine. I won't see him, Noah. Are you happy?"

He lifted my chin up and forced me to look into his eyes. I stared at him, focusing on the fact that this man in front of me knew me better than I knew myself. If I could get past him, I was in the clear from anyone else.

"Yeah. For now at least."

I lightly punched him in the abdomen. "Now get out of my face. You smell like cow shit." I shrugged him off as he came at me, trying to get me to smell his nasty pits. "I'm not kiddin'. I hate it when Shalan's out of town, because you never shower."

"That's a lie. I shower once a day. When she's home I don't work so late, so you just notice it more. It ain't like you haven't smelled manure ever in your life. For Christ sakes, we both grew up around it."

"That doesn't mean *I* have to like it, Noah."

He shook his head, while laughing at my comment. I knew he didn't like it, but still had to deal with it. Part of running a ranch was dealing with animal fecal matter. That's why I steered clear of going anywhere near it. Thankfully, my great aunt had gotten me a job in an office, because there was no way that shoveling up shit was going to work for me. I had a degree in business, and used it to my advantage.

"You may not like it, but you've dealt with your fair share of shit, whether it's the kind that stinks or not." He left me to be alone and sit on his comment. I hated when he got the last word in edgewise. It was a ploy to somehow win every bickering battle between us. Noah was more like my brother, than my cousin. We had the same blood flowing through our veins, since his dad and my mom were first cousins. It just so happened that my dad was also his cousin on the other side of his family. Though my parents had no relation to each other, because that would be totally weird, they'd grown up spending holidays, and summers hanging out. It was bizarre, and extremely hard to explain to people. Either way you looked at it, I was Noah's cousin, through both blood and adoption.

Noah was right about one thing, his last words becoming an echo as they sunk in. I was tired of dealing with the bullshit. My trip home was going to tell me once and for all if Tate could be trusted. When I could make that determination I knew I'd be able to make the right decision for what might come of my future.

My only problem was sneaking around to be able to make it happen. In less than twenty-four hours I'd be in his arms, and that was enough for me to be excited about.

Isabella Mitchell

Chapter 2
Isabella

After being on the long highways for hours, I was ecstatic to pull down the dirt road to my family's farm. Ahead of me was my grandparent's house. I hadn't seen them in months, and looked forward to being able to give them both huge hugs. My grandfather was battling with his heart, and the idea of being so far away always scared me.

Just as I went to pull in next to my father's pickup truck, a dirt bike came racing in, stealing the spot before I could get there. Jax, one of my younger twin brothers, took off his helmet and flipped me the finger.

I smiled to myself. "So great to be home."

This was only the beginning. Between my dad,

my brothers, and my uncle Conner, I was bound to be amused for my entire stay.

He approached the car, covered in muck from head to toe. I hesitated stepping out, in fear of getting filthy. Of course, the first thing he did was drag me out and pull me into his welcoming arms. "What's up, sis? I missed you so much," he said in a sarcastic tone.

I shoved him away, looking down at my now dirty attire. "Seriously, Jax. Was that necessary?"

He slapped me on the backside when I tried to saunter past him. "You bet your ass it was."

"Where's your girlfriend?" I inquired, making all attempts to get him to go away, quickly.

"I don't have a woman anymore. There's way too much pussy out there for Jake to have all of the fun," he snickered. I looked my brother up and down. Even through the filth I could see that his once scrawny body had changed. His shoulders were now broad from years of playing football and working out. By the age of thirteen they both towered over me and my mom, and somehow even though I was years older, they made me feel safe.

Their new idea of womanizing wasn't something I wanted to stick around and hear about though.

"You've got to be kidding me. What is with you two?" My brothers were in college, still learning how to be human, obviously. I tried to avoid them like the plague, failing at every attempt, usually.

"Nope. Last night we went out and took these sisters home. You should have been there."

I put up one hand to motion for him to cease, while tossing him my suitcase. "No, thank you. I'll pass on those details."

He followed behind me, walking straight into the house covered in muddy clothes and boots. My mother smiled when she saw my face, only to look disgusted when she peered behind me. "What the hell, Jax? How many times do I have to tell you to change in the barn before bringin' that mess in here? I just scrubbed the floors."

Jax dropped my bag and went back outside, while my mother came toward me. She lifted her arms and stretched them around my back. "Hi, honey. How was the drive?"

"Long and boring." Kind of like every day had been since being away from home.

"Come in and sit down. Daddy will be out in a minute. We went into town to pick up groceries and ate at this new place. He's been havin' problems ever since," she snorted.

"Well, as much as he jokes about poop, he probably brought it on himself."

"Exactly." She grabbed my bag and walked toward the bedroom hallway. "I'll put this in your room. Everyone is comin' for dinner tonight. We're goin' to eat in the barn so there's room. Your dad installed a new floor last month. Wait until you see it. I can hardly recognize the place, except for the pool table. I tried to get him to toss it, but you know how much he likes to go out there and shoot balls around."

I giggled to myself as she disappeared into the hallway. It was horrible that I was so used to pranks that the mere mention of balls caused me to lose it.

I heard the powder room door opening and saw my dad coming out. A huge grin could be seen when he spotted me across the room. Even under a face full of hair, I could see it. "Hi, Daddy." I only called him that during endearing moments like this one, or when I wanted something.

He walked over and hugged me tight, pulling away to look at my face. "Yeah, you still look the same."

I laughed and held him tight. "I missed you."

"I missed you more. Mom's been cooking all day to welcome you home." He leaned near my ear. "If it tastes like shit just pretend it's amazing. She got this new cookbook and everything tastes the same."

My mom came up behind him and put her hands on her hips. "Seriously, Ty? You told me you liked dinner the other night."

"I did," he cackled. "It was good. I just asked if you didn't make it ever again."

My mom pushed him out of the way and wrapped her arms around me again. "It's good to have you home. Ignore your father. When he gets the shits there's no tellin' what he'll complain about."

"Nothin' changes, does it?"

My dad grabbed my mom and started rubbing his whiskers over her face. She screamed and pulled away. "Seriously, your father has decided that he wants a beard like those men on television. You know the ones that hunt? Wait until you see your uncle's face. They are competing on who can grow it the fastest. I wake up every morning havin' to look at that."

"She thinks I'm sexy," my dad corrected.

My mom faced me and gave me a look. I smiled knowing that she hated the beard, not that she could do anything about it. Once he and my uncle had a bet going, it wouldn't end until someone was declared the winner. This could go on for years.

My poor mother.

"You look like a mammoth already, Dad. Can't you trim it up a little?"

He rubbed the hair and smoothed it under his chin. "This is how it's supposed to look."

"It's creepy. You look like a pedophile," I joked.

Dad took a magazine off the kitchen table and mumbled something as he headed back into the bathroom. "That's it! You hurt my feelings," he stammered before shutting the door behind him.

"Wow." I turned to face my mom. "I've been here for five minutes and am already exhausted. How do you do it?"

She started working in the kitchen again. "When you've been married as long as we have you kind of learn to ignore it. Your dad means well. He is how he is, and we love him for it."

She was right about that. "True." I played with a crumb on the counter. "So, what's up with Jax and Jake? No girlfriends?"

My mom rolled her eyes. "Let's just say that I'm glad I have a daughter, because the two of them may never settle down. I tell ya, just as soon as we start to like a girl, they're bringin' home someone else. I've given up on it. I just call every one of them honey, so I can't hurt their feelin's when I mix up names."

We both snickered over it. I would have been devastated if someone I was seeing took me to meet their parents and they called me their ex's name.

"It feels good to be back, Mom. I miss bein' home. All jokes aside, it's wonderful to sit here in the kitchen and talk to you face to face."

She wiped her hands and leaned over the counter. "Is there somethin' you want to talk to me about?" I smiled thinking about my mother's southern drawl from growing up in Kentucky, which never seemed to fade away. Mine was the same; according to everyone I talked to, but never as strong as my mom.

"No. My life is as borin' as it can get."

"No new man to tell me about?"

"Mom," I gave her an annoyed sort of grin. "Seriously, you know the answer to that."

"Do you hear from Tate?"

I placed my hands flat on the surface and faked a smile. "So where's Jake?"

Her eyebrow cocked right up. "Bella? Don't tell me you're talkin' to him again. Your father will be cleanin' his guns if he finds out."

"Finds out what?" I heard him coming up behind me.

"Nothin'." I looked from one parent to the other. "I'm not talking to Tate. I swear." My lies were getting easier, but the horrible feeling in the pit of my stomach was becoming worse.

"You better not. That guy is a piece of work." My dad offered me a threatening gaze.

I peacefully folded my hands together.

"I didn't come here to be lectured like a child. I'm single, so you both can drop the subject now. Are you happy?"

"We just want to see you with someone that respects you. That's all. It has nothing to do with you, sweetheart," he said in a reassuring way.

"I get it."

"No rush, though. It's okay if you don't marry until you're at least thirty seven." He rubbed my head as if I was a kid at the ball field, who'd just struck out and needed to be cheered up.

I shoved him away, annoyed by his teasing already. "Go away or I'm goin' to stay with Mimi and Poppy."

My dad put his hands up, surrendering to my promise. I'd won the battle for now, making the conversation about me and Tate get dropped. Still, knowing how adamant they were about the whole situation made me worry about how I was going to sneak to see him. I felt like a teen again, but knew it was the only way. For some reason my parents found it necessary to worry about me more than usual. I wondered why they hated him so much, especially considering that they only knew half of what had happened when I was assaulted over a year ago. Then I started wondering if Noah's mother, my aunt Van, had spilled the beans to my mom or dad. They spoke all of the time, and didn't keep secrets. For all I knew it could have been my uncle Colt, Noah's dad. At any rate, I was almost positive that they knew more than I wanted them to.

Dinner with my family was wonderful, and with my poppy around my dad backed off on the relationship talks, and the comedy show. He and my uncle Conner talked shop, while my brothers and my cousin Josh played pool. I sat playing cards with my mom, my grandparents, and my aunt Amy. As much as I wanted to see my three female cousins, Callie, Cassie, and Cammie, I appreciated having all of the attention for once. Those three were drama queens, and at the age where everything out of their mouths was ridiculously annoying, even more than my brothers.

Once everyone started to clear out, I pretended to be exhausted so that I could retreat to

Jennifer Foor

my bedroom. The sooner I got everyone to go to sleep, the faster I could sneak out and meet Tate. Realizing that they couldn't exactly punish me if I got caught, I put on my planned outfit quietly, just waiting for all of the lights in the house to turn off. I was twenty-four years old, and worried about getting in trouble. What was wrong with me?

Two long hours later I was climbing out of my window and running down the lane, dialing his number while getting further away from the house. Tate picked up after four rings.

"I was wondering when you were going to call. I've been waiting for hours."

"Sorry. Just come get me. I had to wait until they were all asleep."

"I'll be there in ten minutes. Start walking. I'll see you and pull over."

Did he know how dark it was in these parts? "I am not walkin', Tate. A trucker could hit me or kill me. You can come and get me. I'll wait at the end of the lane for you. Hurry up!"

I hung up the phone and looked back at the farm. My family would be so disappointed in me, especially Noah, if he ever was to find out. This was something that I was going to have to deal with if I wanted to be with Tate. My heart was telling me one way to go, while my mind was fighting with that same decision. I was so confused, and had nobody to talk to about it, because there wasn't one person on the planet that understood how much I was in love with

43

him.

I looked down at my phone to check the time. He'd already been twelve minutes. Then I told myself that if he didn't show up in the next five I was going back to my house and telling him to go to hell.

He pulled up three minutes later.

Chapter 3
Isabella

When I climbed into the

passenger seat the first thing I noticed was the smell of one of those hanging tree air-fresheners. It was so overwhelming that I almost considered holding my nose. "What took you so long?" I leaned over and hugged him, waiting for a long awaited kiss. His hand reached into my hair, pulling me toward his lips. It was just as I'd remembered kissing him a million times before, but I was taken aback by the way it made me feel to be able to do it again after so long.

Tate pulled away, and we both began opening our eyes. The smile on his face let me know that he was just as happy to see me. "I missed the hell out of you, Bella."

I bit down on my lip and felt a wave of

butterflies rush into my stomach. "I missed you too. It's been way too long."

He started to pull away from the shoulder of the road. "I need you naked."

I started lifting off my shirt as we drove away from the ranch. If he wanted me without clothes than he was going to get that wish, because nothing was going to stop me from being intimate with him. I'd waited too long to see him, to touch him, and to be alone with him.

He took one quick look at me and realized what I was proceeding to do. "In a hurry?"

"Yeah, you could say that. You'd better drive faster, or else we're goin' to have to have a quickie before we even get where we're goin'."

I slipped my shorts down off of my legs, sitting there in only my underwear and bra. Tate reached over and started running his fingertips across my thighs. He traced the lace to my panties and growled with anticipation. "I'm going to fuck you so good that you're never going to go back to Kentucky."

In so many ways I hoped that would happen. Even though I'd moved my whole life to get away from him, he'd be the deciding factor for me to come back home to stay. In fact, I knew that if Tate asked me to, I would never leave again.

We pulled up at his apartment, quickly exiting the car. I managed to grab my clothes before running towards the door, so that nobody would see us. I don't know why I was worried. His neighbors had moved out months ago, and there wasn't another house for at least two miles. Since there were no street lights, there wasn't any way for someone to notice that I wasn't fully clothed, anyway. He opened the door and I walked inside, waiting for my eyes to adjust to the light again. Tate picked me up, grabbing both of my legs and wrapping them around his back. I knew where we were headed, and it didn't even bother me, because I wanted precisely the same thing.

Admittedly, it was probably the first time that we'd been on the exact same page.

We fell down easily onto the mattress of his bed, and I immediately got to work ripping off his shirt, then using my legs to tug down on his shorts. Time had stopped and nothing existed except for the two of us. This man that I'd fallen in love with so long ago had captivated my soul, teaching me everything that I understood about love, and especially sex. I needed him to be inside of me, reminding me that once again we were really together.

I felt my panties being tugged on, then heard the sound of the elastic giving way. He continued doing it until I knew they'd been ripped off of me. Tate then took his hand and grazed it over the smoothly shaved skin of my pussy. I let out a loud moan as our lips came in contact. His hot breath fueled me to seek out his tongue and mingle it with mine. The obvious erection he now had pressed into my leg as our embracing intensified rapidly. I jerked when his finger slid inside of my folds for the first time. He pulled away from our kiss to speak. "You're so fucking ready for me, Bella. I knew you'd be back."

He was being cocky, not that I cared. His words were like the mumbled ones you hear on a cartoon. I knew that he was speaking to me, but nothing he actually said mattered. I was too caught up in having hot sex with him again.

With us both finally naked, he reached down and positioned himself to be pressing on my sex. Right away I began to worry. "Wait. What about protection?"

Tate let out this sarcastic laugh. "Baby, come on. How many times have we done it without a condom?"

I shoved him away and rolled over. "This is different. Things have changed." In no way was I going to let him stick that used thing inside of me without covering it up. I skidded off the bed and put my hands on my hips. "You knew I was comin' over. How could you be so careless?"

He cackled again, showing me that my concerns didn't amuse him. "Bella, come on. Don't get all whack about this. Nothing's changed. I want you and you want me. Come back in this bed, and I'll make you forget all about it." He went to grab me and I pulled away, hugging my arms around my body.

"No!" Tears filled my eyes. It may have not been a huge thing to him, but after finding out he'd cheated on me I'd felt dirty and violated. "It's not happenin'!"

Tate got up on his knees and reached for me again. I backed up against the dresser, as far as I could go. He hopped off the bed and went from cocky to annoyed in just seconds. "I didn't drive out to that farm to pick your ass up for you to reject me. Get back in this bed with me, right now. Quit playing these head games. I know you want me, and I want you. I've waited a long time for this."

I pushed him hard onto the bed, feeling like for the first time I was uncomfortable being alone with him. "Seriously, Tate. How hard was it for you to get a condom? I know you keep them in your drawer. We bought a new box right before I left." I should have said that I'd purchased them, because his pussy ass refused to go to the local pharmacy and do it himself.

He tossed his hands into the air. "You know what? If you want to be a fucking bitch than I'm taking you back home. I ain't got time for this bullshit."

My heart jumped at the mere mention of going home. I'd come all of this way, waited so many months to see him again, and he was telling me that he wanted to take me home. I couldn't let that happen. In a matter of two short minutes he'd changed my mind, with little effort. Out of my own stupidity I fell into his arms. "I'm sorry." We looked into each other's eyes, and I caught him forming a half-smile over his lips. "Don't do that."

He leaned forward and kissed me softly.

"What?" After placing a few more pecks to my lips he let out an air-filled laugh. "I want you, and I know you want me. We've waited a long time to have this again. I'm sorry about the rubbers. I threw them all away a couple of months ago. Since we never used condoms before I honestly didn't think it was a big deal. Now, can we please get back in this bed and be together?"

The butterflies were back in my stomach, giving me the nervous push that I needed to proceed with our night. I could have remained standing there adding up all of the reasons why I shouldn't have gone through with it, but I knew if I didn't I'd regret it. He was right. I wanted this, and the longer I complained about the little things, the less time we'd have to be together.

I shoved Tate back down on the bed, climbing on top of him. My legs spread apart, hovering over his stiff cock. I rocked myself back and forth, teasing him with the base of my entrance. While biting down on my lip, I moaned and threw my head back, giving into the temptation of intimacy.

He penetrated me with little effort, getting into a pace easily. While he thrust himself inside of me, I became over emotional. Tears streamed down my eyes, so much that I couldn't see clearly. There was no question whether I wanted to be with this man. I just needed to figure out how to make it happen. I had to find a way to make my family see that he'd changed; that he deserved a second chance.

Tate buried his face in between my breast, licking the underneath of my skin there, before sliding his tongue up to the tips of my nipples. They hardened immediately, forcing me to cry out while the sensations traveled throughout my body. He lifted my legs, holding them up on his shoulders as he began pumping at a rapid pace. Immediately he started to tighten up, holding me still while he filled me with his release.

I nestled my head on his neck and kissed him on the chin. "I missed you so much. Sorry about earlier. If we're goin' to be together again I need to learn how to trust. I want this to work between us, because I feel so empty without you in my life. I'm so in love with you, Tate, and I'm tired of denyin' it."

"Don't worry about it, baby. All is good. We're going to work everything out." He kissed me on the top of the head. "You know you're my one and only, right?"

It felt so good to hear him say that. I wanted to believe it. Another bout of emotions took over as I started to sniffle. "Yeah, I know that."

He sat up and moved away, as if we weren't having a serious conversation. "I'm just going to take a piss real quick."

After he'd made that announcement, he climbed out of the bed and went into the bathroom, saying nothing else. I sat up and looked around for something to put between my legs to clean up with. That's when I spotted his phone blinking on the floor.

It was half hanging out of his pocket. A message had just come through and the name from the sender displayed Jennifer. Once I'd checked to make sure he wasn't coming out of the bathroom, I opened it up to peek.

I can't wait to see you, baby. I'll be home in two more days. My parents keep asking about you. They love my engagement ring. – Jenn

I put my hand over my mouth to keep Tate from hearing my shock. While trying not to sob, I scrolled through the old messages. He'd deleted everything except the last few, which he probably hadn't had time to do yet.

I hate that I had to take this trip without you. My whole family is so excited for us. – Jenn

I can't wait to watch you walk down that aisle. It's like we always planned. – Tate

Loving you is so easy. I'll be the best wife. I promise. – Jenn

I've loved you every single day of my life, Jenn. Come home soon. I can't sleep without you in my bed. - Tate

I was in such shock that I hadn't heard him come out of the bathroom. He startled me when he called out my name. I dropped the phone on the floor and turned to him with tear-filled eyes. "You're engaged to her?"

He put his head down and shook it. "It's not

what you think. I planned on telling you."

"What? When? After we had sex?"

"Oh, come on, Bella. It's not like that."

"Does she live here now?" I stood up and looked around the room. It was dimly lit, but I could clearly see no evidence of a female in plain sight. So I walked to the closet and opened the door. Right away I noticed dresses that were hanging. I held my lips tight to prevent from feeling them quiver. Then I rushed over toward the nightstand and pulled it open.

Tate grabbed my arm and spun me around. "Bella, please. Listen to me, baby."

I pulled away from him. "Don't you dare baby me."

Looking in that drawer and seeing the slew of pictures that had been removed for my visit made my stomach turn. I picked one up and looked at the happy couple. "Is this really happenin'? You hid her stuff so that you could fuck with my head again? You did this to be able to fuck me?"

I slammed the picture down on the table, listening to the glass shattering all over the place. Tate hugged me from behind, desperately attempting to get me to calm down, but the damage was done.

"My family was right about you. They saw what I was too blind to see." I started putting my clothes on, silently thinking of ways to get home without his assistance. "Don't you ever try to contact me again, Tate. We're done."

He fell back on the bed and rubbed his hands

over his face, as if this was all some kind of joke. Little did he know that I was about to walk out of his life forever, no matter how much it hurt to do.

Before walking out of his bedroom, I leaned over and picked up his cell phone, sticking it in my pocket so that he didn't notice.

Tate stood up and grabbed his pants, pulling them on. "Just wait, Bella. I'll drive you back. Don't do anything else stupid. You know we can work this out. We always do."

I pointed toward his face. "No. This time I'm done, for real. You've destroyed me for the last damn time. If you try to follow me, I'll tell my brothers. Hell, I'll tell my father. I'm sure he'd like to light your ass up for what you've done to me."

Tate put both hands up and backed away. "Whoa. This is between us. Don't go getting your crazy family involved."

I kicked him in the balls so hard that it injured my ankle. After watching him fall to the floor beneath me, I turned and walked out of the apartment, hoping that he wouldn't be able to follow me.

Isabella Mitchell

Chapter 4
Isabella

The first thing I managed to do

was dial my brother, Jake. Since I knew he hadn't come home, there was a good chance he was in town, close to where I was stranded.

It rang five times before the machine picked up.

I tried again, getting no answer for the second time.

When I started to dial my father I began sobbing. He was going to be so disappointed in me, the whole family was. Before I could hit the send button, my phone started to ring.

"Jake. Where are you?"

"Jesus Christ, Bella. I'm fucking sleeping. It's three in the morning."

"I know." I started to cry even harder, and I was sure he couldn't understand my next sentences. "Are you home? I need you to come and get me without mom and dad findin' out. Please, Jake."

"I ain't home. I'm at this chick's place. Where are you?" My little brother's tone had changed from annoyed to worried.

"I'm on cross street, right outside of town. Are you close?"

"We're five minutes away. Hang tight, sis. I've got to find Jax and get him up. We'll be there in a few. Stay outside."

He hung up before I could make that promise, but it wasn't like I was going back inside with Tate. If I never saw him again it would be too soon.

After I put my phone back in my purse I pulled Tate's out of my pocket. That cheater wasn't going to live happily ever after if I had anything to do with it. So I did what every distraught woman would have done in my situation. I made a video.

"Hi Jenn. Sorry you're gettin' this so late. As you can see I'm sendin' this from Tate's phone. We just slept together in the bed that you're about to come home to." I started to cry and looked away from the recording camera. "Sorry, this is all so hard to do. You see, I've been talkin' to Tate for a while now, and he told me that you weren't together. I found his phone and saw your messages. He's a liar, and if you know what's good for you, you'll leave his lyin' ass. I'm sorry that you had to find out, but I thought you'd like to know."

Once the message was sent and delivered, I stuck the phone in the mailbox and put the red flag up. By that time I saw my brother's truck coming toward me. Jax jumped out of the passenger seat and rushed to my side, before Jake could put it into park. "What the fuck are you doing here, Bella?"

I shoved Jax, and felt Jake pulling me into his arms. "It's going to be all right. Calm down and tell us what happened."

"I just want to go home," I cried against his chest.

In that moment I heard someone calling my name. Before I could yell to Jax, he was running after Tate. They fell down onto the damp grass and punches were being thrown, none of which were Tate's. I watched him shielding himself from taking my angry brother's blows, while Jake held me close, preventing me from jumping in between them. "Come on Jax. Let's get out of here," he yelled.

I had to look away, unable to stand watching the man that I had wanted a future with to be beaten to a pulp. I knew he deserved it, but it was still hard to bear.

Jax stood up and said something smart before walking in our direction. When I turned back I saw Tate lying on the ground crying, whining like a little bitch. A smile formed across my face as I realized that he'd be crying for a different reason when he found his phone. Finally he'd get what was coming to him, and lose both Jenn and me.

When we got in the truck and pulled out of town, both of my brothers started on me. I was still crying, trying desperately to convince them not to tell our father. It wasn't like I was actually worried about him going after Tate. I was worried that he'd tell Noah, and all hell would break loose back in Kentucky.

"Guys, please."

Jake pulled over and put the truck in park, halfway home. "Give us one good reason why we should keep this shit a secret. Did he lay a hand on you?"

"No. He didn't hit me. I snuck to see him and discovered that he's engaged to be married. That's all. It's over. I swear. I'm done with him for good. That's why I want you to keep your mouths shut. Please. I've covered for you a million times. Just do me a solid for this one time."

Jake put his hand on my knee. "Your secret's safe with us, right, Jax?"

Jax kissed the top of my head. "Unless I find out more happened. Then I'm going to stick my foot so far up that fucker's ass he'll puke it out of his mouth."

We sat there for a little while so that I could calm down. The three of us were afraid of having to explain to our parents how I'd gotten so messed up. By the time we pulled down the lane the light was on in the kitchen. Jake turned off the ignition and opened the door, sticking his hand out to help me get down.

Jax got out and came around to our side. "Bella, let us go inside. You can come in through my window."

"Seriously? I haven't done that in years."

"Do you want them to know what happened?" Jake asked.

"No." I looked down, realizing it was the only way to keep the peace. "Fine. I'll meet you at your window."

I marched out back while they went inside. It felt like it took them forever, but finally the light came on and I watched the window sliding up. Jax leaned out and took me into his arms. With ease, he pulled me inside. Jake was standing there behind him with his arms crossed.

I sat down on Jax's mattress and covered my face with my hands. "Sorry about all of this, guys."

Jake touched my shoulder, causing me to look up. "Everyone was in bed when we came in. They must have left the light on for us." He kissed my cheek before heading out to his room.

I stood up and followed. "Thanks again, Jax. See you in the mornin'." In all of the years that my brothers had annoyed me, I'd finally gotten to a point where I could appreciate that I had them. They'd saved my butt, and comforted me when I needed it. If there was some way to tell my parents how they'd come to my rescue, I would have done it. Though, I knew I'd never let them know about what had happened, not after I'd sworn to them all that I was done with Tate.

He caught me before I could get all of the way out of his room. "Make that afternoon. My ass isn't getting out of bed until after lunch. Oh, and by the way, you owe me big for tonight. I was about to get my dick wet when you called."

I scrunched up my face, imagining my brothers being old enough to actually have sex with a person instead of their hands. "Spare me the details. I probably kept you from makin' a mistake you'll soon regret."

"Like you just did?"

I flipped him the finger and pulled the knob behind me. Of course he'd bring that up. Once I was out of his room I crept through the hallway quietly. I walked down the hall and opened my bedroom door, flipping on the light before closing it back up. When I turned to head in the direction of my bed I saw my dad lying above the covers, as if he'd been there waiting for me. I had a sudden flashback of being a teen and sneaking out with Tate my senior year. I didn't climb in my window until the sun was coming up, and boy was he pissed.

He opened his eyes and looked around the room, finally catching my stare. "Iz. Where have you been?"

I placed my hands over my hips. "Dad, I'm not a little girl. Did you come in here to punish me?"

He brought his feet to the floor and started to stand up. I could see how he was looking at me. "What are you crying for?"

I opened my mouth to talk and felt the door opening behind me. My brother handed me my purse. "You left this in the truck." He looked over and saw our dad standing up. "Oh, hey, Dad. Did we wake you up?"

"No."

"Well, I'm hitting the sack. Bella drank us under the table tonight. Jax is already passed out."

"Where'd you three go?" His questions were making me nervous, as if he was giving me the third degree.

"Out to a bar, then to the barn. Don't worry, we didn't drink any of your good bourbon," Jake looked to me after his explanation, as if to make sure I was going to agree with him.

"I'm glad you all had a good time, but do you mind telling me why your sister's been crying?" I closed my eyes, knowing he could see right through me.

Before Jake could get us into a deeper lie, I spoke out. "I got a little emotional. It's just that bein' home makes me miss this place even more. I love Kentucky, don't get me wrong, but it's never goin' to be home to me, not while you're all here."

My dad walked over and put his arms around me. "This will always be your home, no matter what. I know you're an adult, but I still worry. It's late, Iz. Why don't we all head to bed and we can catch up more tomorrow. I know you've got to be exhausted."

I nodded and watched the two men leave my room. Once I changed and climbed into bed, I cried myself into a desolate stupor. I'd been so optimistic about my relationship with Tate, never even considering that it would end so horribly. My biggest regret was sleeping with him. I hated myself for letting him get into my pants, especially without a condom. If he was sleeping with me and Jenn, there was no telling how many other women he might be involved with.

I was going to have to get tested to be sure he hadn't given me anything. The idea of getting some kind of STD was revolting to think about. It made me hate him even more. The emotional pain consumed me, driving me to curl up in a ball, and think about all of the time that I'd wasted loving Tate. He'd destroyed me from the inside out, leading me on to only end up destroying me with his web of lies. The fact that I'd let myself fall to his prey again left a bad taste in my mouth. He was the epitome of a man, who didn't deserve to ever be happy.

All I could hope for was that Jenn would wise up and leave him too. He didn't deserve her devotion. For the first time I felt sorry for the girl, realizing that he'd played us both. At least I didn't have to tell my family what a lying cheater he was. There was no way that I could let them know I'd made such a horrible mistake, after they'd warned me time and again not to.

I thought about all of the nights that I fought with Noah. I didn't heed his warnings to stay away from Tate, or to stop talking to him. The idea of admitting to everyone that they were right and I was wrong annoyed the shit out of me. I'd been in such denial, letting my heart blind my judgment. The signs of his ways had always been there, I'd just been too stupid in love to notice.

At least there was one good thing that could come out of this horrible evening. Tate and I were done forever, and this time I wasn't going to regret it.

Isabella Mitchell

Chapter 5
Isabella

The next couple of days went by too quick. I kept my phone on silent, trying to avoid the slew of messages that Tate was leaving. What started out as threats quickly changed to begging. I ignored them all, determined more than ever to be done with him forever.

The night before I left, my mom made my favorite meal. While my brothers shoveled the food into their mouths, like it was the end of times, I savored every bite. My aunt Van could cook and bake up a storm, but there was always something about my mom's cooking that made it the best. I looked down the long table, taking in my immediate family, including my mimi and poppy. It had been good to spend time with everyone, and I knew I'd see them again in a couple of months. It still scared me with them getting older, never knowing when I'd get that call telling me something bad happened.

While deep in thought I felt something slap into my face. Jax ducked down behind my other brother. I took a napkin and rubbed mashed potatoes off of my cheek. "Seriously? Are you five?"

"He's going to miss you, Bella. That's all," Jake explained.

Instead of firing back I simply sat there and smiled. This was my crazy family that I loved more than anything in the world. No matter what happened they'd be there for me, and protect me from myself if I needed it. Knowing that would give me the strength to move on and accept the things in my life that I couldn't change.

Saying goodbye to all of them was always bittersweet. As an adolescent I would have said different, but as an adult I'd learned to appreciate just what I had; two loving parents that were willing to risk their lives to keep our family together. Two brothers that drove me crazy, but always kept a smile on my face. Two grandparents that had paved the way for it all. Grateful wasn't even enough to describe all of them.

That's why when it came to driving away from it all, I lost my shit, every time.

This was the worst by far, considering that I was already holding back the tears of being heartbroken.

The moment my dad wrapped his arms around me I just about broke down. "I love you, Iz. You better call us as soon as you get to Kentucky." He refused to call it home, not when he knew where I'd always belonged.

"I will, Dad. I always do."

I pulled away to hug my mother, but he tugged me back. "One more hug."

He was so silly, although I didn't fight it. There was no comparison to the way it felt to be held by my father. No matter where I was in life, I knew he'd support me. They said that blood is thicker than water, but that's bullshit when it applies to my dad. Blood meant nothing, not anymore. He'd been my father since the moment I took my first breath. Sure, it took him a while to make it happen officially, but we'd always known, somehow in a fate kind of way. My mom used to tell me that I chose him. There's no real explanation for it, but it was definitely there. "If you squeeze me any tighter I am goin' to explode everything I had for dinner."

"That accent is getting stronger. It's driving me crazy."

I giggled and turned to my mother, who apparently sounded just like me. I'd never really noticed it that much. "Do you hear this guy?"

She held me tightly in her arms. "He loves it. Don't let your dad fool you."

"I'm going to call as soon as I get home, I

promise. Thanks for puttin' up with me this weekend. It's still hard being here and knowin' that I can't stay."

"You're always welcome to come home," she added.

I knew that, also knowing my life was now in Kentucky. I had a great job, and even new friends that didn't know Tate or the history that we'd shared.

After saying the rest of my goodbyes, I hopped in my car and started on my journey. The first few miles were filled with sobs. For so many reasons I wanted to turn the car back around. For a different set of reasons I wanted to get out of the state as fast as possible.

I arrived home around nine at night. Noah was watching a football game on television and nodded when I came in carrying my suitcase. I sat it down and wheeled by him quickly. The last thing I wanted was a third degree the moment I stepped in the door. I'd spent the past five hours torturing myself. That was plenty of enough time to accept that I'd been a fool.

All I wanted to do was get a long, hot shower and wash away all of the shitty decisions that I'd made. It was time to start over new, to reinvent myself to be the woman that I deserved to be. In the morning I'd change my number and only let my family know what it was. My times of being vulnerable were about to end.

After grabbing some clean clothes, and a fresh towel out of the hall closet, I opened the bathroom door to display a shocking reveal. My eyes tried to adjust to what I was actually seeing. In my personal bathroom, that nobody else used, was a naked man, desperately trying to cover himself with a small towel.

It took me a second to be able to cover my eyes, turn around, and scream all at the same time. "What in the hell?"

I heard Noah yelling from the other room. "Oh yeah. I forgot to tell you. Rusty's water heater went up in his trailer. I told him he could stay in the other bedroom until we got it figured out."

Rusty, a ranch hand that had been around for a year or two, lived on the property in one of the single-wide trailers that our family provided the full-time workers with. I didn't know much about him, except that he was in his thirties and kept to himself. Aside from seeing him naked, in all of his glory, I'd always been creeped out by the way he stared at me. Sure, he was easy on the eyes. His dark, almost black hair was so wavy, and his irises were a blue-gray. For being in his thirties he was obviously in great shape, not that I was paying that much attention, or maybe I had noticed.

"I'm real sorry, ma'am. Noah told me you wouldn't be home tonight."

He approached me in the hallway with a towel finally wrapped around him. Water glistened over his rock hard chest, and it took a lot for me to not peek at it longer. I moved away from him, finally making it inside of the bathroom before closing the door without a reply.

Perhaps I could have said something kind to the man for his apology, except after seeing his dick just hanging out, I couldn't bring myself to say anything at all.

Once in the shower, I let the water fall down over my face. As much as I'd enjoyed my visit to the Carolinas, it was good to be back in Kentucky, far away from Tate and all of his lies. The distance was going to help me to be strong. Hopefully, I'd be able to forget about him this time, considering that he'd shredded my heart apart.

If it weren't for my dad, and maybe my uncle Colt, I'd think that men couldn't be faithful. Although, Noah had even proven that men could change. Even if it were to happen for Tate, I wouldn't believe him. He'd gotten his last chance.

When the water became cool, I stepped out and dried off before getting dressed. Noah and Rusty were both in the living room when I came out. I said nothing as I walked past and went into the kitchen to grab a bottle of water. I'd no sooner reached in the refrigerator when I felt a presence behind me.

Rusty was standing there, his eyes looking at me like he was peering into my soul. It gave me the immediate chills. "Did you want somethin'?" I scooted to the side to move away from how close we stood to each other.

"I just wanted to say that I'm sorry you caught

me in a bad way. I mean you no disrespect. Your cousin was kind enough to let me stay here while my trailer gets repaired. The water leaked all over the floor and now there's a hole we have to fix. I'll make sure to stay out of your way while I'm a guest."

I tried to keep my cool, just in case the weird vibe was just me being overcautious. "It's fine." I took a sip of my water before continuing. "I'm tired from drivin' and didn't really see nothin' anyway. Don't even worry about it. As far as stayin' out of my way, you probably won't need to work hard at it. I plan on stayin' clear of Noah until his fiancée gets home. He acts like a dickhead when she ain't here, and I'm not his momma." I left the room before he could reply back. Having a conversation would only imply that I wanted to talk, in which I did not.

I passed by Noah again on my way back to my room. He gave me this look that annoyed me. "What?"

He lifted his bottle and pointed to me. "You know what. Did you see him?"

I played it off like I didn't know he was talking about Tate. "See who?"

"You know who. Did you see him, because the way you're actin' is makin' me feel like you did?"

"Shut up. You don't know what you're talkin' about." I rolled my eyes, trying to play off the fact that he was right.

Rusty came back in the room with a water in his hand. It caught my attention since I noticed a few beer bottles on the table in front of Noah. "Excuse me," he said as he passed me and sat down in the chair. I avoided eye contact with our creepy guest and waited for Noah to respond.

"If I find out you saw that douche bag, you're never goin' to hear the end of it. You got me?"

I threw my hands up in the air. "Yeah, Dad. I hear ya." Annoyed, I went back to my room and locked the door. If he wanted to control me like that, I was going to be difficult.

That night I lay in my bed with so much on my mind. The pain and humiliation of what Tate did to me was still too fresh to let go of. The guilt of going against my family was chastening. I was pretty sure that both of my parents knew something had happened. They at least sensed that I was different after that first night. My brothers may have covered for me, but at some point I had this bad feeling they would spill. It was only a matter of time.

Speaking of that. I'd have plenty of time to get over my cheating ex. If they ever discovered the shameful truth at least they'd know that I learned my lesson the hard way. Hopefully they'd feel sorry for me and pity me, instead of letting me know how stupid I was for going against all of them and doing it anyway.

While staring at the empty side of the bed beside me, I wondered if I'd ever be able to find someone that could be faithful to me. Maybe I had this hidden sign on my head that told men they could cheat, lie and treat me like dirt. It was possible that I'd be one of those women that never found true love. It was hard to consider when the adults in my family were all so happy. To long for that kind of life was realistic, but unreachable.

It was heart wrenching, to say the least.

Chapter 6
Rusty

She was so beautiful, but the resemblance was uncanny. I couldn't stop looking at her and seeing my old life; the one I'd walked away from years ago. Seeing Isabella was like reliving it over and over again. On one hand I couldn't look away when she came into the room. On the other, I wanted to be as far from her as humanly possible.

It wasn't just her figure, or the color of her blonde hair either. Those eyes, green and pure, brought back so much regret.

As much as I tried to keep my cool around her, I knew I was freaking her out. If she only knew what I was thinking she'd hate me more.

The Mitchell family had been so kind to hire me without doing a background check. I don't know if they saw something desperate in me eyes, or maybe they just needed help that bad. Either way it was a job that offered me a roof over my head. After all, I wasn't just running from my old life, I was running from everyone that had ever known the man I used to be.

Having secrets came with consequences. It forced me to start over, with nothing to show for. To the Mitchell family I was a drifter. They couldn't know what I'd been through, and I was determined to make sure the truth never came out. This was my fresh start; my second chance.

After Isabella walked into the bathroom on me, I felt overwhelmingly conscious. It was hard to be sensible on an average day when I saw her walking by, but standing naked in her bathroom was unimaginable. The shock on her face said it all, and then our encounter in the kitchen let me know that she wanted to get as far away from me as possible.

I couldn't blame her. It wasn't as if I had anything to offer someone like her. She came from such a great family, and even if she didn't succeed on her own, they'd be there to support her financially and emotionally anyway.

I knew all of this because a long time ago I'd had the same kind of life. It saddened me to think about it now, but there was no way to go back and change things. I'd tried doing that for years, with no result except for constant misery.

That night while lying in the next room over

from Isabella, I listened to her crying. She was clearly in a bad way, seemingly distraught about something she neglected to tell her cousin. I wondered if it was their little argument, or something else all together. The idea of her being so close to me, but not being able to offer her support was disappointing.

For hours on end she sobbed, until finally everything became silent. All that could be heard was the insects that were outdoors. I stayed awake a little while longer, not that it was anything new. I hadn't had a good night's sleep in as long as I could remember.

Nightmares were a constant for me, so avoiding rest was necessary. On most nights I'd take walks, or drink coffee to avoid being tired. By the time I rested, I was so beat that I didn't dream. I'd gotten used to it, and in some ways it was just habit.

The next morning Noah neglected to wake me. Since there was no alarm in my room I only opened my eyes when I heard someone moving around. I headed for the bathroom to relieve myself and was met with Isabella in a towel. Her hair was wet, and I think the shock of seeing me again displayed on her face. "Mornin'," I said in my best voice.

She never even flinched a smile. "I forgot you were here."

"It's all good. I just need to use the bathroom. Do you mind?" I pointed toward the bathroom door and watched as she went into her room. When I was done brushing my teeth, I headed out to go to work, hoping to catch another glimpse of her. Unfortunately, she'd gone into her room and had the door shut. I could hear the hairdryer running, knowing for sure that she wouldn't be out for a long time.

After grabbing some coffee, I headed out to work. My daily chores were hard and strenuous, but I enjoyed the way they kept me busy. I'd taken a liking to working with some of the horses that Shalan, Noah's fiancée, had purchased. The newest one, named Titan, was acquired as a wild colt and hadn't been broken yet. It was going to take me a while, but I was determined to make it happen. In fact, I spent most of my evenings with that horse in the stables, resting against a bed of hay, reading. Aside from the training, I felt that it was best to make the horse feel comfortable around me. To be honest, I enjoyed the solitary of it all. The less people I was around, the less I had to pretend who I was.

When the plumbers arrived at my trailer I knew my time staying in the same house as Isabella was about to end. Determined to make a good impression, I decided to cook them both dinner for their hospitality. Grilling had always been something that I was good at, so I picked up some corn, zucchini, and chicken and got to work.

She pulled up just as I was finishing up, giving me a questionable look as she exited her vehicle. I could already tell that my being around annoyed her.

For the most part she never talked to me. I knew it was for the best, still I yearned for her to notice me, just so I could look into those beautiful eyes with little effort. Her dress was tight around her ass, forcing me to fight with myself to not stare. By the time I found her breasts in the low cut shirt, I knew I was doomed.

I focused on the chicken before she could notice and call me out. Her presence alarmed me, causing me to stiffen my stance. "What's all this?" she asked.

"Just a little supper to say thanks for putting up with me. I hope you like chicken and vegetables."

"I love them. That's real kind of you, Rusty. Considerin' that I worked through lunch, it's perfect."

I threw her a smile, and couldn't take my eyes off of her beautiful face. Right away I knew it was a mistake. She looked down for a second and then back to me. "Why do you look at me like that?"

I let my eyes fall to the grilling food. "Like what?"

"I don't know. It's weird, but you're always doin' it."

I knew I was going to come across as creepy. "Sorry. It's just the way I look at people, I guess. I don't mean to offend you in any way."

"What's your deal anyway?" She sat down on a chair near the grill and crossed her legs. I tried so hard not to notice the way her thighs lifted at the bottom, almost displaying the skin of her ass.

"I don't have a deal. I work the ranch, and train the horses."

"No," she was determined to keep digging. "You've got to have a back story. My cousin told me you're in your thirties. Obviously you've been doin' something for all these years, so spill. Who is Rusty?"

I finally looked in her direction, clenching my jaw as I contemplated making something up. "There's no back story. I've traveled different places and decided to settle down here in Kentucky. It's beautiful, and the hunting is good."

She raised her brow, seemingly trying to read me. "I hardly think that you're tellin' me everything. You're sayin' that you've been traveling for your whole adult life?"

"There's nothing to tell, I can assure you."

"You were in jail weren't you?" Her question offended me, even though she had every right to assume that.

"No. I haven't been in jail." I couldn't even laugh about it.

"Are you runnin' from the law?"

I put the tongs down and let both of my hands fall to my sides. "Why do you want to know about me? Are you interested or something?"

It was sure fire way to make her leave me alone. I could tell from her vibes that she wanted nothing to do with me that way.

"No. I'm not interested what so ever. I'm done

with men in general, especially after recent events. Besides, my father would die if I was datin' a mysterious ranch hand that was much older than me. I reckon I'm just bein' nosey, that's all."

"You've got nothing to worry about, ma'am. I can assure you that I mean you no harm. I'm not a criminal, or some kind of stalker." I chuckled to myself knowing how creepy I sounded. "I'm simply living a quiet life off the beaten path."

"You're weird, that's for sure. I'm goin' to go change for dinner, and leave you to be alone, like you obviously prefer." With that statement she headed into the house.

If she only knew that I longed for the company of a beautiful woman. I just knew that I didn't deserve it. This was my punishment for my past. There was no way to rectify what had been done, therefore I refused to give myself hope.

Noah pulled in on a Gator moments later. "I made dinner," I announced proudly.

"Damn, I wish I could stay. My girl flew in early and I'm on my way to pick her up from the airport. We'll probably get dinner in town on our way home. Thanks for the sentiment. I appreciate it, but I can't pass up seein' my woman."

I understood completely. If he only knew how envious I was at the life he had, especially considering that mine used to be so similar.

"Go on and get out of here then. I'll make sure to save you both a plate anyway."

"Sorry for leavin' you to deal with Bells. She's been such a bitch lately. I swear that chick's had her period for the past month."

I laughed to myself. "I'll be sure to eat in silence, just in case she plans to attack."

Once Noah went inside I stood there happily cooking, knowing that in just a little while I was going to be in the company of a gorgeous woman for a meal that I prepared. Sure, it certainly wasn't a date, but it was probably the closest that I was going to get to one, with her especially.

Chapter 7
Isabella

I heard my cousin come into the house when I was pulling on a pair of shorts. He knocked on my door before just helping himself to opening it. "Seriously, I'm tryin' to change in here."

"Whatever. I ain't lookin'. I just wanted you to know that I'm headin' in town to pick up Shalan. She caught an earlier flight. You're goin' to have to eat dinner with Rusty tonight alone."

"What?" That wasn't going to happen. "He's creepy as shit. Have you seen the way he looks at me?"

He laughed. "Get over yourself, Bells. He's a nice guy. Just eat the fuckin' meal and then you can come back in here and sulk in your room all night."

"Screw you, Noah."

"I'll see you later." He waved as he closed my bedroom door behind him.

I was pissed, especially because the man outside made me leery. Something about him was off and I couldn't put my finger on it. Normally I could care less who my family had working for them. Hell, Mr. Harvey had been working for my poppy since before I was born. If anyone had a secret past it was him, seeing as he was in the country illegally. He'd snuck over the border when he was twenty, and still sent money back to his family.

My judgment over Rusty was nothing like that. He had secret written all over his face, and it bothered me. I didn't want to think that my family was harboring a fugitive, or maybe even worse.

Knowing that I'd hear a wrath of shit when Noah got back, I threw my hair into a ponytail and decided that it was just one meal. I'd eat the food, and lock myself in my room afterwards. No harm, no foul.

By the time I came back outside with plates and silverware, my cousin had already left to pick up Shalan. Rusty stood over the grill, placing the food on a large tray to the side. I sat down at the picnic table and laid out the forks and knives next to the plates. He walked over and sat the tray down. "What would you like to drink? I can go grab it."

I sat down in front of one of the settings, promising myself that I was going to be nice to the guy, for the small amount of time it took me to eat.

"Sure. Tea is fine, or a beer. Whatever you're havin'."

He brought out two iced teas, and then sat down across from me. I helped myself to the hot food, and smiled when he pushed the glass in my direction. "We're never going to eat all of this food."

"I'm starvin', so you may be wrong." It was the truth. Sometimes when I got busy at work I'd forget to eat. This had been one of those days. My stomach rumbled as I poked my fork into the grilled vegetables.

They tasted delicious. "These are amazin'."

He smiled and took a bite himself. "Thanks. Cooking is a hobby of mine."

After tasting the chicken I was convinced of one thing. "You're wastin' your talent workin' on this stinky ass ranch, that's for sure."

He laughed and kept eating. I took a sip of tea, while watching him. Once he was finished chewing he took a drink and then replied to me. "I happen to enjoy what I do. As far as the cooking goes, whenever you want some, feel free to stop by my trailer."

I think he and I both realized exactly at the same time what he'd just offered. I didn't know what to say, or even if we were on the same page. Perhaps he was just being a nice man, or it was possible that he was asking me to join him because he was interested. "I, don't, um -."

"I didn't mean it the way it sounded, Isabella. Maybe it came out wrong. All I was saying is that you were welcome to eat dinner. I meant nothing else by it."

"It's not that." I felt bad for acting so stuck up. "Sorry. I'm just all messed up right now. I wish I could explain things more, but some people around here like to get all up in my business. That's why I refuse to discuss it."

He placed the silverware down on his plate and folded his hands. "I'm not an open book either, as you've probably been able to tell. Some things aren't anyone's business but our own."

For the first time I saw something different in this stranger. We could relate, obviously from secrets that we both kept, but it was enough to catch my interest. "I agree."

It was quick, but I could have sworn that I saw a smile form in the corner of his lips. As fast as it was there, it disappeared. "Noah tells me that you visited your family this weekend past. How did that go?"

It was small talk, and for the time being it was okay. "Fine, I guess. I saw people that I missed a lot."

"I bet it's hard being so far away from them. I heard you crying the night you came home. Was it because you wish you were home with your parents?"

Immediately I was offended. He'd listened to me crying and now he was prying. "That's none of your business. Look, I agreed to have dinner tonight because you obviously took the time to cook it, but we're not friends. I'm not goin' to sit here pretendin' we're friends. You work for my family. That's it."

I stood up and rushed toward the kitchen

door. He came after me, meeting me inside. "Isabella, I didn't mean to -."

I cut him off. "Just stop."

"What? What did I say?"

"First, you can stop calling me Isabella. It's weird. Nobody calls me that."

"Okay. What do you like to be called?"

I threw up my hands. This guy wasn't getting it. Couldn't he take a hint that I was damaged and not interested in being buddies? "This is pointless. Thank you for dinner, Rusty. Just leave the dishes in the sink. I'll clean them in a little while."

I began to walk away when I heard him talking. What he said stopped me dead in my tracks. "I hated hearing you cry. It reminds of something in my past. I wish I could talk about it, but like you I know I can't. Sometimes we need to walk away from what we want. I guess it's part of life, even though it feels like torture."

I turned around and tried my best to relate to whatever he meant. "Look, we don't know each other. You seem like you're a nice guy. If I was lookin' for a friend this might have gone differently. Right now my life is too messed up to even consider it. I enjoyed dinner. None of this is about you, Rusty. I've got demons that I'm tryin' to get rid of, and so do you obviously. A friendship between us would just add fuel to the fire."

He went back outside, only to come in to put his plate in the sink. I watched him walk outside and start cleaning up again. A part of me wanted to apologize. He seemed like I'd offended him, and I probably had. For someone that didn't want to be a jerk, it was exactly what I was being.

Rusty stayed away from me after that night. Shalan came home and things got back to normal. We were planning her wedding, which was keeping me busy enough to not dwell on my ex. Noah was finally off my back, and for the most part I felt better about everything that was happening in my life.

I'd seen Rusty in passing, but with the exception of a couple waves from him, he'd steered clear of me. I didn't blame him after I'd been such a bitch. Honestly, nothing would ever come out of a friendship with him. I knew my family, and what they'd say if I got involved with someone like him. Since I wanted them as far out of my business as possible, I chose to push him away. Sure, he was handsome, even for being ten years older than me. His almost black hair and gray eyes were very easy on the eyes, especially when riding by and seeing him shirtless. Just because he was good to look at didn't mean I wanted to hang out.

Before I knew it two months had gone by. Noah had built a house for Shalan, and they were about to move in it. I was actually looking forward to taking over the house, and redecorating. The deer heads were cool when we were kids, but Noah's once bachelor pad needed a makeover.

Everyone on the ranch came to lend a helping hand on moving day. My aunt Van and my grandma Karen came to help make food for all of the men while they did the heavy lifting. I was carrying one of the last boxes over to the flat bed trailer when I spotted Rusty walking toward me. I sat the box down and stood up straight to face him. "Noah sent me over here to grab this stuff. Is this all of it?"

"This is it." I pointed to the boxes.

He wiped beads of sweat off of his forehead. "Do you mind if I have a glass of water? They picked up some beer, but I don't drink."

I'd noticed that, but been afraid to ask him at the time. "Sure. Be right back." I ran inside and got two bottles of water. After handing Rusty one of them I stood there quenching my own thirst.

"It's hot as hell out here today," he said before finishing off the water. Then he wiped his face with his shirt. I caught one glimpse of a rock hard stomach before he saw me. With nothing to say to get out of it, I changed the subject.

"So, how come you don't drink?"

"Personal reasons. For the most part it's because I grew up around alcoholics." When he didn't get into further detail I knew I had to back off.

"That's understandable."

We stood for a moment in complete silence. When it got to be too awkward Rusty handed me his bottle. "Thanks for the water, Iz."

I opened my mouth but nothing would come

out.

He smiled, as if he knew that name was special to me. "Is that okay? I mean, you told me not to call you Isabella."

"I guess. Only my father calls me by that."

"Have a good afternoon then." He left me standing there, and I wasn't sure if I liked it. It was as if he was giving me the cold shoulder. I certainly deserved it, especially after the way I'd been cold to him. Still, each time I was around him things were weird. I was determined to figure it out, even if it required me to have more conversations with the mysterious man. Little by little he was revealing things about himself. If I gave him the chance, I might be able to get to the bottom of it.

Knowing that it was going to require me to be nice, I decided that it was as good as any time to change my attitude. I'd been withdrawn for too long.

Getting to know Rusty a bit more would help me make that push I needed to be able to go out and consider dating again. One day I'd find someone that cared about me, who wouldn't ever want to be with anyone else. I had to stay positive and believe that it would happen.

In the two months that I'd gone without talking to Tate I was starting to finally be able to accept that we were never meant to be together. My pain was replaced with resentment and hate, which I was finally okay with feeling. He'd hurt me in the worst way possible, and even though he'd always be my first love, I knew he wouldn't be the last. No matter where he was in the world no longer mattered to me, because my future was mine to make.

Chapter 8
Rusty

Day after day I would see her.

Even if it were only seconds, it was enough to satisfy the constant ache. I'd tried several times to be nice to her, only to get shot down repeatedly. Keeping my distance was getting easier, especially when imagining being with her was less hard than the real thing. Isabella gave difficult a new definition.

I woke up one Sunday morning and noticed that it was raining. My chores were going to suck, and I wasn't going to be able to work with Titan until it cleared.

Just as I'd started in one of the chicken

houses, I got a call on my cell phone.

"Hey, it's Noah. Listen, can you head over to my old place and give my cousin a hand? She's bitchin' about something with the plumbin', and I'm tryin' to get this paintin' done over here."

"Yeah, sure. I'll head over there as soon as I'm done."

"Take your time, man. The longer she has to wait the more it will annoy her. After the way she's acted for the past few months she deserves it."

"I'll take care of it."

We hung up and I picked up my pace. Little did Noah know that I wanted to be around his cousin. He may have wanted to wait, but I couldn't get there fast enough.

A little less than an hour later I was knocking on the kitchen door. Isabella spotted me standing there in the rain and hesitated before unlatching the lock to let me in. I could tell that she expected to see Noah, and was annoyed that he'd called me instead. "Noah says you need some help."

Right away I could smell puke. She started to walk away before I could ask. "The clog is back here. I've tried to get it out, but it's makin' me sick. I've thrown up three times today."

I wasn't going to let her know that the house reeked of it. "Hopefully I can get it fixed for you."

She led me to the bathroom and tossed me a towel. "Here. You look like you just jumped in the pool."

"It's really coming down out there."

Isabella smiled, making me do the same, as if it was contagious. "Anyway, the clog is here. It's full of hair, and gunk. I've tried using the scrub brush to pick it, but every time I get close I start heavin'. I don't know what's wrong with me. I've seen blood, snot, and every other kind of bodily fluid and never been bothered."

For a couple seconds I wondered if she could be pregnant, though I'd never seen her with a gentlemen, or noticed her going out anywhere. Besides, that was definitely not my business to ask about. Knowing her, she'd probably slap me for bringing it up.

I sat down the towel and got on my knees to address the problem. The moment she saw me picking up the lump of hair she fell against the toilet and started vomiting. Quickly I grabbed the trashcan and discarded the wad of nastiness. Then I turned all of my attention to her. I wet the towel and handed it to her. "Put this on the back of your neck. It will help with the nausea."

She did as I told her, but lingered over the toilet. I made my way out of the bathroom and sat down on the bed to make sure she was all right. When she finally walked into the room her face was pale. I'd never seen her look so bad before. She sat down next to me and slowly let her head fall down on the pillows. "I feel horrible. It must be somethin' I ate."

"I'll get you some water." I headed into the kitchen and grabbed her a bottle before returning to the room. Her eyes were closed, but opened when she heard me coming in. "Here. Sip this slowly."

She took a sip and sat it down on the table next to her. "Thanks. I'm actually glad you came instead of Noah. He'd give me a hard time about being creeped out so much over a glob of hair."

I wanted to reach over and grab her hand, but I knew it wasn't going to happen. She didn't know me, and as much as she reminded me of someone, I had to keep telling myself that she wasn't. "Do you need me to stick around for a bit? I can go watch television or something. With the rain I can't exactly work with Titan today."

"I don't care if you stick around. I probably won't be good company though."

"It's fine." I stood up and started to head out of the room. "If you need anything just let me know. I'm just going to turn on a movie."

Once I was in the living room I sat on the couch wondering what I was actually doing. This woman didn't want me sticking around bothering her. Clearly she wasn't feeling well. Still, I couldn't bring myself to leave her.

A couple minute later she surprised me by coming out and joining me on the couch. I pulled a blanket down over her legs and rested her head on the opposite end of the furniture. I flipped through the channels until I found a movie, and was content with whatever it might be about.

I'm not real sure how long I was there before I fell asleep. Isabella must have dozed off before me, otherwise she probably would have asked me to leave. Instead I woke to someone yelling at me.

It was Noah, and he didn't look happy.

In the doorway between the kitchen and living room he stood, both hand on his hips. "What are you doin'?"

I sat up, realizing that I was leaning over on her knees. It was an honest mistake, but he wasn't seeing it that way. "We were just watching a movie, that's all. I must have fallen asleep."

It would have been easier to explain that she'd been sick, but from the look on her face I could tell that she didn't want him knowing anything. "What's the big deal, Noah? He helped me fix the bathroom and I told him to stay and watch a movie."

He got up in my face and pointed his finger. "You need to leave."

I stood up and smiled at her before walking outside. Honestly, I'd never seen Noah so upset, and certainly hadn't done anything to deserve that type of response out of him.

I could hear screaming coming from the house, but refused to go back in. A couple minutes later Noah came out and walked toward me. "You need to back off when it comes to her, Rusty. You do a lot around here and I appreciate it, but my cousin is off limits. I don't' care how many chicks you take to your trailer. Your business is your own, but she's my business. I've protected her our whole lives, and I won't have her hurt again, especially by someone that works for me. Are we clear?"

Even though I hated what he was saying, I valued having a roof over my head, and to be able to hold a job without question. I had to abide by his rules, no matter how hard they were to do. "Yeah, I get it. Just to be clear, nothing happened. I've never even tried to touch your cousin."

"Keep it that way, man. She's got issues with guys that you don't even want to begin to understand. To keep the peace in my family I've got to be a dick about it. I hope you understand."

I did. Noah loved her like she was his sister. Him protecting her was an instinct. If I'd only had that kind of instinct before my life may have been different. "I do. No worries, man. I'm just going to head home."

That night it was harder than ever to not think about her. My mind went back to being alone with her, and how for the first time she'd appreciated my company. It may have been nothing but a few hours, but it meant more than she'd ever know.

A knock at my door well after midnight caught my immediate attention. I grabbed a bat and headed toward the door, being extra cautious. When I opened it up and saw her standing there I pulled her inside the trailer. "What are you doing out in the rain?"

She put her hood down and reached inside of her pocket. "I figured you need this in the mornin'. I found it in the couch earlier." My phone was placed into my hand, but I never took my eyes from hers.

"Thanks. I appreciate that."

"Look, I'm really sorry about Noah earlier. He's got a hair up his ass when it comes to me."

I pulled out a chair and offered it to her. "Sit down for a minute?"

She sat and took off her jacket. "I probably shouldn't be tellin' you this, but I was involved with this guy who cheated and lied to me. We started datin' in high school and I thought he was my future. We attended the same college, and talked bout being married and having a life together. It all turned to shit when I found out he was still havin' relations with his first love. He may have been mine, but apparently I wasn't his. When I went home a couple months ago I promised Noah that I wouldn't see this particular guy again, and the first thing I did was run right to him. I ran right back to his bed and gave myself to him completely. Only minutes after it was all said and done did I realize that I'd become the other woman. He actually had pictures of them hidden, so that I wouldn't see them. Anyway, you can imagine how fucked up it made me. I had to call my little brothers to come pick me up that night. One of them gave him a good beatin'. I thought it would make me feel better, but it didn't. That night you heard me cryin', it was because of that. Anyway, that's the reason that Noah's bein' irrational. He doesn't trust me to make the right decisions, and even though I lied to him, he still thinks I snuck and saw Tate. He knows me better than I know myself, which is why he's always determined to be my keeper. So don't take it personal. It's not you at all."

This was more than she's ever talked to me before. I couldn't let her leave, not when she was opening up like this. I reached over the table to touch her hand, but pulled away right before. "It's not a big deal. He loves you, that's all."

"Sometimes Noah loves me too much. He forgets that I'm an adult too. If I wanted to have some hot affair with you, I don't need his permission. Not that it's ever goin' to happen. I'm just sayin' in general."

Hearing her say that sent a jolt right to my cock. I knew if I tried to stand up she'd notice it immediately. I clenched my jaw and tried to stay calm. "I appreciate you telling me. It probably wasn't a good idea to fall asleep next to you. I can't imagine what he must think."

"He thinks we're fuckin'. Noah has a one-track mind."

"We both know that's not the case." Not that I would be against it happening. Imagining her soft skin against my hands was something that I'd been doing for as long as I'd known her. If she knew that she'd be so creeped out that I was sure to get fired. It was something I'd have to keep a secret.

"Of course it isn't. I'm real sorry if it caused problems for you. I know you like to keep to yourself."

"I keep to myself to avoid drama, yes. That doesn't mean that I'm not willing to help out a friend. I know we're strangers, but I can assure you that your secret is safe with me. I don't plan on causing you any trouble."

She seemed to be pleased with my response. After standing up she held out her hand. "Thanks for listenin' and helpin' me out earlier. For what it's worth, it was nice to sit in a room with someone that wasn't judgin' me."

No. Instead she was sitting in a room with someone that fantasized about being with her. I don't know what was worse.

"It's not a problem."

"I better get goin'. It's startin' to thunder." I watched her putting on her jacket and walking out the door. I couldn't help by peer through the window as she pulled away on a golf-cart.

Isabella had confided in me. It meant that in some way she trusted me. Against Noah's threats I had to find a way to know more about her. Even if I had to sneak around, she was worth the risk. I had to figure out why I felt so drawn to her, so I could come up with a solution to make it stop.

Chapter 9
Isabella

For the next week I threw up each morning, and sometimes during the evenings. My stomach turned, and every single smell made me gag. It wasn't until I was driving home after the fifth day that I realized what it could be. I almost drove my car off the side of the road into a ravine because of it.

It couldn't be true.

There was no way.

It had only been one night; one time.

I turned my car around and went into the pharmacy, determined to prove my theory wrong. After buying three different tests, I went straight home. It took me a while to build up the courage to walk into the bathroom and pee on those sticks. A part of me wanted to just think I could wish myself not to be, and it to work.

When I'd run out of reasons to not do it, I took two of the tests and ran out of the bathroom. My heart was racing, and I was certain that I was about to pass out. Silently, I sat on the couch staring down the hallway at the bathroom door. My fate sat on two sticks inside of it, and I was too afraid to see what they said.

Then my cousin came barging in my kitchen door. He had company too. Behind him came Rusty, who was helping him carry this cabinet that was supposed to sit on the back of my toilet. I panicked.

I excused myself into the bathroom, desperately trying to find a place to hide the tests. When I heard the door closing I looked out the window to see Noah standing outside on his phone. I looked down at the tests, seeing the results. A lump formed in my throat as I gathered the two stick and all of the rest of the garbage and packed it into a white plastic bag. I tied to top and ran out into the kitchen as fast as I could. Tears were streaming down my cheeks when I got to where Rusty was standing. "I need a favor before he comes in here."

"Sure, What do you need?"

"Take this out front and hide it somewhere. Once he tells you to leave pick it up and throw it in the dumpster that gets picked up tomorrow."

"What's in it?"

I shoved it against his chest. "Rusty, please don't ask me any questions. Just get rid of it. I'm begging you."

I heard Noah walking up the porch steps. Rusty gave me a concerned look but rushed toward the front door. He came back inside before Noah walked into the living room. To hide my sudden emotional breakdown, I retreated to my bedroom, acting like I was indisposed.

"Just set it up for me, will ya?"

I could hear the guys moving it around, and then the house got quiet. A knock on my bedroom door alarmed me. I opened it slowly, trying to come up with a reason to be crying. That's when I noticed that it was Rusty. "I took care of that thing for you. I'm ridin' back with Noah, so I'll come back by in a few minutes to pick it up and throw it away."

I reached over and touched his arm. "You're a life saver. Thanks so much."

"You all right?"

"I will be. I promise." I was lying. Nothing was going to be okay. My life had just taken a turn for the worse and I didn't know what I was going to do about it.

"Okay. If you need to talk you know where to find me."

He left without another word, which I was grateful for. The last thing I wanted to do was stand around talking when my whole life was falling apart.

Once everyone was gone I fell to the floor and

let the real tears come. I'd been careless one time, and now was faced with the most horrifying decision of my life. How I was going to be able to face my family was beyond me. Not to mention what I was supposed to do with my future.

Both of those sticks had read the same. Two lines gave me a positive result. I was pregnant with Tate's child, and I had no idea what I was going to do. I didn't even know who I could talk to about it. My family would all do the math. They'd warned me about seeing him, and I lied to every single one of them. Now I was in this predicament with nowhere to turn. To make matters worse, this was going to force me to contact Tate, which I promised myself that I was never going to do again.

If I knew anything about him I knew he'd want to be a part of his child's life. The idea of sharing custody with me made my stomach curl. Instantly I was running to the toilet, throwing up what I left in my stomach.

For the next several hours I cried to myself alone in bed. I'd made the wrong choices and now I was being punished for it. My parents were going to lose all respect for me, not to mention my cousin. He'd never forgive for this; for lying to him of all people.

This secret that my brother's had promised to take to the grave was about to bite us all in the ass and I didn't see any way around it.

The next week flew by. I contacted my doctor, but already knew how far along I was. I'd been with one person one time in the past year. The life growing inside of me was a result of that night, and even though it had ended terribly, I couldn't bring myself to consider abortion. There was no way that I could go through with something like that and be able to live with myself. Life was too precious to me, and had my mother felt that way than I wouldn't even be on the earth right now to be going through all of this.

The ground was dropping out from under me, which wasn't surprising considered the predicament I was in. As the days went by it got harder to accept. I knew it was only a matter of time before someone found out, and then I'd have to face the music. My secret would be out and the whole family would know. They'd never look at me the same, and I'd never be able to forgive myself. I'd pride myself on being honest, and this little lie had resulted in a life. The idea of being a mother scared the shit out of me, and being a single mother was even more frightening.

The only thing I was sure of at this point was that I wanted my baby, and I didn't want to have to tell Tate. I wondered how long I could get away without him finding out. My family would only be able to protect me for so long. I imagined walking down the road one day and passing him. I thought about my child seeing his father, and them having them same eyes.

With everything going on inside of my head, I refused to hang out with my cousin and his fiancée. After a week they were starting to ask questions that I didn't have answers for. Unfortunately, with everything on my mind I'd forgotten about going dress shopping with Shalan and aunt Van. They showed up at my house on a Saturday morning and I was in the bathroom throwing my guts up.

Right away they started asking the one question that I didn't want to answer. "Sweetheart, you couldn't be pregnant could you?"

I shook my head. "Of course not. What would give you that idea?"

My aunt Van handed me a paper towel. "Well, you're throwing up. You look like death, and you're tired all of the time."

I turned away, unable to face her when I lied my ass off. "I'm not pregnant. I just have a virus or somethin'."

"We'll just go without you today. If we find something we'll send you a picture. Is that okay?"

"Yeah. It's fine. Sorry I can't go, Shalan. I promise that I'll be there for everything else."

She hugged me and they both headed out.

That's when I think I started to panic again. I needed to know that Rusty had thrown all of the evidence away. If they were asking if I was pregnant I didn't want it to be because any of them saw the tests in the trash.

It took me a while to hunt him down. When I found him, he was too preoccupied with Titan to call out his name. For a couple minutes I sat there watching him with the large horse. Rusty had this gentle side of him when it came to being around Titan. He was patient and gentle, which made the horse respond positively, instead of aggressive. When Rusty spotted me he started walking in my direction. I met him halfway. "I need to talk to you."

"Are you okay?" He seemed concerned.

"Just tell me that you got rid of that bag I gave you. Tell me you hid it in the trash and that it was picked up before anyone could see it."

"I did what you said, Iz." It still gave me chills when he called me that. "I threw it away that night, just like you said to do."

"Okay. Just checkin'. Sorry I bothered you." I looked down at the ground and started to walk away.

Rusty came running after men. "Iz, wait. Is something wrong?"

I probably should have kept walking away, except I knew that he was the one person around that would listen to me and not go crazy. "Not really. I'm in trouble, and I don't know what to do."

"What kind of trouble are you in?" His concern made me feel like he was way off with theories.

"Not anything illegal, if that's what you think. It's personal. I really don't know what I'm goin' to do. Everything's a mess. My family is goin' to freak out." I started to sob, and felt strong arms wrapping around me. He smelled like sweat and after-shave, reminding me that a man was comforting me. Instead of being freaked out, I let my arms wrap around his back. "I'm so scared. They're never goin' to forgive me, Rusty. They'll never trust me again."

He pulled away and looked right into my eyes. "Tell me. What's really going on, Iz. I won't say anything."

I looked away, feeling ashamed to even admit it out loud. "I'm pregnant. I'm pregnant with my ex's child, and I don't know what to do." It was all I could get out before I lost it.

He pulled me back into his chest and held me tight. "It's going to be okay."

He had no idea how bad it was going to be for me, but I appreciated the temporary comfort. "Thanks, but it's not. I can't lose my family over this."

Rusty grabbed the sides of my face and looked right into my eyes. "Just try to calm down. You're going to be okay, and I'm goin to help you make sure of it."

Chapter 10

Rusty

She had no idea what I meant

when I'd said it, and neither did I. All I knew was that she was in trouble and something inside of me was determined to be the one to help her.

I held her there in that pasture for a long time. Her hair smelled so sweet, and I couldn't help letting my lips linger against it. This was the closest I'd ever been to her. Though the circumstances were desperate, I knew she needed me.

I helped her back to her house that evening, and stuck around for a while until I got her settled down. It was hard to leave when I knew she'd fall apart as soon as I was gone, but I couldn't take the chance of getting caught by Noah.

That next morning I got up early and snuck

over again. She answered the door and let me inside. I could see that she hadn't gotten much sleep. "I'm just checking on you."

"I'm still the same." She tried to conjure up a smile, but failed horribly. "I never imagined that my life would be like this. I've never had to make a decision without everyone in my family before. Just knowin' how upset they'll be is makin' it even harder. How am I supposed to do this?"

I reached for her hand. "You've got a friend, Iz."

She looked up at me with such sad eyes. "I don't deserve it. I've been a bitch to you since we met."

"Well it ain't like anyone else is knocking on my friend door. Besides, you had your reasons to steer clear of me. I'm not saying that I'm a good influence, but I sure as hell can't stand seeing you so distraught. Your family is going to come around. It may take them awhile, but they'll understand."

She shook her head. "No. They won't, Rusty. They hate Tate that much. They'll want me to abort the baby so that I don't have anything to do with him. This pregnancy forces me to let him back into my life. Don't you see? This is the worst thing that could ever happen."

I understood why she was scared, but this was a baby, a miracle that she'd been given. No matter what her family thought, it was always going to be her decision. "What can I do for you?"

She shrugged. "Nothin'. The damage is done."

I brought her hand up to my lips and kissed it. "If you need to talk, you know where to find me. It doesn't matter if it's in the middle of the night."

"Rusty, I appreciate that. Are you just bein' nice to me because you think I might give you a chance?"

This time I was the one shrugging. "Would it really make a difference?"

"No. I'm sorry. I wish I could offer you some kind of hope, but we both know that's not goin' to happen. I'm just not interested in being with anyone. After this, I'll probably never be interested. It's not you. I just can't dig my grave anymore than I already have."

I understood, but it was still a kick to the balls. "It's fine. Friends then."

She seemed reluctant, but knowing that I was all she had, she couldn't refuse.

I can't say that it didn't bother me. I wanted more from her, and it was never going to happen.

For the next few weeks the more I tried to be a friend to Isabella, the harder she tried to push me away. I saw her falling down a wormhole and couldn't seem to figure out a way to pick her back up out of it.

Her cousin was too focused on his new house, and the wedding to be able to notice that something was seriously going on with her. To make matters worse, she was doing a great job keeping it a secret from everyone.

I stopped by at least once a week to check on her, only to hear the same load of crap about her trying to handle things herself. It wasn't until I overheard her on the phone that I decided I needed to step in. I'd stopped by to give her dinner one night after work. She was standing on her porch on the cell phone. Since I approached the house from the opposite direction, she never knew I was standing there.

It was obvious right away that she was making an appointment at the clinic. She was responding to questions that they'd ask when one was planning on terminating a pregnancy. Right away I had to clench my fists and fight to keep my cool. She didn't know how lucky she was to have something so wonderful growing inside of her. She had a chance to give life, which was precious in it self. I couldn't allow her go through with it.

So I did what every person in my situation would have done. I listened to the rest of her conversation, and waited to hear her confirm the date and time. With that information I followed her on the day of the appointment.

She parked her vehicle and sat in the hot car with her head down. That's when I realized that she was broken up over it. The weak woman didn't want to end her pregnancy, but she didn't see any way around it without losing her wonderful family.

I couldn't sit in my truck and observe her over there in so much pain. My feet hit the pavement, and I started walking across the parking lot before I even knew what I was going to say to her. I knocked on the window with my knuckles and waited for her to respond.

Mascara was running down both of her cheeks. "Isabella, please get out of the car."

"What are you doin' here? Did you follow me?" I could tell she was both frantic and pissed off.

"Does it matter? I can't let you do this, and I'm not leaving here unless you're coming with me."

"Who are you to tell me what to do with my life? This is my decision. Don't you get that? Stop trying to fix my problems, Rusty. I don't want to be helped. You obviously either spied on me or followed me. Both are appalling to me. How could you invade my privacy, after you of all people know what I'm already goin' through? What is with you? Just get out of here and leave me alone!"

"I'm not who you think I am, Iz."

"Don't call me that. Do you hear me? Don't you dare call me that."

She was offended, and it hurt my feelings. Sure, I'd overstepped boundaries, but only because she was making a terrible mistake. I couldn't sit around at the ranch knowing what she was about to do. I couldn't let her make a mistake that she'd carry for the rest of her life. "I'm sorry you're pissed. It's not what you think. I would never hurt you."

She began to sob, making it hard for me to understand her words. "You're hurtin' me now. Don't you get that? I just want it to be over. I can't do this anymore. I can't ruin my life."

Her anger was only making her communicate with me, and I was almost happy about that. I crossed my arms over my chest. "Get out of your car. I need to show you something. You need to know why I'm not going to let you go inside of this building."

She laid her head on the steering wheel, exhausted and furious. I waited, and when she realized that I wasn't going to leave, she finally climbed out of her car.

After grabbing her purse and locking the door, I drug her gently by her arm to my truck and helped her inside. "Where are you takin' me? Hopefully it's to kill me, so I don't have to deal with this anymore. Maybe if I'm gone they'll never know what a disappointment I am to them."

Once I had her inside of the truck, I walked to my side and entered the vehicle. I closed the driver's side door and looked at her before turning on the ignition. "Look here. Nothing about your life is a mistake. Your family ain't going to disown you, and they sure as hell don't want you dead. Buckle up. It's a long drive."

I didn't tell her where we were going, even after we crossed state lines and hours started to pass.

While Isabella cried to herself, I thought about what I was about to do. This wasn't something I ever thought I'd be able to tell someone. This pain that I'd felt for so long was about to get worse.

I couldn't let her give up on her baby, or her life, not when it meant so much to so many, especially me. She needed to know she was worth something.

The sun was starting to set when we made it to the destination. My hands clenched the steering wheel as the sleeping companion next to me opened her eyes and looked around. Even though I was having second thoughts, I knew I wasn't going to be able to turn around without seeing this through. If I could save a life because of this, it was worth the pain.

She was about to see the real me.

She'd know my secrets.

She'd know my pain.

And she'd know why I had to leave it all behind.

This hardheaded woman, that kept rejecting me in every way, was about to find out that I wasn't at all who she thought I was. She could take my new life away from me if she wanted to. This could all backfire in my face.

I had to risk it.

She was worth it.

Chapter 11
Isabella

To be honest, I had no idea what I was thinking when I got into the truck with this guy. He was obviously stalking me, and now we were in a different state, too far from anyone that would be able to save me when he started murdering me, and cutting me into a million pieces. In all of the times that he'd offered to be a friend, I'd never felt so uncomfortable as I did now.

The long drive to wherever he was taking me gave me time to think. It made me realize that no matter what happened with my family, I'd never be able to get rid of my baby. He or she was mine. I could do it without ever telling Tate and deal with the consequences, even if they were too harsh to imagine.

A part of me couldn't stop thinking about my

mom and dad, and the look on their faces when they learned the news. They'd be so hurt, and I feared seeing that.

More than twenty years ago my mother was in this same situation. She prided herself on letting us kids know what it was like to go through, and that she'd never want us to have to do it. Here I was repeating history. The only difference was that I didn't have someone that was going to sweep me off my feet and show me what real love feels like. I was in this alone, and I was so afraid.

When we first pulled to make a stop in front of an old church, I wondered how far I could get before he caught up to me. I looked around at the landscape wondering if there was something I could pick up and hit him with if I needed to.

It was horrible, but in my head, I was considering that this might be a fight to stay alive.

Rusty remained quiet in the seat next to me. I finally got up the nerve to turn and look at him and noticed that his eyes were already on me. I swallowed the lump in my throat. "Are you goin' to kill me? I read somewhere that a cemetery is the perfect place to hide a body." Why was I feeding him with ideas? He already had a plan for me. I wondered if there was a shovel in the back of the truck.

He didn't move his head from the steering wheel. "I told you before that I wasn't going to hurt you. Is that what you think of me? You think I'm a murderer? I've done nothing but been nice to you, and still you think I'm a terrible person. What do I have to do to prove that I'm not?"

"What am I supposed to think? You just drove me to Bumfuck. There ain't a house around within yellin' distance. Just so you know, my family will find out. They'll kill you if you harm me in any way."

He started to laugh at me and shook his head. "You're hopeless, Iz."

"Isabella," I corrected.

"Whatever. Get out of the truck. There's something I need to show you."

I was reluctant, but had a feeling he was going to force me if I didn't. Just because he was saying he wasn't going to harm me didn't mean it wasn't going to happen. I hopped down from the truck, and watched him start walking way from me.

For a few seconds I looked behind me, wondering if somewhere inside of the old church in the distance I'd be able to find help. I certainly didn't want to drive home for hours with this guy. He'd clearly lost his marbles, and I didn't want to help him find them.

This was probably why he worked on the ranch. Maybe his family had him declared insane and he had to run away to elude the insane asylum. Obviously he wasn't taking any of his prescribed medicine. If he had been I was sure he wouldn't have practically kidnapped me from the clinic.

"Are you coming or not?"

My heart jumped when I heard him talking to me. I turned to see him standing there waiting for me. "Yeah. I'm comin'."

I hated that he waited for me to get close before he started walking through the graveyard again. At first I wasn't sure what he was doing. We walked for a while and then he started looking down at the ground, as if he'd lost something. Then I noticed the tiny headstones getting bigger in size. The dates on the graves were becoming more recent.

We walked past a few more before coming to a stone bench. He circled around it and ducked down, wiping off where a name would be. I sat on the bench, still wondering what he was doing. "Are you lookin' for somethin' in particular?"

"No. I found them."

"You found who?" I was at least a little bit curious.

"I'm glad you're sitting, because this is probably going to take me a while. You say you don't know me, so obviously you refuse to trust me. That baby growing inside of you needs to be protected. I know you're probably thinking I've lost it. The truth is, I did lose it, but it was a long time ago. Now I just live my life the best I know how to do, because I know there's no going back."

"What did you do, Rusty? Tell me why you brought me all the way out here, because I've tried to keep calm, but this had gone far enough. If you don't

start explainin' right now I'm goin' to start screamin'."
Was this the graves of people he'd killed?

"My family is...," he said in a whisper. "Sorry, this is harder than I thought." When his body sort of collapsed onto the ground, I started to realize that this wasn't really about me at all. This poor man was in pain and I had no idea why.

"Your family? Do they live near here? Is this your parents graves?"

He shook his head. "No. It's not my parents. My precious little girl is buried here, Isabella. She was three when God took her away from me." He wiped the edge of his eye, causing me to look at his face. His lips trembled as he began talking again. "She was my everything. I lived and breathed to be near her. She was so beautiful. Her pretty blonde hair was always so full of curls, and it would bounce when she would walk or run." He looked into the distance, trying to compose himself to carry on. "Her eyes, were so green, just like her mother's. I'll never be able to get them out of my mind, even if I wanted to. One look at either of them and I was pudding in their hands."

I heard him sniffle and take another break from talking. In a matter of minutes all of my fear had dissipated. "Oh my God. Rusty, I had no idea." Imagining anyone losing their child was awful, but this man was clearly in so much pain that he'd tried to bury it, by running away. "How did it happen?"

He sniffled and wiped his face again. "Honestly, I don't even know if the doctors were certain. They called it bacterial meningitis. She was fine in the morning and dead by dinner. We had no warning. I still remember that day. She came into our bedroom and woke us both up. She kept begging for us to take her to the park, but I had yard work to do, and I told her no." He broke down, making it difficult to speak. "All she wanted to do was go on the damn swings and I couldn't give her a few minutes of my time. How could I be so selfish?" His sad eyes were so lost.

My body lurched forward until my arms were around his crouched body. "I'm so sorry, Rusty." I could feel hot tears building in my own eyes. I pictured this healthy little girl smiling, and then her being gone. The agony that he must have gone through every single day since then had to take a toll on him. "I can't imagine what you must have felt that day."

"I just don't understand why. I was a good father. I protected her, and made sure she wasn't ever scared. To this day it haunts me when I think about the way she looked in that hospital bed. It was like she knew I couldn't save her. I've never felt someone's fear before that day. I've never felt pain until that moment she took her last breath."

My cheeks were wet as I continued to try to fight my own emotions. Being pregnant didn't make it any easier. Then I realized why he'd brought me here. I knew exactly what he was trying to force me to see, and any ill feelings I had for the man were suddenly gone. "She knew you were there with her, Rusty. That has to count for somethin'."

"This is the first time I've been here. I couldn't come before, because it only makes it all play out in my head again. I hate myself for wanting to forget her. I just don't want to hurt anymore. I don't want to feel the constant ache that I have for her."

I pulled him closer and let the grown man cry. "I get it, Rusty."

He moved back and looked up at me. His eyes were so glossed over I wondered if he could actually see me as he spoke. "Do you? Can you understand how life is precious?"

"Of course. Look, I wouldn't have gone through with it. That's why I didn't go directly inside." He was questioning my ability to be compassionate. I had to stay calm to be able to comfort him without getting defensive.

"You don't know how lucky you are. A child is a beautiful blessing. When you think your life is over, you'll have that one person that's going to love you unconditionally. There isn't anything that I wouldn't give to have just more day with her. I'm begging you, Isabella, please don't give up that chance at happiness. Even if it's only for a little amount of time, being a parent is the most wonderful gift."

A rush of painful emotions hit me all at once. The fact that I'd even considered making that appointment said a lot about my faith in my family, and myself.

Then Rusty moved to the side. There wasn't just one name on the headstone.

Tillman

Simone & Sydney
Mother & Daughter

He looked from me to the gravestone and I watched his body sag. "My wife couldn't take the loss of our daughter. She couldn't handle any of it. On the day that our daughter passed away she fainted. The doctor gave her some pills to relax, so we'd be able to make arrangements and such. When we arrived at the funeral home she used the ladies room and never came back out. She took the whole bottle, and sat on the cold floor with a picture of our daughter in her hands."

I covered my mouth with my hands. "Oh no."

He cried harder as he attempted to finish. "She just wanted to be with our daughter again. She couldn't live without her."

What was I supposed to say to him? I didn't know where to begin. He'd brought me our here to save a life, while drudging up the memories of something that no person should ever have to endure. "I am so so sorry." It was all I could come up with. While fighting my own tears I sat there watching him break down over the loss of his family. I wondered how many nights he'd sat awake wondering what could have been if they'd both lived. I thought about him being alone in that old trailer, and how he'd preferred to bottle up all of that pain for so long.

It made me feel like the devil. I'd flaunted my perfect life in front of him, while he desperately tried to communicate. He'd been so kind to me, while living with a secret that ripped him apart.

A wave of regret hit me, causing me to get up and leave him sitting there alone. I couldn't handle it any longer. It was as if I'd known them and watched it all fall apart. I was living through his memories of them, experiencing what he went through firsthand. It was all too much to bear.

One thing was for certain as I watched him from afar. I was going to keep my baby, and treasure every single moment of that child's life, because it was a blessing. My family was going to have to help me, and they wouldn't be happy about it, but I didn't care.

Chapter 12
Rusty

When I started driving, I hadn't considered what it would be like for me. I couldn't have known that I'd break down in front of her like that. Even when I was losing control of my emotions, I could feel her responding in a way that she'd never done before.

For the first time she trusted me. All it took was for me to bear my soul to her.

She needed to know, though. She needed to know how precious life was, so that any inclination of wanting an abortion would be gone forever.

After I'd broken down and told her about my

family, she gave me some time to be alone. It was difficult for me to be there, knowing that beneath me in the ground were the two people that I'd loved more than life itself.

I wished that I could hate my wife for taking her own life, but understood why she felt it necessary to do so. Living every single day, waking up and knowing they were gone, was my own personal hell. For so long I'd been alone, never wanting to get close to anyone, in fear of losing them. I'd made peace with living in seclusion, because it gave me a sense of security.

Then I saw her one day from afar. She was feeding one of the horses an apple, while I stood in the stables watching. Even before I peered into those familiar green eyes, I was attracted to something else. She had this contagious smile, and when she was all by herself, she'd hold her head up high, as if nothing could bring her down.

Things had changed since that first day she'd caught my eye. Isabella had gone through a lot, and it had taken a toll on the way she carried herself.

I don't know why I thought taking her to my family's gravesite would somehow bring her to change her mind. I suppose that for a little while I lost my ability to rationalize with what I was doing. The moment I saw her so torn up in front of that clinic I knew that nothing was going to stop me until I had my point across.

The problem with my theory was that there were going to be after effects. Isabella knew my secret, and it was only a matter of time before the whole Mitchell family found out. Then I'd be faced with a decision. I could face the life that I'd left behind, or move on to another place where my past wouldn't come back to haunt me.

For the time being, my focus had to stay on Isabella. She wouldn't admit that she needed me, but I knew otherwise.

When I finally gained enough courage to move, I noticed that she was standing against my truck. I walked slowly, trying to think of something to say the lighten the mood. In my sudden situation I knew that nothing was going to work. It was a good thing that she took the lead. "Hey. How about we get somethin' to eat. My treat."

In that moment I knew that this whole ordeal had turned the tables on who was the vulnerable one. Isabella felt sorry for me, and she was willing to be nice to make it easier to cope.

At any rate, I wanted to be around her as much as possible. "Sure. That sounds nice."

My old hometown remained the same as the day I'd left it. I drove on the outskirts, avoiding passing by where I used to live with my wife and child. I'd already suffered enough for one day. To make sure that I didn't see anyone I knew, I took her to an old truck stop that served breakfast twenty-four hours. I could tell that she was fine with it when she started talking about one that she'd been to a long time ago with her parents.

By the time the waitress came to our table I'd heard all about their road trip that they took one summer. It was nice hearing her talk about details in her life. Had it been one day earlier I would have only gotten a wave. Somehow confessing my tragedy had changed the way she acted around me.

"I'm sorry again for today. I had no right to put you through that. I'm embarrassed to say that I don't find it comforting that you saw me lose it like that."

She reached cross the table and touched my hand. "It's okay. I totally understand."

I could have played the hand that I'd been dealt with two ways.

I could take advantage of the situation and manipulate her into liking me, or I could face the facts and understand that she was doing this out of pity. Either way it was a loss for my ego. No matter how I tried to spin it I knew she didn't like me, and that she'd never be interested. If I wanted this girl's attention, I was going to have to get it some other way.

"This town is pretty nice. I would have never pegged you for living in Indiana."

I took a sip of soda and laughed at the way she was looking at me. It was strange to have her trying to read me.

"This was where my wife's family is from. I

lived in Maryland up until I was fifteen. We moved to Indiana when my father sold his company. I met Simone in college."

She cut me off before I could continue telling her my story. "Wait. Did you just say you went to college?"

"Yeah. I went to college."

"And you're workin' on a ranch, shovelin' shit for a livin'?"

I chuckled and messed around with the glass, trying to avoid answering. When I looked up she gave me this look like she wasn't going to let up until I told her everything. "I left that life behind me a long time ago, Iz."

She put her head down and sighed. "I don't blame you. I don't know what I would have done if I were in your shoes, Rusty. I feel like this whole day is my fault."

"It's not. I think it's something I needed to do for myself."

"Does my cousin know about any of this?"

I didn't want to be considered a liar, but I certainly couldn't make up enough excuses to justify keeping my past from my employer. If anyone should have known what I'd been through it was him. "He doesn't know anything, and I'd really appreciate it if he didn't find out. Some things are left buried, especially when they pertain my sanity."

"I get it. I can't blame you. My family can be nosey. You're lucky Noah isn't like his daddy. He's more withdrawn. I think as long as you keep doin' a good job he'll never ask."

"What about your secret," I quickly changed the subject. "When do you plan on telling him, and the rest of your family?"

She shrugged, and I watched her face scrunch up. "I don't know. I suppose that I could tell Shalan, or maybe my grandmother, but everyone else won't support me. I think it would be best if I just waited until after my first trimester was over. That way they can't try to talk me out of it. If I'm really goin' to go through with this pregnancy than I have a lot of things I need to figure out. I'm not ready to deal with their added stress. This is too big of a change to have to adapt to."

I folded my hands and leaned forward. "I'm going to let you in on a secret about becoming a parent. No matter how much you try to prepare, you're never really ready. You're going to be a great mother. The moment you hold him or her in your arms for the first time you'll know what I'm talking about. It really is the most beautiful moment of my life."

Right away I thought about the worst moment of my life. I still wasn't sure which hurt the worse; losing Simone, or Sydney. I'd never want to compare one to the other, but it was literally an unforgettable prolonged pain. To deal with their losses at the same time was horrendous. I went through the motions, with no real life coming out of me. For the most part I was dead inside. How anyone expected me to pick up those pieces and move forward was beyond my reasoning. They obviously had no idea what it was like to wake up one day and be without air. They couldn't fathom what it felt like to look around my house and see only reminders of them everywhere.

I had to leave it all behind, because I couldn't handle it any longer. It was either leave that life or put a bullet in my skull.

"Do you have a picture of them?" Her question sent immediate chills to my spine. Opening my wallet had become a chore, because I knew their faces were always inside. Reluctant, I pulled it open and pushed it across the table.

Her eyes increased in size when she saw in the pictures what I'd been seeing every time I looked at her. The resemblance was so similar, and there was no denying it.

"Oh my God. We could be sisters."

I played with my hands, contemplating the notion of talking about it further. "Yeah. You can imagine what it was like for me to see you from afar on that first day. I was a bit freaked out."

"I bet. They're both very beautiful." She started to laugh. "Is that conceited?"

I actually found humor in her question, enough to break a smile myself. "No. Even though you resemble each other, you're very different. Simone was a wonderful mother. In fact, there was nothing she wouldn't do for our daughter, but she was quiet, and somewhat shy. She liked the idea of the three of us living in a secluded cabin, where we didn't have to associate with society."

"That sounds like a beautiful life."

I paused. It would have been beautiful, and I would have tried my best to give it to her, had she not taken her life. "I reckon it would have been, had she stuck around."

"I'm sorry again for what you've had to endure. There's no real words I can say to you that will put a dent in the pain you've suffered." She looked down at the table, just when the waitress brought us our food.

For a couple minutes we both got started eating. I supposed I could have left the conversation alone, and forgotten about the way it was getting to me again, but opening up to someone after so long, especially with Isabella, made me feel alive. It reminded me that I was still living and breathing.

"It's been hard for me, Iz. Can I call you that now?" I waited for her response.

"Sure. I'm gettin' used to it."

"Anyway, it's been trying at times. For the first few months I completely shut down. My parents did their best, but it was a lost cause. I stopped working, and eventually lost the house. I let it go into foreclosure; lost everything because I couldn't cope. Once I had to move back into their house they did everything they could to get me out of my coma-like state."

She took a bite of food and spoke at the same time. Some would have been offended by her table mannerism, but I found it cute how comfortable she instantly felt being around me. "How did you get better? What made you up and leave?"

"I heard my parents fighting. They were discussing how I'd ruined my life. I know they didn't mean it to be offensive, but I took it the worst way possible. In the middle of the night I packed a bag and left. For a while I just drove around, doing odd and end jobs to stay afloat. Then my bank account ran dry, and I knew that I could either be homeless or find something more permanent. I've always loved horses, and spent my summers working with a trainer, so I knew enough to make an impression on your cousin. He gave me a week to show him progress, and after I did he offered me the position. I never looked back after that, and even though they're still on my mind almost every second of the day, I was able to start living again, well the best I could of course." I looked down at my food and shook my head from side to side. "I can't believe that I'm telling you all of this."

"It's okay. Really. I'm glad you're able to talk about it. That's got to be progress. Don't you think?" I shouldn't have looked into her eyes. The moment I did I felt all kinds of confused. She must have sensed it too. "I have to ask you somethin', Rusty, and I don't want you to take offense to it."

135

"Ask away." I already knew the question. I could see it in her body language. I'd watched her enough to know when she was nervous, scared, or confused.

"It's obvious that you have some kind of attraction to me. At times it's been a little creepy, but I get it now. I guess I'm just wonderin' if you feel the way you do because I look so much like her? I wouldn't blame you if it was true. I'd probably feel that way if I was in your shoes. It's like gettin' a second chance in some ways."

I couldn't look at her when I answered. It wasn't just a personal question she was asking. My answer could affect our friendship in the future. I had to be careful with my choice of words. "At first it was. I'm not going to lie. One look at you and I did feel like I was getting a second chance with Simone. It was short lived though. I mean, I knew you were someone else. Then I saw you screaming at your cousin and knew for sure that you were nothing like her. It only took me being around you a couple more times to realize that my attraction to you went beyond the resemblance. I wanted to know that indecisive woman that spoke her mind, and yet always seemed confused. I wanted to be there when you were down, and do whatever it took to make you smile. Being around you helps me want to live again." I put up my hands so she wouldn't get freaked out, or try to cut me off. "I get that you're not into me that way. I know I'm ten years older than you, and that your family would send me packing if I tried to pursue anything more than a friendship, but I also know that I'd be lying if I tried to deny it."

Isabella put her fork down on the table and placed her hands flat on either side of her plate. "I would have thought that gettin' knocked up by another man would change your opinion of me."

"You're in love with the guy. Why would that change the way I feel?"

"I was in love with him. There's a huge difference. As far as he goes, I hope his dick falls off. He doesn't deserve to be happy, not after the shit he pulled on me."

I started to laugh. She smiled and cocked her head to the side. "What's so funny?" she asked.

"It's that spunk that I think is fascinating. You don't hold anything in. Sometimes you're so brutally honest that it's painful." I continued to laugh after explaining, and she finally joined in. This was pure enjoyment for me. I needed this kind of connection, and it reminded me again why she was so different from Simone.

Then she did something that I wasn't prepared for. Her smile faded away and she peered into my eyes with some kind of intent that I'd never seen from her before. "Today has opened my eyes to the person behind the mask."

"Is that a good thing or bad?"

She smiled and cackled to herself. "I'm still decidin'."

I took a sip of my tea, never taking my eyes from hers. "Let me know when you've reached a verdict."

"Okay." This half-smile formed at the corner of her lips and she looked down at her plate. "Doesn't it gross you out that I'm pregnant?"

"Why would it? You're still you."

"I'm about to get terribly fat. I already have killer mood swings, and most of the time I have puke in my hair from mornin' sickness. Sorry for rainin' on your parade, but I'm not very desirable."

"It's true. You are going to gain weight. Some days you may become so crabby that nobody wants to be near you, but the morning sickness will soon pass. You're going to get this glow to you, and as your body transforms from a young woman to a loving mother, you'll rediscover yourself in ways you never knew possible."

"Is that what happened with your wife?"

I laughed. Simone was a happy woman when she carried Sydney. "No. I read a lot."

"You read pregnancy books?"

"In med school I did."

"What? You went to med school? Were you going to be a doctor?"

"A veterinarian. I had my own practice that I ran with my dad. He retired, and I took on the whole thing. That's why I can't go back. I ruined my father's legacy without a single apology."

She changed the mood by throwing me a compliment. "I can see you in one of those white lab coats. I bet you were a little sexy."

Her comment honestly made me blush. I'd never heard her compliment me in that way. "You think I'm sexy now, after everything I've told you?"

Isabella folded her hands and shot me a ornery grin. "Maybe."

"So old men can be sexy?" Something was happening between us. I could feel it, though I had to wonder what the reasoning behind it was.

"You're not that old."

"You didn't answer the question."

I watched her sipping the tea up from a straw. "I'm not goin' to."

I waved for the waitress to bring us our check. It was going to be a long drive back to Kentucky, and since I wasn't full of rage anymore it was certainly going to drag.

I paid for our meal and we started walking out to the truck. While I kept my eyes focused on where I was heading, she asked something that stopped me dead in my tracks. "You must hate me. I wouldn't blame you for it. I've been so shitty to you. If I'd have known..."

I didn't let her finish. "No. Of course I don't hate you." I paused and looked down at my hands before proceeding. "It's the opposite actually. Listen, I chose to keep my life a secret. I suppose I scared you with my stalker tendencies. I can assure you that it wasn't on purpose. I just didn't know how to go about getting you to notice me."

Her cheeks reddened as she looked away, seemingly embarrassed at my confession. "Doesn't it bother you that I'm ten years younger? I mean, when you were in elementary school I wasn't even born."

I let out a chuckle in light of her question. "If you haven't noticed, I am a man. Though I try to be a gentleman in most circumstances, I'd have to say that having a younger woman is sort of every man's dream, at least once."

I realized right away that they could have been construed as a come on. Before I could retract the statement, or at least rephrase it, she asked a question that changed everything.

"So, I was wonderin', are we goin' to drive home tonight, or get a room somewhere? To be honest, I'm kind of tired."

I never saw it coming, and wasn't positive what she was implying.

Chapter 13
Isabella

I couldn't believe that I'd said it. One minute I wanted to be as far away from him as physically possible and the next I was asking him to spend the night out of state in a hotel room.

To say that I was confused would have been an understatement.

There was no denying my attraction to him, though I wasn't sure if it was out of feeling sorry for him, or something else all together. Obviously I'd found him attractive before, and I think that's why it was so confusing to me.

Was my sudden interest in him something that was building, or something that had come on for my utter guilt of what he'd endured?

Rusty scratched his head, and I could tell he

had mixed feelings about my question. "We could get a room with two beds, for sure."

Right away I realized he was trying his hardest to make me feel comfortable. Little did he know that I was fighting a losing battle with my conscience. "That's what I thought, too." Far be it from me to give him false hope about hooking up. I was in no condition to lead him on, but I was also the one sitting silently imagining what it would be like if we did do something.

"Yeah, I guess it would be fine if we stayed somewhere local and made the drive in the morning. I apologize again for bringing you so far from home. My intentions were in the right place, I can assure you."

I smiled, still wondering if he was blowing me off, or being kind in fear of how I'd react. "If I had any doubts about my decision, they're all gone. I'm goin' to have this baby. Even if I'd made it inside of that building, there was no way I would have been able to go through with it. The decision to make the appointment wasn't my highest moment. You can imagine that it's been difficult for me to cope with this news."

"I can understand how one would think that an abortion is an easy out."

I appreciated his sympathy. "Thanks. It means a lot that you aren't lookin' at me like I was a monster."

He reached across the table and touched my

hand. I didn't pull away for two reasons. The first was that I knew he was being genuinely kindhearted. The second reason was because his touch gave me chills throughout my body. "I would never see you that way."

I had to look away when the heat of his words overwhelmed me. I could feel my heartbeat increasing, and knew that my reaction was only verifying what I could already feel was happening between us.

After our conversation I felt even more eager to be alone with Rusty. I wanted to know everything about him, and this night, being away from home, was going to give me the chance.

We drove a for a while before he pulled into a nice hotel. He started to get out of the truck and stopped to say something to me. "Wait here. It's probably best if you let me pay for the room. I don't want your cousin knowing that we're together, so go ahead and call someone at the ranch. I don't care what you tell them. I sent Noah a text this morning when I followed you. I knew I wouldn't be in any condition to work either way it went, so I told him that I had a family emergency."

"Clever. He's probably going to ask you about it."

"I'll make up something. Just take care on your side." He walked away, leaving me alone to think up a good excuse that would keep me away from home. After a few minutes I had the perfect idea.

Can you get Rusty to check on my house tonight? I had to drive all the way to West Virginia today to meet with our partner company. It was last minute and I'm just going to spend the night here. I'm not sure if I turned off my coffee pot. –Bella

He responded immediately.

I'll do it. Rusty took the day off. The house hasn't burned down, so that's a good sign. – Noah

Okay, thanks. See you tomorrow then. - Bella

Rusty came outside with a key card in his hand. "You ready?"

I climbed out of the truck and followed him inside, where we took an elevator up to the fourth floor. Once inside of the room we both plopped down on the two beds and laid there in silence for a few seconds. "I'm so tired," I announced.

"Yeah. It's been a long day." He hopped off the bed and started walking toward the door. "I'm goin' to run out and find a place to get us some waters. Do you want anything else?"

I sat up and looked at him. "Do you want me to go?"

He shook his head. "Nah. Just relax."

"Okay. I think a toothbrush would be nice. Do you want some money? You paid for the room. The lease I can do is buy you a toothbrush."

He laughed at me. "I'm pretty sure the hotel has toothbrushes if you call housekeeping."

I watched him leave before getting up and going in to use the bathroom. After I was done, I started the shower. Rusty would be at least fifteen minutes, so I had time to clean up and crawl into bed. I could sleep in my bra and panties, and make him turn his head when I got up to dress in the morning.

The shower felt wonderful after such an emotional day. While I stood there letting the beads of water run down my body I thought about Rusty. It was possible that he'd used the store as an excuse for some alone time.

The man had been a mystery up until a couple hours ago. I could only imagine that his head would be a little messed up. For so long he'd kept his past a secret. Telling me could have opened up wounds he thought had healed enough to go on.

I felt so bad for him. Even though I wasn't yet a mother, I still couldn't imagine what it would be like to watch my child die, and not be able to do anything about it. To some she took the coward way out, but I felt like I would have done the same thing. Her mind wasn't on Rusty when Simone took her life. All she wanted was to be with her daughter again.

I hadn't meant to start crying again, but that's exactly what began to happen. Waves of tears started pouring out of my eyes until I let my body sink to the tub bottom. I brought my knees up to my chest and let the sobs continue.

I thought about that man being so in love with his family, and what it was like to wake up one day without them. My heart ached, and I knew that everything I'd ever thought about him had been untrue. This man wasn't just running, he was doing his best to get by. Meeting me had changed something in him, and now after all this time he was beginning to feel again.

Whether I wanted to admit it or not, there was this connection that I felt to him. It wasn't just because he'd tried to save me from making a terrible choice. It was more. When I needed him, he'd always seemed to be there. He'd been trying to know me for a while and I'd pushed him away.

I thought he was a creep.

Little did I know that he was yearning for a friendship. He longed to feel needed by someone again. Whether he picked me because I looked like her, or for other reasons, I had to help him. I wanted to do it.

Whatever I was feeling for this guy needed to be addressed. My head was spinning with such confusion.

Time got away from me, because the next thing I knew the bathroom door was opening. "Iz, are you all right?"

"Yeah," I stood up and turned off the water. "I'm just finishing up."

I don't know why I tried to play off being upset. He'd obviously heard me crying, or else he wouldn't have asked. "I got you a t-shirt and some shorts. They aren't anything special. The pharmacy was selling them."

I stuck my head out from beyond the curtain and looked at the clothing in his hands. "Thanks. You didn't have to do that."

"I figured you'd want to be comfortable when you slept."

He left me alone to change, and when I came out into the room he was staring out the large window. He turned to acknowledge my presence. "I figured they'd be huge on you."

I looked down at the oversized top and rolled up shorts. "It's fine. They feel nice."

His eyes traveled to my chest, where my hard nipples made it obvious that I'd left my bra off. I could feel my cheeks getting warm as I looked up at him. He met my gaze and smiled.

Since it made me uncomfortable, I crawled under the covers on one of the beds. "I'm so tired that I could go to sleep now." Since it was just starting to get dark I knew it was still pretty early.

Rusty sat on the edge of his bed and started taking off his boots. "I feel the same. Do you want to watch a movie?" He stood up and pulled his shirt over his head, then dropped his jeans, leaving me to stare. Even though he'd still had on a pair of boxers, it left little to the imagination. His chest was perfectly sculpted, as I'd already known. The V in the front of his shorts caught my eye. I couldn't take my eyes off of him. He made Tate look like a scrawny teenager.

"Iz, did you hear me?"

"Huh?" I looked up realizing that I'd missed everything.

"I asked you if you wanted to play cards." He held up the deck that he'd just purchased.

How was I supposed to reply when he knew I'd been mesmerized by his body? The room became quiet as I brought my feet to the floor and stood up. Our eyes stayed fixed on one another, and I was beginning to shake as I took a step in his direction. "I don't want to play cards."

He watched me take a couple more steps, breaking that distance between us. "What do you want to do then, just go to bed?"

I licked my lips as I brought my face closer to his. "I'm suddenly not tired anymore."

To be honest, I have no idea what had gotten into me. I'd never come onto a man in my life, and here I was taking advantage of the situation. Heaven help me but I couldn't stop myself. I wanted to feel what it was like to kiss him, to feel his lips kissing me back. I needed to feel what it was like to be wanted by a man again. Pregnant or not, I had needs that I'd been neglecting.

Our lips brushed for the first time and I closed my eyes, preparing to go further. He grabbed my shoulders and pushed me away, turning his head while looking pained. "I can't."

I felt rejected. "I thought you liked me."

"I do." I started to back away, but he pulled me closer. "It's not that, I can assure you."

"Then what?"

Rusty looked away and closed his eyes. "Isabella, I do want you. It's just that I haven't been with anyone in a very long time. I don't want you to do this because you feel sorry for me."

"I don't want you to want me because you miss your wife and I remind you of her."

At the same time we both said, "I don't." It may have been a lie for both of us, but it didn't matter. The moment was already happening.

We both sort of smiled and looked away again. Rusty lifted my chin and looked deeply into my eyes. "You deserve to feel wanted."

"So do you." It was the truth. He needed to feel alive again, because he was. "We're both adults. I know this is unexpected, but we're in this hotel together and we're both obviously attracted to each other. I'm not sayin' that we have to make love, but -." His lips were on mine before I could answer. My hands found his hard chest and I ran the palms of them over his skin. Our mouths connected several times before I found the courage to use my tongue. It was as if I needed to test the waters before jumping right in.

This man was so fragile. He'd confided in me, and it had caused us to connect on a level that I'd never experienced with anyone before. I thought I knew Tate, but really our childhood relationship didn't compare to this at all. I craved to be touched by this man, who in turned yearned to feel something real again. If all we had was this one night and nothing else, I wanted it to be memorable.

We both pulled away to catch our breaths. I ran my hands over the elastic to his boxers. He pulled away, as if he was embarrassed that he was forming an erection. "Sorry. I'm not –."

"Shh." I pulled the elastic toward me and let my hand slide down beneath until I felt his warm, smooth skin with my fingertips. "Close your eyes."

He did as I asked and I leaned forward brushing my lips over his. Right away I felt his body beginning to tremble. He began shaking so bad that I couldn't ignore it. His eyes shot open and I took one step back. "Are you okay?"

He just stood there staring at me, like he'd done before when I thought he was a stalker.

"Rusty?"

He came at me, shoving our lips together, and pulling us both down on one of the beds. It was so sexy to be with a real man, someone older that was still nervous. The more I fought with myself over my actions, the more I knew I wasn't going to back down.

Chapter 14
Rusty

I couldn't believe that she was on top of me, pressing those perfect lips against mine. Her hands remained on my chest as our tongues mingled together. I hadn't felt this way in such a long time, but worried that at any minute she was going to stop.

For so long I'd felt as if I'd never be able to feel something for anyone again. I'd given up hope that good things could happen for me.

I was afraid to keep closing my eyes, in fear of her not being there when I opened them back up. I was scared to death that it could have all just been a dream. For so many nights I'd imagined what it would be like to touch her soft skin, to smell the fragrance of her body lotion, and to feel the way her lips felt when they pressed over mine.

Now it was happening, and I couldn't slow down my trembling body. My nerves were taking over, and I wasn't sure whether to stop or push on.

When I knew that it was apparent to her again, I pulled away. She lay there under me on the bed, waiting for me to respond in some way. "Sorry. I just need a minute."

Isabella reached up and ran her fingers through my hair on the sides. "Do you want to stop?"

I moved my head slowly from side to side. "You're asking a man whether he wants to stop kissing you."

She shrugged. "Yeah, so?"

"You already know the answer to that. It's just...it's hard to not feel like I'm cheating. I know it sounds ridiculous." I looked down, ashamed to break the moment with my emotional guilt.

"She'd want you to be happy."

I traced her bottom lip with my thumb. "That's just it, Iz. I know she'd want that. The question is whether this is going to end once we go home. Is this the start of something new, or just a one-time thing, because I'm going to be honest with you. I don't think I can be with you one time and be happy."

She sat up on her elbows and I backed off the bed to kneel in front of her. I could tell she was thinking about what to say. "I don't have an answer to that. Up until today I would have told you that you'd be the last person on earth I'd want to sleep with. Contrary to my first impressions of you, I've learned that I never really knew the real you at all. Somethin' changed between us today. I'm not goin' to even try to deny it. Kissin' you feels so good, and I'd like to continue, but I don't know what will happen when we get home. My cousin's a big problem, and I don't want you to lose your job."

"You really think he'd fire me?"

She shrugged. "I think that once the family finds out I'm pregnant they're goin' to have a real problem with me sleepin' with the help. No offense. They obviously don't know the real you, and since you don't want to share it with them, I can't see this workin' out."

She was right. The truth hurt.

Still, I wasn't ready to let the whole world know who I used to be.

"And don't even get me started on my dad and brothers. They like to be in control of everything I do."

I traced my fingers over one of her knees. "So we should probably just stop while we're ahead then?"

She leaned forward, inching her mouth to touch mine. Her kiss was so gentle. "Probably."

Had I been in control of my sex drive I probably would have handle things much differently. My body was reacting to hers before my mind could catch up. I had to continue kissing those soft lips.

When her arms reached around my neck, I was immediately pulled back down onto the bed. My hands traveled up to her loose t-shirt, inching their way to touch one of her soft breasts. I was taken back when it finally coursed over the nipple, feeling that hard bud beneath my fingertips. She pulled me closer, kissing me harder. I began holding my breath to prevent from pulling away from her.

As the petting intensified, so did my increased need to feel her bare skin. Before I could lift up her shirt, she was doing it for me, sitting up and pulling it over her head. I'd imagined what this moment would be like. There'd been so many nights when I'd thought about getting her naked; many nights where I'd relieved myself thinking about an encounter just like this.

Isabella reached down and touched both of her breasts, using her manicured fingernails to pinch the nipples.

A sudden spark hit my dick, awakening a deep desire that I'd locked up to prevent from feeling. I watched her top lip dragging over her bottom, leaving a trail of glistening saliva as it moved. My need to kiss her only increased when she reached her hand down into her shorts and moved it up and down. Her eyes closed, and I knew exactly what she was doing, even before she said it. "I want you to want me, Rusty. I want to feel needed."

I pulled her off the bed making her stand up.

She looked directly into my eyes as I ripped her hand out from inside of her shorts. Her confusion was short lived when I tugged down on them. To my surprise she'd not only gone without a bra, but her underwear as well. My mouth watered as I crouched down to be face to face with her pussy. Just as my hand brushed over the shaved skin, I looked up to see her watching me. The expression on her face let me know that she wasn't about to refuse me. I inched my way forward, smelling her fresh skin before grazing my lips over it. She dug her hands into my hair, not to guide me but to hold on to something while she closed her eyes.

I couldn't believe this was happening; that I was here with her in this room, alone and unclothed. I'd dreamed of this moment.

My focus went back to the task at hand. While my throbbing cock continued to beckon, I licked that sweet spot for the very first time. She let out a soft moan as I continued, letting my moist muscle slide in between her folds until it reached her clit. I sucked it in between my teeth and tugged, listening to her body reacting to me.

It was hard for me to stay focused, knowing that at any second I was going to prematurely lose it in my shorts. I lapped her pussy up again, over and over, sucking and flicking her clit with my tongue until she began to cry out. Even still, I kept going, wanting nothing more than to bring her pleasure for awakening a dead part of me again.

Isabella became weak in the knees and let her

ass fall down on the mattress. I craved more of her pussy and put her legs up high for her to hold. I gave her a final stare before diving in again. The taste of her filled my mouth, and I savored it as if it were the best flavor in the world.

For the first time since the day I lost my wife I felt whole again. It was as if this connection was bringing me back to life. When her body began to crash again, I pulled away, kissing the inner part of her thighs, before looking up to see her expression. She played with my hair and let out a deep laugh. "Wow. That was intense."

I showered her with tiny kisses until our lips met. She pulled away, shocked from tasting herself. This got to me, making me realize that she'd been with one person since high school. Her experience was limited, which meant that I could show her things she couldn't imagine existed. I could make her feel like no other man ever had before.

The knowledge of that excited me more. To be able to bring her to the brink of ecstasy repeatedly was an unimaginable high. Isabella flipped us around. I grabbed her fingers and intertwined ours together. It was something that I used to do with my wife, and even though I wasn't trying to think about being with her again, little details kept occurring. I must have only closed my eyes for a second, but it was enough for her to read that something was wrong. She released her hands and sat on top of me with worried eyes. "What just happened?"

"It's nothing."

"Do you want to stop? We can, if that's what you need to do."

I shook my head immediately, before she even stopped talking. "No. This is where I want to be, here with you. Didn't I just prove that to you? Do you have any idea how many nights I've thought about being like this with you?"

She slid over to the side of the bed. "It's not that. Rusty, right now I want to be with you too, but we can't do this today. You and I both know we need to stop while we're ahead."

She was right.

This encounter was only happening because we were both so emotional. Had I lost my shit we never would have ended up remotely near each other. It was a sad truth. I backed away from her, distancing myself from being able to touch her beautiful body in any way. "You're absolutely right. I can't let this happen in a shitty hotel room." I reached my hand out and touched one of hers. "What just happened between us is only the beginning. I have to believe that. What you felt is just a piece of what I have to offer you, when the time is right." I stood up and looked down at her still body. "If you don't mind, I'm just going to go take a cold shower, because if I have to look at that amazing body for one more second all bets are going to be off."

I didn't wait for her to argue with me, and I

knew she would because she was famous for getting the last word in edgewise. This decision had to stick, because if I wanted her to be with me, the reason couldn't be that she felt sorry for me. This day was about saving her, and I'd done that. Sure, we'd almost made love, and one day I hoped we still would. At least I got to find out what it felt like to kiss her, and to know what it felt like to give her pleasure. At the end of this awful day, it was at least something to smile about.

Chapter 15
Isabella

Confusion wasn't my best

attribute. I was trying so hard to rationalize with what had taken place in the past hour and I couldn't even begin to understand how I'd gone from hating someone, to craving his touch.

I was able to accept that my judgment had been blurred in light of learning about Rusty's heartbreaking past. I knew it was too late for any meaningful condolences, but longed to give him some kind of hope that he could live again. From the moment his lips touched mine for the first time, I knew that being with him physically would prove dangerous for both of us. In that instant I was willing to overlook my set boundaries and do what my body was telling me to do.

Unfortunately, there are consequences to every premature decision, mine being the fact that I hadn't considered what would happen between the two of us from that point on. The thought of alluding my family filled my mind, as I desperately clung on to the way this man had made me feel. I knew I wouldn't be able to deny our connection, whether it be for the sake of both of us getting some kind of emotional release, or something more than that. All I knew was that us stopping wasn't what I had wanted.

While Rusty showered, I leaned over and lifted his wallet out of his pants. I wanted to see a picture of his family again, and observe the uncanny resemblance I had to his two girls. Sure, our hair was around the same color, and they both seemed to have green eyes, but that was it. What bothered me so much was knowing that all along Rusty had found interest in me because of this resemblance. It only made me think that our connection was superficial at best. Obviously it wasn't me he was after, but some remnant of his late wife.

I closed the wallet and put it back in his pants before the water stopped running in the shower. By the time the door opened, I tucked myself under the covers of my own bed. He entered the room in only a towel, holding it close to his hip as he set down on the edge of my bed. "Are you okay, Isabella?"

"Yeah. I'm fine," I lied, knowing that I was more confused than ever before. Then I knew what I wanted. Seeing him so close to me, knowing that his arms brought me so much comfort, I knew exactly what I needed. "Lay with me tonight. Please. I just want to hold you."

He never removed the towel until he was under the covers beside me. A part of me felt the need to put my clothes back on, but we'd already been there and experienced that. I had nothing to hide from this man, and longed to be close to him.

We lay side by side for a while, staring into each other's eyes. In so many ways it was like we were having a silent conversation, sharing all of our emotions while doing nothing at all. I'd never connected on this type of level, and didn't know if it would ever be like this again. Rusty reached over and stroked my hair. He smiled and leaned over to kiss my forehead. "You make me want to live again."

I'd never had so much sentiment on my shoulders before. This broken man found contentment in being around me. I couldn't deny him that, nor refute my own growing desire to be with him.

My hand stretched to connect with his scruffy cheek. The palms coursed over his skin while I watched the lids of his eyes slowly closing. He leaned into my touch, accepting the comfort. "Kiss me."

Our lips united, sending waves of delight through every inch of my body. Quickly I responded to the way his tongue matched mine. I climbed up and straddled his body, feeling his growing erection beneath me. In an immediate comeback, I began to rock forward, meeting his welcoming mouth for more of what was fueling me to need more. Our tongues blended, while his hands came up and possessed my hips. As they continued traveling up I realized that we were instantly right back in the same place as before. He traced the Mitchell tattoo that was written vertically on the left side of my ribs. It tickled there, feeling him so close to the underneath of my breasts. A time out had only heightened my hunger for this sensitive man, and thankfully he wasn't persuading me to stop again.

My lips trailed over his, while words began coming out; words I knew would take us to the next level. "Make love to me."

He reached up, running his full hands over both of my breasts. I kept moving around, letting him know I was ready and willing. Everything I was experiencing, all of my emotions were fading with the new revelation of becoming one with this man. He sat up, switching our positions so that he was lingering over top of me. Our eyes convened, and I could sense the deprivation that he'd been living with for so long. He needed this more than I did, not that it was a competition. We both had issues that had brought us together, that was no secret.

Gentle kisses trailed over my body, and his hand traveling over my most sensitive of areas, while I patiently accepted him getting familiar with every inch of me. I may not have asked to find someone new, but he was lying on top of me, offering to make me forget, even if only for a little while. His hand swept over my sex, and I watched a smile forming in the corner of his mouth. "You're so warm, and I can't get the way you taste out of my mind."

Waves of sensitive tingles rushed through me, hardening my nipples and giving me butterflies in my stomach. I was about to be with a real man, someone older, who knew exactly what he was doing. The idea of it all was frightening, but electrifying at the same time. I accepted his mouth as he came down to kiss me again. Our tongues met, and as the pattern of our movements increased, I understood his hunger was only intensifying.

I reached down, prepared to stroke his cock with my own hands, but he stopped me, replacing mine with his own. With one swift undertaking he toyed with my entrance, gliding his stiffness over it. I nodded, silently letting him know that it's what I desired. "Are you sure you want this? If you'd rather me hold you, I'll do it."

"Stop givin' me choices. I told you what I want," I whispered.

My body beckoned to be filled, and slowly it happened. Rusty never moved his lips far from mine as he started to enter me. I watched him closing his eyes, appearing to have been swept away by something he hadn't felt in so long. I noticed him trembling even before he was fully inside. My arms wrapped around his back, as I prepared to keep him as close as possible. This wasn't like a quickie, or just regular sex. I wanted to experience all of him; to share his pleasure, and his pain.

He leaned his forehead on mine, and stopping moving the lower part of his body as he spoke. "I'm sorry. I need to take my time with you, but I'm afraid I may not last that long. It's been years since I've felt this."

I reached my mouth to his and sucked on his bottom lip. It was easy to reciprocate my affections, knowing that I welcomed whatever he was offering. I didn't care if he lasted ten seconds, or ten hours. I'd never experienced such emotion with sex, and knew it wasn't all about intercourse. There was something deeper between us, and I felt it necessary to explore every aspect of it.

Our first encounter didn't last very long. Rusty pulled out of me, refusing to finish inside, even though we both knew I couldn't get pregnant from this encounter. However, hours later when we woke in each other's arms, he wasn't so concerned. He fulfilled me, taking me to heights, and then held me afterwards, placing sensual kisses over my body. The chemistry between us was undeniable, and I realized early on that this thing wasn't going to end when we got home. Pregnant or not, Rusty wanted to be with me. We'd talked about it while lying naked together in bed. The comfort of his touch let me know that I didn't have to be alone. Whether we were friends, or remained lovers, he wanted be around. In a perfect world I would have loved to go home and announce to everyone that we were going to be a couple. In that same world they'd accept us, and the fact that I was carrying my ex-boyfriend's child. I wasn't living in that perfect world though.

As the sun rose I lie awake watching Rusty sleep. He seemed so peaceful, and I appreciated what we'd shared. It almost made me wonder how I was going to be able to see him every day, without anyone finding out that I'd be reminiscing on the night we'd shared. When the time was right I'd tell the family about the baby, but didn't know how Rusty would fit into it all. They weren't going to be happy with me, so I couldn't spring both things on them, and expect acceptance. It literally wasn't feasible.

A low snore came out of his mouth as he slept so close to me. I ran my fingers over his lips, smiling when he never opened his eyes. He seemed so peaceful, reminding me that I was the reason for it. It only made me feel worse, because I knew I'd have to give him up.

Since I'd planned on being off of work for an extra day anyway, I snuggled up closer to his hot body, and closed my eyes. In truth I knew I didn't want to be anywhere else. Never in my adult life had I ever felt so comfortable before.

Things were much different on the ride home. Instead of refusing to speak to him, and keeping my distance, I sat in the middle seat, with his arm wrapped around my shoulder. He let me sleep for most of the way, every once in a while kissing me on the head, reminding me of how sweet he was.

It killed me that he didn't want anyone to know the real him, because he truly was a wonderful soul. His secret was safe with me, no matter how many obstacles it caused me to go through. In the upcoming months I'd need his friendship, so no one, especially my cousin, was going to be able to find out about us. Knowing that hurt me so much, because it also reminded me that our time like this was about to end. I'd made my choice though, and there was nothing anyone could do to change it.

Chapter 16
Rusty

It was funny how she felt like she was broken, but I was the one that needed all of the saving. Being with her, feeling her touch, it brought me back to life again. When we arrived back to Kentucky things didn't go as I had assumed they would. It all started that first night when I stopped by to check on her. I'd dropped her off earlier to get her vehicle, and purposely took my time going back to the ranch so that we didn't arrive at the same time. After checking in with Noah, and making sure that Titan, and my trailer, were all the way I left them, I snuck over to visit Isabella. I'd gone for a few hours without seeing her, and already was feeling as if it had been too long.

It was hard to not think about the night

before, and how she'd finally been in my arms. I think I'd deprived myself for such a long amount of time that I'd forgotten how to control these types of emotions. I definitely wasn't mad that they were happening. For so long I'd waited for her to notice me; to give me a chance to know her better.

I hadn't expected that we'd end up in bed, but I'd given her plenty of time to reconsider the decision before going through with it.

I knocked on her front door, which was more hidden than the kitchen entrance. She answered and smiled, but I could tell from her body language that something was off. She didn't make me wait long to figure it out.

She motioned her hand toward the living room furniture. "We need to talk."

I sat down on the couch next to her, silently wondering if I should try to kiss her, or even hold her hand. When I reached for hers, she pulled it away. "Rusty, I can't do this with you. There's too much goin' on in my life to be able to start somethin' with you. What happened in that hotel room was –."

"Perfect," I interrupted.

"Don't say that."

She looked away, causing me to question the connection that I could have sworn we had. I reached for her arm, only to be rejected again. "What's wrong? Is it something I said?"

"No!" Her alarming expression let me know

that we definitely were not on the same page. "I can't do this, okay?"

"But you and I..."

"There is no you and I, Rusty. There can't be. I'm pregnant with another man's child, and I can't even begin to grasp what's to come. I need to be able to make the right choices, and last night was obviously not the kind of choice an expectin' mother should have made."

"So what?" I was going to fight to prove my point. "You're just going to deny this attraction, and pretend that last night didn't happen at all?"

Isabella got up and walked into the kitchen. When I followed she leaned her hands against the kitchen counter facing the cabinets. I wanted her to look me in the eyes as she let me down, but she refused. "I know what happened between us. That's why this is so hard for me. We were both so emotional. Things happened because we were in a fragile state. I'm not goin' to make it out to be somethin' it never was. Last night two people came together to comfort each other. It wasn't about attractions, or feelin's."

"You're wrong. At least, that's not what it was for me." I couldn't deny how hurt it made me feel when she said these kind of things to me. She was forgetting that I was in that room with her. I know what I was feeling was mutual. "You can sit there and act like this was a one-night stand, but we both know that ain't true."

"Please don't do this." She turned around and rubbed her eyes. " Don't make this harder than it already is."

I walked over and put my arms around her waist, waiting to see those eyes looking up at me. This wasn't just a fight to change her mind, it was also my happiness hanging by a thread. While waiting, I brushed the long blonde hair away from her cheek. Slowly, she raised her head and looked at me with tears falling down. I let my lips come down, almost to where they brushed over hers. "I want to -."

Before I could finish the door was flying open and I was being shoved across the kitchen. Noah looked from me to Isabella. "What the fuck? He pointed toward me. "I told you to steer clear of my cousin, didn't I?"

I threw my hands up, trying hard to defend myself. "I-."

"He was just leavin'," Isabella announced.

I didn't know how to react. My job wasn't more important than finishing our conversation, but she'd ended it for me.

"You heard her. Get out, before I say somethin' I might regret." Noah was my boss, and I had to be respectful since this ranch belonged to his family.

I turned to Isabella, noticing right away how hurt she seemed. Her forehead was creased, and one hand was over her mouth. I nodded to her and walked out of the house. Even when I made it onto the long lane I could hear him yelling at her. As sorrowful as it was, I knew I had to keep walking. She'd pushed me away, and he'd made sure I'd gone.

For the first time in forever I wanted a drink, so that I could numb myself from feeling anything at all. I'd opened my heart to her, and showed her a part of me that I'd kept hidden. In the end it had only gotten me exactly back where I started.

Alone.

There was no use tryin' to avoid Noah, when I knew his next move was to locate me and let me have it. I took a quick shower, and sat down at my kitchen table waiting for him to arrive. When he entered it was without a friendly knock. He could do it that way because he owned the place. The chair across from me made a loud screech as it was being pulled out to allow him room to sit down. He cleared his throat before beginning. "I want you to be straight with me, Rusty. What's goin' on with you and my cousin?"

I considered telling him everything, even about the life I'd given up. "It was nothing. I was simply inviting her to share a meal with me and I crossed a line. I'm sorry, boss. It won't happen again."

Some guys my age would have had a problem dealing with a younger boss. At the end of the day it wasn't Noah that I had to answer to, well not completely. His father still ran the show. "Listen, I'm not tryin' to be some hard ass. I get that you think she's pretty, and you'd like to get to know her more. I've seen and heard it all before."

I put my hand up in the air. "Noah, I wont go near her, okay? It was a mistake." The lies were piling up. Every second with Isabella wasn't a mistake. I only wish I had the strength to tell him how I really felt about his cousin. "I meant nothing by it. I just figured we could enjoy a meal with conversation instead of eating alone. That's all it was."

He raised his brow for a moment like he didn't believe me. When I didn't flinch, he finally calmed. "Whatever. If you need company than get a dog."

"You really care about your cousin. I can appreciate the way you're always looking out for her. If I had a cousin I think I'd be the same way." I was trying to get back on his good side. There was no telling how long Noah had been watching us, but from what I gathered it hadn't been long. If anything he saw us standing face to face, and from the angle of the kitchen door he wouldn't have been able to tell if we were close enough to kiss or not. Plus I think if he'd had seen that he would have come after me and things would have gone from bad to worse.

Instead he was being cordial, calm almost.

"I've been raised like that, Rusty. Family is the most important thing in life. I don't know much about you, or your upbrinin', but it's just how ours is." He stood up and tapped the table with his hands. "You do a lot for me and my dad, and we appreciate it. I'd like to keep you around for a while."

He was warning me. I supposed I should have taken heed, but instead I felt offended. Perhaps if he heard my story he'd back off. At any rate I knew I had to keep calm and let him leave in a good mood. I liked living on the ranch, and there was no way I was willing to give up being able to see Isabella everyday. If I had to go back to being a creepy stalker to get her attention that's what I was going to do.

Chapter 17
Isabella

It was extremely difficult looking into my cousin's eyes and telling him that there was nothing going on between Rusty and I. It was even harder lying to myself about it. In my head I knew that being alone was the right decision, yet my heart ached to feel that attention he'd given me.

As the weeks passed, I felt even more regret when it came to pushing Rusty away. He consumed my thoughts, and left me in a state of depression knowing that it wouldn't happen again. Exactly one month after I slept with him, I'd woke up on a beautiful Saturday morning and decided that I wanted to work outside in my little garden. It wasn't anything fancy, just a bunch of marigolds and some hastes, that were definitely in need of some pruning. Every day my little belly seemed to be getting bigger, but that could have just been my imagination. At any rate, I put on a baggy t-shirt and headed outside into the breezy morning sunshine. I'd been down on my knees for a good thirty minutes when I realized that my back was feeling stiff, so I stood up to stretch, and noticed Shalan and Noah riding horses towards the tree line. In that instant I don't know what got into me. Before I even thought to wash off my dirt-filled hands, I was walking toward the stables with one thing on my mind. After countless hours of lying awake at night, and even more daydreaming at my job, I knew I had to see him again. I felt like if I just gave myself a couple of minutes to be around him, I'd be able to focus on my life again.

It would have been better if I'd found him shoveling large piles of manure, or bailing some hay. Instead I walked into to find him pouring a bottle of water down his bare chest. All I could do was stand there and watch, as if it were in slow motion. Even only having been with him for one night it was hard to not picture my hands on his skin, and the way he'd touched me over and over again. I licked my lips, and tried my best to slow down to rapid breathing. It was no use. As I stood there spying on the man who should steer clear of me and my problems, I knew one thing for sure.

I had to make my presence known.

After crossing my arms and leaning against the old wooden door, I cleared my throat. Rusty looked up, tossing the bottle in the trash can to the side. "Iz, what are you doing here?"

I didn't move from where I was standing. "I needed to see you."

"Is something wrong?" He immediately started to walk in my direction. My arms dropped to my sides, but my feet never left where they stood.

My teeth drug over my bottle lip while contemplating how I should answer. "Maybe."

His strong hands grasped both of my arms, holding them while his eyes focused on mine. "What is it?"

"Just kiss me."

His lips were on mine so quickly that I barely had time to take a breath. His mouth, that I'd been so perplexed over before, placed gentle kisses all over my lips and cheeks. Our mouths clashed together again, this time allowing our tongues to dance in a harmonious pattern. I could feel my heart beating rapidly as my clammy hands reached up to touch that bare, sweaty chest for the first time. His skin, so hot and sticky, was just as rock hard as I'd recalled it to be. From the moment my fingertips coursed over his smooth skin, a fire ignited between my legs. The burning desire that I felt for this man was only being heightened, and I wasn't sure how I was going to be able to stop myself until I had everything I wanted from him.

After a few moments of reconciliation, Rusty picked me up and carried me into a stall filled with hay. He stood me up and grabbed an old horse blanket to lay out over the pile. I didn't wait for him to motion for me to lay on it. I already knew what was about to happen, and I didn't care if we were outside, or in the open so that anyone could walk in us. The only thing running through my mind was being able to be satisfied by this beautiful man.

Before Rusty laid down beside me, I lifted off my top. He leaned forward to lay me down with such ease that it felt like I'd floated back. Our lips met again, this time honing in on the focus at hand. I let my foot lift up until it stroked over his growing erection. My need to remove his fitting jeans had become very apparent.

Rusty lifted his body. His boots came off first, while never taking his eyes off of me. While he worked on himself, I removed my bra and fell back down on the thick blanket for comfort.

I watched his belt buckle unclasp as he proceeded in dropping the denim he had on, to the floor. From that moment I knew there was no turning back. The intent in his eyes let me know we were on the same page, and as he crouched down to be close to me, I knew that he was going to make me regret ever pushing him away.

Rusty smiled as his lips came down over mine. His slow, passionate kisses filled my body with such anticipation. I longed for his touch, and soon got a lot more than I could have bargained for. He pulled a piece hay out from the large stack beneath us, while leaning up on his elbow. At first he drug it over my lips, causing them to part. The dried plant skated across my chin as it slowly brushed the tip of my ear lobe. The tickling sensations overwhelmed my skin, sending chills all the way down to my toes. My nipples hardened even before the tip of that hay was being circled around them. One at a time he traced those sensitive buds, causing me to moan out little cries of sheer bliss.

I could feel myself becoming soaked with expectation. Rusty wasn't just teasing me. He was deliberately memorizing every inch of my skin, while giving me pleasure as he did so. This wasn't like our first encounter, as neither of us were over emotional. Our drive to be together was fueled by need.

When that long stem ran across my abdomen my body began to shiver. Rusty, still focused on watching my reactions, leaned down and kissed it tenderly. I touched his hair and smiled, knowing it was meant to comfort me in my obvious condition.

We didn't speak to each other, and I was glad of that, considering I had no idea what to say. This was premeditated, and I couldn't let myself rationalize about what was happening, because I knew I'd overthink it and want to stop.

The piece of hay stroked over my pussy, causing sporadic jolts of delight. I gasped again, taking

177

in a deep breath and exhaling while trying to keep my body from trembling. Rusty moved down, rubbing his hands over my dirtied knees. He kissed one of them before moving unhurriedly up my thighs.

I had to sit up on my elbows to be able to watch as he teased my pussy with that same piece of hay, rubbing it over the smooth folds, and then finally lightly brushing it over the crease. This time I couldn't contain the amount of sexual tension that it was placing on me. I knew I was wet, probably soaked with eagerness, so he continued teasing me on purpose.

Rusty licked his own lips and turned the strand of hay around so that the thicker end was now at the top. He pressed it ever so gently over my clit, moving side to side to get me aroused. I couldn't stop watching him, so focused on what he was doing to me. His stiff erection was apparent, and I'd never wanted to satisfy a man the way that I was feeling at this very moment.

He blew onto my sex, while tracing my clit with that stem. My hips jerked and I could feel that tingling burn starting to overwhelm me. I closed my eyes and felt his heated tongue lapping over my deprived bud, as if he were using some kind of centrifugal force to guide him. I screamed out while waves of ecstasy besieged me, causing me to become dizzy and lightheaded. Never before had I experienced such a heightened orgasm.

Rusty laughed with his mouth still lingering

over my swollen bud. He used his chin whiskers to tickle me there, prolonging the frenzy that he'd bestowed. I clenched a chunk of his hair with my fist and pulled, expressing the physical attributes to losing control. The euphoric moment finally slowed, giving me a few moments to gather my breath, and open my eyes wide.

He still dawdled there, right over my pussy, with no regard for how sensitive that area had become. In lieu of what had occurred, I pulled that handful of hair up, until his body was even with mine. His stiff erection pressed against my thigh as our lips met. The immediate connection was undeniable. Rusty moved his tongue with precision, as I matched his movements. I felt his hand tracing over the smooth skin of my pussy, gliding one finger inside the folds to feel just how ready he'd made me. He pulled away from my lips and stared at me for a second before grabbing another strand of hay from behind my head. With one quick movement he'd ducked back down, focused on playing again. Before I could think of anything to say I felt something different. I looked toward his hand and noticed that this stem didn't just have one strand at the top. It had four. He spun it between his finger, causing a windmill effect. While doing it, he let those buds at the top smack over my clit. Every second they hit that same spot. My body flailed as I lost control again, so quickly that I was almost embarrassed to admit. Finally, when it got to be too much to bear, I pulled his arm away, begging him to stop. "Please. I can't take it anymore."

His smile let me know that he's succeeded in what he'd sought out to do. It was no surprise that he'd be content with leaving me wanting so much more than I was willing to admit. He wanted me to know what I'd been missing, and I was well aware of everything that he had to offer, even before this encounter.

Rusty took his entire palm and cupped my pussy, He held onto it while moving his arm slightly up and down. My sensitive area began to throb, and it felt like it was on fire. It ached to be touched again, and I couldn't stop myself from taking hold of that same arm and moving it harder. His finger slipped in between my wet folds, penetrating me as I controlled it. The faster I moved that arm, the more pleasure it gave me. I was fully aware that this was me pleasing myself, but Rusty didn't seem to mind. He watched my face as I bit down hard on my bottom lip and cried out again.

My eyes became focused on his as he pulled that finger out of me, sucking it in between his lips. I gasped, feeling so turned on by his actions. "Do you like the way I taste?" The words seemed to purr.

"Mhmm. I need more though." He took one hand and grabbed the skin where my hip meets my ass. In an instant he was positioning himself overtop of me. I could feel his cock pressing my entrance, without being guided there. "Is this what you came for?" Sweat was running down the side of his head, dripping on my neck. I flinched each time it hit me, even while trying to remain focused on what was about to happen.

I refused to answer him out loud. Instead a simple nod let him know the truth. I may have not anticipated this happening when I woke up this morning, but I certainly knew exactly what I wanted.

He entered me with ease, sliding inside gracefully, while bringing his lips down against mine. The sheer fulfillment I got from him being inside of me was unexplainable. The foreplay was amazing in itself, but this was utter delight. In no time at all I was overtaken with reoccurring waves again. I dug my nails into his back and clung to his skin while feeling yet another release.

Rusty kissed me once softly, before pulling out of me and flipping me around. His pent up predicament left him without another ounce of patience. He needed to explode and I was going to help it happen.

The next thing I knew his chest was coming over my back, while his hands reached around, pinching at both of my nipples. He entered me, fully, working up a pace immediately. His hands slid down my body until my hips served as handles. He pulled my body into his so hard that loud slapping sounds filled the area around us. My breasts bounced around as Rusty continued pumping me. I knew when he was being overwhelmed by his eruption when his body tightened, and he held me completely still. Though I wanted him to continue, his body was spent.

He gained his breath back and rolled off of me, letting the breeze hit our soaked skin. I was at a loss for words, simply devoured by sexual satisfaction. There was nothing that could bring me down from this high.

Nothing but hearing my cousin's voice getting closer.

Chapter 18
Rusty

My legs were still weak as I jumped up and started pulling my jeans on over my sweat-soaked legs. Noah's voice was getting close, as was the sound of the horses canters. I hooked my belt just as I saw him coming through the stable entrance. Isabella gathered her clothing and covered up with the blanket, while positioning herself in the corner of the area we were in. Since the walls were only chest high, if Noah looked hard enough he'd see her hiding there.

I walked far away from where she was crouched down and picked up a shovel, as if I'd been hard at work. Shalan appeared behind Noah, both of them caught up in their own conversation. I nodded when Noah acknowledged I was inside.

"I figured you'd be in here in the shade. It's

hotter than hell in that sun."

"The breeze is nice today at least."

Noah jumped off his horse and offered his arms to Shalan to catch her when she climbed off. She wrapped her hands around his neck and pulled him in for a kiss as he sat her down on the ground. He smiled as he pulled away and kissed the top of her nose. "I love you, darlin'."

She giggled and turned to me. "Hey, Rusty. Sorry I missed you this morning. I wanted to thank you for all your hard work with Titan, and let you know that my new horse will be here in about a week. Are you sure you're ready to take on another project? I can get another person to help."

I put up my hands. "No need. I enjoy it. It actually gives me something to stay busy. Besides, what man doesn't love a challenge?"

It was hard to not think of Isabella when I said it. She was the biggest challenge in my life. I could only hope that this time had changed her mind about me. It was ridiculous for us to not be together, when we obviously both felt the same about each other.

"We're goin' to head back to the house and grab our bathin' suits. Shalan wants to get in the pool."

"Sounds nice."

"You should join us," she added.

I smiled, trying to not talk so much that they'd end up sticking around. "I've got a lot to do before I'm done for the day. Enjoy your swim. Maybe I'll come next time."

Noah took off the first saddle and started carrying it over toward where Isabella was hiding. I panicked, rushing over and taking it out of his hands. "I've got this, boss. Go ahead and enjoy your day."

He walked over to grab the second one. "Nah, I can help. It's only a saddle."

When I hung the first one up I spotted her out of the corner of my eye. She was bawled up in the corner ducked down. If Noah came in this direction he was going to see her.

I spun around quickly, holding out my hands for the second saddle. "Go on now. I've got this taken care of. I'll brush down the horses, and make sure they're watered before I do anything else. The farrier is coming later on anyway, so they'll be ready for his arrival."

Noah finally let me take the saddle. For a second I swear he looked behind me like I was hiding something. Just as it appeared he was going to say something, Shalan came and grabbed him by the hand. "Come on. You promised me a whole day with no work."

I waved as they finally left the building, and then sighed as they disappeared on a golf-cart. "The coast is clear."

She stood up and starting putting on a bra when I heard another voice coming from the doors. A female entered, and it took me a second to realize that it was Addison, Noah's younger sister. "Whoa. Put some clothes on Bella. If Noah catches your ass in here he'll flip out."

She threw her shirt over her head as she frantically started on her other cousin. "Oh my God, Addy, you can't tell anyone. Please, you've got to promise us that you will keep quiet about seein' us together."

She lit up a joint and exhaled before answering. "Whatever. You keep quiet about this, and I never saw nothin'."

I walked over and grabbed the paraphernalia out of her fingers. "You won't be needing this, young lady."

"Hey, Give that back. I paid good money for that. Besides, you wouldn't want my daddy findin' out what his help has been up to, would you?"

Isabella rushed over, grabbing the joint out of my hand and delivering it to her younger cousin. "We won't say nothin' either. You have my word."

In a second's time I was being pulled out of the stable. "You're just going to let her smoke pot like that?"

"If it prevents my family from knowin' that this happened, then yes. That's exactly what's goin' to happen." When she started to walk away I pulled on her t-shirt, causing her to stand still. I took a few steps in her direction, breaking that distance she'd made between us.

"Don't leave like this. We need to talk about what we're going to do."

She turned, with a shocking grimace. "What we're goin' to do? There is no we, Rusty."

"You just...I can't...come on now. You know that wasn't nothing." It shocked me that she'd showed up out of nowhere, allowed me to make love to her, and was already denying that it ever happened.

Isabella covered her face, like she did when she was thinking or frustrated. "For the past week I've been melancholy. I just needed to unwind, Rusty. You know that's all this was for us. You're lonely, and I'm all messed up. We did each other a favor. That's all."

I refused to let her walk away. "No. That's not all it was. Why do you keep denying yourself the pleasure of being happy?"

"Because I can't be with you. Please, don't ask these questions. I enjoy your company. I ain't even goin' to try to lie to you about it, but you know my situation. You know we can't be together, and the sooner you accept that, the sooner we can both agree that this can't happen again."

"You came onto me this time. I did what you said and kept my distance. You're the one that stomped in here on some mission to fuck. This is on you. What's your excuse this time? Is it your hormones? Did you just need to get off? I'm not your damn punching bag. If you say that this is nothing, than I suggest you keep it that way. Don't come running to me, and expect me satisfy you, so you can just walk away. I'm done putting myself out there to be walked all over."

She shot her hands in the air. "Fine! I'll stay away. So sorry I bothered you, Rusty. I didn't mean to ruin your day." When I saw that her eyes were glossed over I knew I'd crossed a line. I hadn't meant to hurt her feelings, but done just that.

Still, she'd used me for the last time. I wasn't willing to let her hurt me, when there was absolutely no way for anything to come of it.

She was already clear across the dirt lane when I called out to her. "Don't walk away mad."

I saw her middle finger shoot up above her head as she continued walking at a fast pace to get away from me. For being angry, I couldn't deny how cute she was when she was throwing an attitude. If I had my way, I would have scooped her up and taken her back into that stable until I could convince her that my feelings were genuine.

For the next week Isabella avoided me at all costs. She was determined to make it clear that we were nothing to each other. I'd stopped by her house several times after dark to try to reason with her, but she refused to answer the door and let me inside. I knew she was in there, probably cursing me under her breath, yet I didn't know how else to reach out to her. I didn't have her phone number, and I certainly didn't know a way to leave her a message where nobody else would find it first.

Day after day I sulked silently to myself, trying to come up with ways to win her over. It was ridiculous that I was a grown man, in his thirties, determined to win over a twenty-something female that was hell-bent on keeping her distance.

When the new horse was delivered it took a lot of the extra time I had used to dwell on Isabella. I focused all of my energy on my new project to try and get her off of my mind. It worked during the day, but at night I longed to see her, to hold her, and to tell her that if she'd give me the chance, I'd be everything she ever needed.

With the soon arrival of the rest of the Mitchell clan, Noah had me doing extra work around his parent's place to prepare for the large amount of people that would be coming into town for the wedding shower. Shalan had even provided me with a list of special requests that she'd come up with on her own. I worked alongside the other ranch hands on our tasks, while trying to come up with a plan to get to know her parents. I thought that if I could convince them I wasn't a bad guy, they'd persuade their daughter to have an interest in me. Of course, they wouldn't have to know that I'd already been in her pants, or that late at night she kept me from closing my eyes. All they needed to see was that I was a hard worker, with kind mannerism. In some ways it felt like I was a teenager again, going to meet my date's parents for the first time.

Since everyone was invited to the dinner, I went out and purchased a new pair of jeans, a button up shirt, and even a new pair of boots. My old ones were starting to wear, and even though they were extremely comfortable, they didn't exactly look presentable. Besides, I was pretty sure that the manure smell was baked into the leather.

With new ideas, and a fresh set of things to put on, I was ready to see her again, and do my best to try to win her over for the hundredth time. She'd soon know that I wasn't going to give up. Being with her had changed my life, and she might not have been able to admit it, but I knew she felt something for me too. Providing it was the hard part.

Chapter 19
Rusty

The day before the big party, I

was running around trying to make sure that
everything was in order. Noah was doing the same,
running after me task after task to double check.
When the workday was over I longed for a long, hot
shower to wash away the crud and sweat.

As soon as I pulled up at my trailer I saw Noah.
He hopped of the Gator and approached me with this
concerned look on his face. I swear I thought he knew
that I'd been with Isabella in the stables. I was certain
that his little sister had spilled our secret. I silently
prepared for him to come at me.

"Did you get things taken care of?"
I nodded. "Yeah."

He gave me that same sneer as before. "Everything all right with you, Rusty? You've been quiet the past couple of weeks. You used to carry on with some of the guys, and even they've noticed a difference. I need to know if you're in some kind of trouble. I hired you without question, but I can't have somethin' shady goin' on. If there's somethin' you need to tell me, I'm all ears."

I put my hands up. "Whoa. There's nothing shady going on. I assure you."

"All right then. I've already taken care of the chicken houses for tomorrow. That kid Johnny is goin' to handle them for us."

"Thanks. I'm just going to get up early and double check things at your parent's house. The tables will be set up in the pole building before everyone arrives."

He started to walk away, but turned around. "Thanks for all of this. This woman of mine is about to drive me bonkers. I'd much rather go to the court house. Don't ever get married, man. It's a pain in the ass."

Once he'd gone, I took a long shower trying to clear my head. Of course, the mere mention of being married had only given me reason to think about Simone. I'd been so focused on moving forward with Isabella that I felt guilty over not spending my nights mourning her and Sydney. I knew she wouldn't have wanted me to do it, but for so long it was how I'd gotten by.

It didn't take long for me to get myself all worked up. A hunger was building inside of me, and I only knew one way to feed it.

I didn't bother taking a golf cart, or looking around as I began my journey across the ranch, and down the long dirt lane. Her kitchen door was unlocked, and I refused to stand outside to get caught, or be rejected entrance, so I headed inside without waiting. I called for her twice, before I began looking around, only to find her in the shower. I knew I'd frighten her, but didn't hesitate pulling the curtain to make my appearance known.

She jumped. "Oh my God. You scared the shit out of me. What the hell are you doin' in my house? You need to leave, Rusty. Is there a vehicle outside? We're goin' to get caught."

"I walked. Relax. Nobody saw me." All I could do was stand there staring at that gorgeous body that I wanted to devour. My eyes showed her the exact reason for my visit, and it didn't take her long at all to decide what she was going to do about it.

Her gaze stayed focused on mine, as she took my hand. I was so shocked at what was happening that I didn't notice her pulling me in the water until it was too late.

I kissed her sweet lips before saying anything else, or arguing with her about being fully clothed. As the water soaked all of the fabric, I stood there, wrapping my arms around her tiny waist.

"So nobody knows you're here?" She needed extra confirmation.

My head moved from side to side, while I studied her reaction. From the shit-eating grin, I already knew she wasn't going to ask me to leave. "Nope. The kitchen door is locked and we're all alone."

Her fingernails trailed over my wet shirt. "You shouldn't be here, Rusty." I let her lift the fabric over my head, then watched as she unbuttoned my jeans, and started the task of pulling them down. They clung to my legs, but Isabella got them off with ease, probably because she had motive. I could feel her own hunger radiating off of that glistening body.

I reacted, pressing her against the cold shower wall, and ducking down to savor her sweet pussy again. The flavor was disguised by the rapid amount of water running over her skin, not that I cared much. My idea was to give her pleasure, before taking some for myself. It was my motto; never being selfish for sexual gain. Although one could describe this moment as exactly that. I'd come for one reason, and she was giving it to me without a fight.

I pulled my face away, only to finally answer her question. "I can't get enough of you. I need more."

With no warning I lifted her up, waiting for her legs to wrap around my back. She welcomed my kisses, and accepted all of me as I entered her. The sheer pleasure of being inside of her overwhelmed me again. I buried my head in between her breasts, pushing her with my body, so that I could run one hand over her hardened nipples. This beautiful woman had finally let me in. I couldn't get enough, and it was hard to control. I wanted to be lost in her, completely, with no concern for anyone else. We were two consenting adults, sharing a connection that was only natural. I'd waited for this woman to notice me, and now that it had happened, I wasn't willing to give it up.

After a few moments of straining to hold her up and do all of the things I wanted to do to her, I soon realized that it would be better if we continued on her bed. Carefully, I carried her wet body out of the bathroom and placed her down on the comforter on her mattress. She pulled me along with her, allowing me to savor her sweet lips.

I took my time, never caring about where I wasn't supposed to be. Nothing else was more important than remaining in bed with this woman, who'd gracefully helped me to begin to heal.

Each encounter we were learning more about each other, like the way she enjoyed being tickled just under her chin, or the way she responded when I kissed the lobe of her ear. I loved the way she laughed, and how she made little moan sounds when I gave her pleasure.

After spending a good hour in her bed, I let her know that I wouldn't be able to stop visiting her. I put my wet clothes back on, and kissed her goodbye, knowing that I'd have to head back to the trailer to change into dry clothes, before I could even settle in for the night.

It was difficult walking out that door, knowing she was still in bed naked. The annoying wet clothes left a smile on my face as I traveled back to my place, because I knew the reason they were still soaked was worth any lost amount of time.

That night it was hard to stay focused on anything. She was so close, yet unreachable in a sense. If I could only convince Noah that I wasn't a threat to his family, maybe he could get past his having to protect his cousin from me.

There had to be a way to get into his good graces, and I was determined to make it happen.

She was passed her first trimester, and we both knew that soon she'd have to tell everyone about the baby. As much as I wanted to be there for her, I knew she wasn't ready to hear that I wanted to be around and help her raise the baby. I'd thought a lot about it, and had made my mind up. Nothing brought me more happiness than being a father. I knew that nobody could ever replace Sydney, but at least I'd be able to feel that kind of love again.

With the upcoming nuptials of her cousin and his girlfriend, Isabella was on edge knowing that the family was coming in for a coed wedding shower. Her little belly was beginning to show, but she did a good job hiding it with baggy jackets, and sweatshirts. Since the weather was getting cooler in the evenings nobody would have questioned it. In fact, she probably could have gotten away with just saying she'd gained a few pounds, and they wouldn't have known any different.

Still, after worrying about it for so long she was ready to come clean. She was too far along for anyone to even suggest that she not keep the child. Even before we became something more, I think I would have lost my shit if I heard someone talking about that in front of me.

On the afternoon before her parents were due to arrive, she came walking into the stable. I hadn't spoken to her since I'd left her the night before. I could tell right away that something was bothering her. "What's wrong?"

She just about fell into my welcoming arms. "I'm scared."

I held her, while kissing the top of her head. "Don't be. They love you, and they'll love your child."

"I hope you're right."

She looked up into my eyes, pulling away from me as she did it.

"It's going to kill me to not hold you tonight. I know you're going to be stressed."

She turned and looked at me with such sad eyes. "If my brother's weren't comin' it would be different. I would probably ask you to come over."

"All you have to do is say the word. I'll sneak in once they're asleep if you want me to."

Isabella pulled away further. Her indecisive grimace let me know she was more confused than ever. "This changes nothin' you know. We're just friends, Rusty."

"I don't give a shit what you label this. It's something, and I'm not going to let you think you're in this all by yourself. That's what's making it so hard. You're doing this all alone. It ain't right."

"Just because I don't want to be in a relationship with you doesn't mean I don't appreciate that. I couldn't have done any of this without you. I hope you know that." She rubbed her belly and smiled. "The only reason I'm able to tell them is because I know I won't be alone, even if they push me away."

"We talked about this already. They won't do that."

"I hope you're right. I just know my dad. He's going to flip."

I smiled, imagining what it would have been like to see Sydney grow up and tell me she was pregnant. A warm feeling of anguish hit me, and it was difficult to ignore. "You better get going. You wouldn't want Noah to think something's going on between us, when obviously it's not." It was cruel to put it out there like that, but I was fighting my own battles with my heart and couldn't take anymore rejection.

I knew what had to be done, and was determined to make it happen. She'd never ask me to step in, and a part of me loved her for being independent like that, but another part of me longed for her to need me.

It had been so long since I'd felt this sort of connection. For weeks I'd spent every minute of every single day thinking about being close to her. The time we spent together was awakening, showing me that it was possible for me to move on. I had a reason to wake up every day and smile, and her name was Isabella Mitchell.

Knowing that I was about to be around her whole family, I prepared myself for what was to come. She was going to make that announcement, and I could choose to stand there and let it all play out, or do something drastic to secure my place in her life.

My choice was always the right thing to do. I really didn't have to think much about it at all. The time for being irrational and overthinking my decisions was long gone. If I wanted this second chance at happiness I was going to have to make sacrifices to have it.

Isabella Mitchell

Chapter 20
Isabella

Once again my mind was in a million places. The day had come that I was finally going to announce to the whole family that I was with child. I'd gotten through the first trimester, the morning sickness, the constant lethargy, and every other crappy symptom I suffered from so far. One thing that kept me from going insane was Rusty. He'd been there already for one pregnancy and knew just what I needed. He took care of me a much as I'd let him, and showed me what it was like to feel needed.

Yes, I said it.

I was admitting that there was something more between us than just sex. The more I fought with myself about it, the more I knew it to be the truth.

Of course, I refused to tell him, because I knew that my family couldn't know about our relationship. It was one thing to tell them that I was carrying Tate's child, but another story to tell them that I was in a sexual relationship with an older mysterious man. Besides, Noah had warned him to steer clear of me, so it only would put his job in jeopardy.

The other thing that bothered me was the fact that I was falling for a man who could never really love me. He'd lost his wife, and daughter, and been sure to let me know how much I reminded him of them. He'd been drawn to me because of that. In my heart I knew I'd never be able to accept never knowing if it was me he loved, or the connection that I had to his family.

After being with Tate, I needed someone that could give me their all, not just what they had left. Maybe it was selfish, but I had a child to think about, so settling wasn't an option.

As much as I was falling for him, I knew what we had was only going to be temporary. I'd start to get huge, and if that didn't scare him way, when the baby came it would change me. At some point he'd realize that I was nothing more than a reminder.

While biting off all of my fingernails, I heard a car pulling down the road. The motor shut off, and I prepared to be bombarded with hugs from someone in my family.

I heard my dad's voice first, beckoning me from the kitchen. "IZZY!"

I got up off the couch and made sure the hoodie I was wearing covered my stomach. The first thing he noticed was my weight. I wrapped my arms around him and watched him pull away and look at my face. "The last time I saw you, you were skin and bones. You look so healthy."

I raised my brows and pretended to be totally offended. "Geesh, are you sayin' I'm fat, daddy?"

"Never. You just look great, that's all. I'm glad to see you put on a few pounds."

My mom gave me this look, and I feared she could see right through my fake smile. She leaned forward and hugged me without addressing my weight. That was a big red flag, considering that she was always more vocal. "Your brothers drove themselves. Callie and Cammie came with them."

"What about Josh?"

"He's got football this weekend in Virginia. To be honest I'm surprised your brothers wanted to come. It's not like they care about a wedding." My dad was being stupid if he didn't know the real reason.

I raised my brow and let out an air-filled laugh. "They like to drink, and they know it's free here."

"Probably," he agreed. "I'll kick their asses if they wreck another golf cart."

"Yeah, get in line behind uncle Colt. He was pissed last time."

My mom grabbed my arm to catch my

attention. "Dad and I just wanted to stop by and see you first. I need to go help your aunt Van with dinner. We'll see you in a bit, honey."

I watched them leave, and out of the corner of my eye something was approaching the house. My brothers whipped around on the golf cart, pretending they were about to run into the porch. They both hopped off laughing, while climbing the steps with their small bags. "What's up, sis?" Jax hugged me first and then waited for Jake to do the same thing.

"You look different," Jake announced.

I pulled away and made sure my sweatshirt was protecting the bump in my belly. "My hair is longer."

He shrugged and went inside, letting the obvious change in my appearance go without a second look. Jax pulled me to the side once we were in the kitchen. The serious scowl on his face let me know that I wasn't going to appreciate what he was about to say. "You heard from your boy lately?"

"My boy?"

"Tate. Have you heard from him?"

I scrunched up my face and sat down at the table. "No. Why would you even ask me that?"

He laughed again, just as Jake came in. "I heard about it too, bro. His ass got shut down."

"What are y'all talkin' about?" As much as I didn't want to hear the mention of his name, obviously I was curious.

"Mom ran into his parents at the salon. His mom said that he'd been in the hospital for an apparent suicide attempt. He drank drain cleaner. What kind of idiot does that shit?"

I swear that my heart stopped beating for a second. All of the hate that I'd felt for my cheating ex was gone. "Why would he do that?" It was sickening to even imagine.

Jake came over and grabbed my arm as he spoke. "Get this. You know that chick he was seeing behind your back?" He paused and waited for me to nod. "Apparently she found out he'd been cheating on her and broke up with him. I guess the dude couldn't deal with it. I mean, one minute he's planning a wedding with the chick, and the next it's all gone. His mom said they'd been dating since elementary school or some shit. Then to add to that, he got in huge trouble at that new job. He showed up intoxicated, and tried to beat up his manager. They fired him that same day."

I looked down at my hands and tried my hardest to not let my brothers see my anguish. I'd been the reason that Jenn had broken up with Tate. I'd caused her so much pain that she'd pushed him away. The worst part of that was knowing exactly what I was doing. This was no accident. Then to imagine how upset he was, it was almost too much to fathom. Then on top of it all, he'd lost his job as a direct result of this all playing out. "So he's okay now?"

205

"Aside from being insane, yeah I guess. Did you know he was with this chick the whole time you were together? That is so fucked up."

I cocked my head from side to side. "Not really. It wasn't until the end of us seeing each other."

"Well like he said, it's fucked up. We would have beat his ass sooner if we knew about that," Jax added.

I knew I had to call Tate. Against my better judgment, I had to reach out to him. Guilt was already eating away at me. I'd taken everything away from him out of anger. Now he'd lost it all, and wanted to end his life. As angry as I was at what he'd done to me, I couldn't live with myself knowing that I was carrying his child and did nothing to make it better. "That's terrible. I haven't heard anything. I've been workin' a ton, and busy with life here. It sucks for him, but he made his choices." It hurt me to lie through my teeth. "Listen guys, I really need to get ready. Do you mind givin' me some privacy?"

As soon as they agreed, I rushed into my room, closing the door behind me. To prevent them from hearing me, I turned on my music and sat inside of my closet. With shaky hands I dialed his number that I'd never been able to forget.

He picked up after two rings. "Bella?"

"Hi, Tate. It's been a long time."

"Yeah, it has."

The line was silent. I knew we both had hard

feelings.

Since I didn't want to bring up my brothers, I came up with another way to let him know that I was aware of his situation. "Listen, my mom's here and she told me that you weren't doin' so good. Is it true? Did you try to end your life?" I could feel the burn in my throat starting and knew my emotions were a reaction to imagining him dead. No matter how much I tried to hate him, something so serious reminded me of all the reasons that I loved him in the first place.

"Yeah. If you're calling to scream at me, don't bother. You're the one who got me into this mess. I was going to be a good husband. She broke up with me, ended our engagement and it's all your fault. Nothing you say to me right now is going to change that. You ruined my life. Do you hear me?"

"Yes," I cried. "I'm so sorry, but you're the one who cheated. I feel bad for what's happened to you, but it's not all my fault. You drove me to that extreme."

"Don't bother apologizing to me. There's nothing you can say to give me back my life. Just lose my number. I can't deal with hearing from you, Bella. No matter how much I cared about you, I can't bring myself to ever forgive what's been done. It was bad enough losing you, but her too? Was it really that necessary to destroy me?"

"Wait," I pleaded. "There's somethin' you need to know." I was still bitter about Jenn, but he had a right to be angry with me.

"Goodbye."

He hung up before I could bring myself to tell him the truth. I'm not saying that he didn't deserve to get caught cheating. He'd hurt me, and obviously Jenn. To be cheated on was the ultimate kind of betrayal, and she deserved to know as much as I did. For years he'd strung us both along.

I stayed in my closet until I was finally able to accept what needed to be done.

After throwing on some clothes that looked presentable, I set out to reveal to my whole family that I was pregnant with Tate's child.

Since the party was located at Noah's parent's house, located on the ranch, I took a golf cart and pulled into their yard. My younger cousins were conversing out on the porch. I scanned the surrounding area, scoping for Noah or Shalan. Out of the corner of my eye I saw Rusty walking toward me. He carried flowers in his hand and smiled when I greeted him. "Hey, have I missed you today."

Right away I felt guilty. Had I not found out that Tate had attempted suicide I would have been head over heels for this kind of announcement. Instead it made me feel uncomfortable. I wanted nothing more than to move forward, but the odds were already against us. I was pregnant with another man's child, and Rusty had been told to steer clear of me. In light of the new information I'd been given, my decision was made. There was no way that I could expect anything to work out in my favor. The damage was done.

"I better get inside."

He grabbed me and held me from walking away. "Are we okay?"

With a quick nod I pulled out of his hold. "You can't touch me around my family, Rusty. I've got enough to worry about."

He threw up his hands. "Sorry. I'll just go give Mrs. Mitchell these flowers and pretend I don't know you."

I tried to think of what to say to make him not feel hurt, but it was no use. As much as I wanted to be with Rusty, I knew it wasn't going to happen. Our summer fling was about to end, and with that knowledge I felt so defeated.

I knew my hormones were making me feel crazy things, but enough was enough. Something had to give. I couldn't want Rusty one minute, and refuse him the next. It wasn't fair to him, or me even.

When I entered the house I found my parents and the rest of my family all conversing together. This dinner wasn't the official wedding shower, so it wouldn't rustle feathers if I announced my pregnancy. Of all the people there, Shalan was probably going to end up being the most supportive.

For a while it was easy to blend in with my family and avoid Rusty. The problem with that was the fact that I actually caught myself looking for him. I caught his stare quite a few times before we all headed out to the pole barn where all of the tables and chairs would fit.

Music was playing as I sat down at the table next to my parents with my brothers, just like I was used to doing. Jax was already doing his normal scheming with Jake. I saw them whispering and pointing toward Christian. With a swift kick to one of their legs I caught both of their attention. "Don't even think about it. So help me God I will beat you to the ground, and then let Noah have a turn."

My parents looked at me like I had three heads. When my dad reached across the table and grabbed my hand I immediately felt our bond breaking. He didn't even know the news and already was concerned about me. "It would be nice if you didn't do that while wearing a white shirt, honey. You know that blood stains are horrible to get out." Even his humor couldn't get a reaction out of me. I was frozen with guilt.

A few minutes later we all stood to say grace. Everyone bowed their heads and I secretly scanned the room to find Rusty. His eyes were on mine. I watched as he winked and formed a smile in the corner of his lips. A part of me wanted to smile back, but it would only give him false hope, when I knew there was none left.

Then the room got quiet. My heart raced, my hands felt clammy, and I swore that if I didn't make my announcement at any second I was going to chicken out and not do it at all. So as the family took their seats I remained standing and blurted out the hard truth I'd been so frightened to share. "I'm pregnant."

My dad laughed for a second, of course thinking it was just one of our family pranks. Since we were known for some drastic shenanigans, he never would have dreamed that I was making this kind of announcement because it was true. It wasn't until I sank down in my seat and watched his reaction that he knew it wasn't a joke. "Daddy, say somethin'." The tears were already running down my face, and as I lifted my hand to wipe them away I could see how much my body was shaking.

The room remained quiet, and I could see Noah coming over near our table. While looking down at the napkins, I repeated my announcement. "I'm in my second trimester. I'm due in March."

My dad kept staring, and I swore that he was about to explode. The pain in his eyes let me know that my biggest fear was happening. My mom caught my attention next. "Honey, why did you wait so long to tell us?"

Jake busted in. "Who is the daddy?"

"Is it that douche, Bells?" Noah's question send chills down my spine.

Just as I was about to accept my fate and be honest, I heard someone yelling from across the room. All eyes turned in that direction.

"It's mine."

Rusty stood there, his hands in his pockets, with a big grin on his face, as if I'd just delivered my family the happiest news of their lives.

I sat there in shock, not knowing what to do.

Chapter 21
Rusty

I'd like to say that everyone welcomed me into the family and accepted that I was the father of Isabella's unborn child, but that's not exactly how it all panned out.

After I'd stood up and blurted out that comment, everyone turned their attention to me. Not that their expressions mattered at all. I was only focused on one person and from the utter disbelief on her face I knew that she wasn't very happy.

A few things happened at one time. The room got loud with everyone talking at once, and Noah started to come after me. The twins, which I knew were Isabella's brothers, both grabbed him and held him back. Mr. Colt Mitchell walked up to me and sat down at the table. While all of the commotion was taken place around us, he motioned for me to join him. I could see her father eying me up, and knew it was only going to be a matter of time before he was hunting me down. For all he knew I'd knocked up his daughter, and it was very obvious that we hadn't come to this party as a couple.

Colt looked me dead in the eyes. "I reckon you need to start explainin' to me what's goin' on here. I never pegged you to be a trouble maker, but I'm sure you can imagine that this predicament my niece is in ain't very settlin'. You see, I promised her daddy that we'd keep her safe, and now I've got to explain to him how my ranch hand has been screwing around with his child. You can see where this is going to be a problem, can't you Rusty?"

I nodded. "I do. Before I say anything more I think it would be best to let you know that I care deeply for her."

We heard yelling and turned our attention back to where Isabella stood with her parents. She had her face covered and I could tell she crying. When she rushed outside, I got up and left Mr. Mitchell sitting at the table so I could chase after her.

Even as I called her name she continued walking. Until we reached the first set of stables she never turned around to address me. Once inside it was a different story. I'd no sooner made it over the threshold when I felt a hand slapping across my face. The burn was already apparent when she began screaming at me. "How could you? This is none of your concern. My pregnancy ain't your business, Rusty."

I tried to grab her arms as I replied. "Will you just calm down and hear me out? I did this so we can be together. Don't you see that this solves everything?"

"What are you talking about? I never said I wanted to be with you, Rusty. You knew that I was strugglin' with my baby's father already, and now you do this. Not only will my family think I'm a whore, but they'll hate me for sure. So thanks for nothin'!"

I didn't know what to say. In all honesty I thought she'd be happy. Every time we'd been alone a side of her came out that screamed to be with me. It made absolutely no sense.

"I'm real sorry that you feel that way. Do you want me to go back in there and tell them all it was a lie?"

She shook her head with fresh tears streaming down her cheeks. "No. They'll fire you for sure, and make you leave the ranch. I might be pissed at you, but I'd never want to cause another man his livelihood. I just wish you would have talked to me. I had everything worked out in my head, and now I've got a mess to figure out."

I reached for her and held one of her hands in mine. She didn't try to pull away. "Iz, I did this because I want to be with you. I could be a good dad to that baby. If what I do isn't enough for you I could start

215

practicing again and get my license reinstated."

"No." She finally removed her hand from mine and took a step backwards. "I refuse to live my life as someone's replacement, Rusty. It's not happenin'. Now can you please just leave me alone? I need to get my head on straight before I go back in there and deal with my family.

I looked down at the ground, only hearing her call herself a replacement. It definitely got to me on a deeper level than she probably set out to do. Before I could consider saying anything else to piss her off, I turned and walked away, passing her mother, and Shalan when I did.

I should have been prepared for Noah to come seek me out. From the amount of anger that was gleaming off of his face I knew it was going to get ugly. As my heart rate picked up I prepared myself for a physical confrontation.

Noah approached me quickly, coming up on me with his arm jacked back. "I trusted you."

I put my hands up, determined that I wasn't going to fight back. Not only had Isabella's words messed me up, but somehow I wanted him to hurt me. I was already feeling pretty low, and without the hope of being with his cousin, I didn't really have anything to be optimistic about. She was most likely already spilling to her mother that I wasn't the father.

Just imagining never being with her again felt like daggers stabbing into my heart. I should have never let myself feel something again, when I knew I wouldn't be able to control how it all played out. "Go ahead. Just get it over with. I know I deserve it."

Out of nowhere came Mr. Tyler Mitchell. I'd been working at the ranch for long enough to be familiar with who everyone was. He looked upset, but not so much angry. Noah looked over at his uncle, and then in the distance we both spotted his father coming toward us. He put his arm down and took a couple steps back. "Uncle Ty. I was just -."

The man put his hands up to motion for him to be quiet. "Go back to the party, Noah. I'll handle this myself."

Knowing that Noah's father was my main boss, I feared what he was walking over to say to me. For sure he was going to have me packing by the end of the night.

Tyler spoke first. "Rusty." He shook his head and scratched it, as if he was trying to refrain from saying the wrong thing. Colt came up and stood behind him with his arms crossed over his chest. "You knocked up my daughter."

"It's not what you think, sir."

"Don't call me sir. You're probably close to my age than my daughter's. Ty is fine for the time being."

"Okay, Ty. Like I said before. This isn't how it seems," It was hard to explain something that was a lie, in order to pass it off as the truth.

"Well the way I see it, you knocked up my daughter and the cat is out of the bag. She's obviously decided to keep the child, being that she's so far along." He looked down for a second, and even I could tell he was distraught. "This is bullshit. Do you hear me? That's my little girl that you put your hands on. Forgive me for wanting to break you in half right now. I'm just not able to control the aggression that I'd like to take out on you."

Colt stepped in, putting his hand on his cousin's shoulder. "I think it's best if we all just calm down before we do somethin' we might regret. Don't you agree?" The question was for Ty, not me. He waited for him to nod before continuing. "Rusty, I've always considered you a good man. Isabella is a beautiful young lady, and I can see where you'd want to get to know her. You're both adults, and things can happen that is beyond our control. Now, I understand Noah had asked you to not pursue somethin' with my niece. Is that true?"

I nodded. "Yes. He did several times."

"And you disobeyed that request?"

My response was more a shrug. "I suppose I did."

"It takes two to tango, and if anyone knows somethin' about forbidden relationships it's this guy here. Once upon a time he was told the same thing as you. So I'm sure he understands how difficult that can be sometimes."

Isabella's dad immediately gave his cousin one of those looks that says 'I'm kicking your ass for this later', while I tried not to smile. It wasn't that I wanted them to immediately accept me into the family. My decision hadn't been based on that at all. I'd done this to protect Isabella, not hurt her. "I can assure you that I'll do everything I can to support your daughter. I understand what Noah had asked me, but the truth is that I care for her. No disrespect to you, but this wasn't about the sex."

"Save it. I can't think about her that way do you understand? I can't picture my little girl with child. I realize it is happening, but it's too new to accept. I came over here to prevent my nephew from making this personal. For now, until I can talk to my daughter, I'm -."

In the distance we all heard Noah. "I want him off this property!"

Near the stable I could see Isabella walking toward us with her mother and Shalan in tow. "Daddy, wait. Please don't let Noah kick Rusty out. This ain't his fault. He's just tryin' to protect me and the baby. He can't lose his job."

Her dad looked from me to Isabella. "Sweetie, I don't know what you want me to say."

She looked right at her father, as if none of us were around. "I want you to say that you love me, and you'll support me. I know I hurt you." Her sobs became apparent and Ty wrapped his arms around her without hesitation.

"I do love you, Iz. That's never going to be a question you need to worry about. You're my daughter. No matter what you do, I'll continue loving you. This is all a shock. I don't even know what to say."

"Say that you and Mom will love your grandchild. Please. I need to know I'm not alone."

I watched an upset father begin to get emotional in front of a crowd of people. He sniffled and leaned his face down onto his daughter's shoulder. My heart broke for the bond that they shared, and I finally realize why she was so afraid. I didn't know their history, but clearly they were close. Her mother joined in, putting her arms around both of them. I could hear Isabella crying even though I couldn't see her any longer. They talked amongst themselves while all three becoming caught up in despair.

Colt put his hand on my shoulder and motioned for me to follow him. Since I assumed that my time on the ranch was about to end, I continued looking back at Isabella. It was so juvenile, but I didn't even have her phone number. If I was being escorted off the property this could be one of the last times I'd get to see her. Surely her family would have her move home, which would make sense. She had nothing keeping her in Kentucky, especially me.

"You need to give them time," he explained. "This isn't about you seein' her, Rusty. To be honest, I think you're probably a good man. It took a lot of courage for you to stand up in front of everyone and admit what you did. Right now we all need time to take it in. Our family doesn't do well with secrets, and you're just about the most secretive man I've met."

He was right. I needed to tell them who I was if I wanted a chance at ever being respected. "Do you want me to leave the ranch?"

"No. However, I do need you to go home. Give her time to talk to them. It's best for everyone."

"Yes, sir. I'll leave now." It wasn't what I wanted to do, but I had no other options. I hadn't thought about the repercussions of such a big confession. Never had it concerned me that I'd be causing a commotion. Isabella was a wreck, and her parents weren't taking the news as being happy. It was to be expected, but still didn't make it easier to understand. They didn't know what it was like to lose their child. I think when that happens you're willing to let little things go. Given the chance to do it all over I never would have told my daughter no to anything she asked.

While walking back to the trailer I thought about what I was going to say to Isabella. She was so angry with me, and I knew if I didn't get back into her good graces she was going to push me further away.

Chapter 22
Isabella

As if things couldn't get worse.

Rusty had made my problems double. Standing there in my dad's arms, hearing him crying, was the epitome of how much of a mess I'd made of my life. That one night with Tate was going to haunt me until the day I died, and I wanted to hate him for it.

Knowing that I still felt guilt about him losing his job, and basically everything else, I was determined to find a way to help him. It wasn't clear how my baby fit into the whole picture, but I was certainly going to do everything in my power to rectify his current situation. For the time being, I knew I couldn't hurt my family any more, so Rusty taking responsibility was going to have to stick. That meant that I had to come to terms with it and treat him at least nice while the family was around.

The bottom line was that I was still pissed at him for doing it without talking to me first.

Because of how everything had played out, our family get together didn't continue as expected. My parents and I headed back to my house, while the rest of the family attempted to pretend that nothing had happened.

I was sure my brothers were getting into trouble, and Shalan was going crazy trying to stay in control. More than anything I wished I could be there celebrating with everyone.

Anything was better than sitting in my living room across from my disappointed parents. I played with the fabric on the out recliner that I was sitting in, trying to think of ways to break the uncomfortable silence in the room. We'd been back for at least a half hour and besides making drinks, none of us had anything to say.

My father was leaning forward with his elbows on his knees. His face was covered by his hands. My mother, who seemed to be in better shape than my dad, rubbed his back, while sobbing to herself.

This wasn't like you see in the movies, where the family is over-ecstatic. My parents were acting as if my entire future was over, and I suppose in some ways it wasn't what they wanted for me. I just knew that someday I wanted to have a family. Yes, I'd gone about doing it all wrong, but I wasn't going to look back and regret it. Every single moment of knowing that I had a child growing inside of me made that choice easy. This was my baby, and he or she was going to be my future, with or without anyone's approval.

"Please say somethin'." I couldn't sit in silence any longer.

My dad wiped off his face and finally sat straight. "What do you want us to say? Were you even planning on telling us that you were shackin' up with the help?"

"Daddy? Do you have to look at it that way?"

"Your father is just hurt, sweetie. We wanted so much more for you. You just graduated college and started a great job. You've got so much ahead of you. We don't understand how this could have happened. You never mentioned that man to us once. Accordin' to your cousin, he was warned to steer clear of you. Is that why you kept it a secret?"

I wish I knew how to explain my relationship with Rusty, but more than that I wished that I could come clean about the real biological father of my baby. Trying to describe my relationship situation with my parents required me to lie to their faces. I felt so sick over doing it, even as the words escaped my lips. "Our relationship is complicated." I looked down and played with my fingernails, knowing I couldn't even begin to look in their direction. "He was around when I was going through a tough time, and to be honest I wasn't lookin' for a relationship. It just sort of happened."

I knew without even looking that my father was cringing at the idea of me being intimate with a man. Both of my parents knew this wasn't just any guy my age, who was trying to make a future for himself. Rusty appeared to be a drifter, with no real future for anything. Had I been able to tell them that he was once a successful person maybe it would have gone in a whole separate direction. "Does he love you?" Of course my dad would want to know that. He'd kill a man for disrespecting me.

When I opened my mouth to answer I thought of my last conversation with Rusty. I'd told him that I couldn't be with someone that compared me to his dead family. A wave of emotions hit me as I realized how awful I must have made him feel. It still didn't change the fact that I'd never be able to know if his feelings were for me, or just because of some sick reminder that I provided him with. "Yes. I think so," I lied.

"You think so?"

"We've never said it out loud. Come on, it's not like you and Mom. I didn't know right away that we were fated to be together forever."

My dad let out an air-filled laugh and shook his head, while my mom gave me her normal confused stare. "Bella, don't be sarcastic. Your father is just concerned."

"I get it, okay? I'm havin' a child. I'm goin' to be a mother. I don't see why it's so hard to be able to hear. You got knocked up and planned on doin' it all alone too. You didn't know Daddy was goin' to step up and take responsibility when you made the decision to keep me."

"This is different. I thought I lov-."

My dad wasn't going to let her discuss my sperm donor. The mere mention of his name gave me the creeps anyway. "Don't you dare compare this, young lady. Your mother made the choice because she thought she was going to have support. Yes, things happened and the rest is history, but her life isn't yours. How do you know this Rusty guys isn't going to disappear on you?"

"He won't." I had no idea if he'd stick around, especially when the truth about Tate came out. Still, I had to appease them for the time being. "He's not like that."

"What do you even know about this guy? Your

uncle always says he's a bit insane. Aunt Van thinks he's creepy and probably has a shady past." Leave it to my aunt to freak out. She'd been through a terrible time with my biological father. After that she'd never trusted mysterious men. "I know he's a good man, and that he'd do anything for me. Isn't that all that matters?"

"Of course he's going to be nice. He's screwing someone that just got out of college." My dad stood up. I could see his fists clenched, like he wanted to punch something.

"Can we just drop the Rusty part for a minute? This is why I waited to tell you. I know I'm not perfect, but I make good money, and if I had to I could take care of me and my baby alone. Now, I don't need your support, but I sure could use it. You're treatin' me like it's the end of the world, and it's not. I'm having a baby, not becomin' a stripper."

"If you became a stripper I wouldn't be this calm. Damn, don't even joke about that." He walked into the kitchen and came back with a beer. I watched him open it and take a sip, all the while I thought about Rusty, and the reason he didn't drink.

"Bella, your dad and I will always support you. We're just in shock, that's all. This baby is our family. Of course we're goin' to love it, and support you. Whatever you need, we'll take care of it, won't we, babe?"

My dad shook his head. "Yeah. Sorry, I'm just trying to come to grips with being a grandfather. I'm old as shit. Next I'll be having a heart attack and keeling over."

"Daddy, don't say that." My overuse of the 'daddy' only made it more apparent that I was desperate. Everyone in the room knew it, but nobody was bringing it up.

"You're making us grandparents before we even turn fifty. It's a bit hard to grasp."

I stood up from the chair and walked over to my dad. My arms wrapped around his stiff body, and finally I felt him reciprocating. "I love you, Daddy. Please don't ever say that. I'm going to need you to stick around, and so is your grandchild. I can't bring another Mitchell into this world without the two of you by my side."

He pulled away and looked me right in the eyes. "We'll be there, Izzy. You know we will."

Things got better after that moment. My parents stuck around for a short time after that and finally headed back to my aunt and uncles to go to bed. I knew neither of them would get much sleep, but at least they didn't hate me like I'd feared.

Since I knew my brothers would need to get in the house, I left it unlocked. Never in a million years would I think Rusty would have snuck over to see me, but as I sat up in my own bed seeing him standing over me, I knew it was true.

"What are you doin' here?"

"I think you know the answer to that."

"If my family finds out they might hogtie and torture you." There was no telling what Noah had imagined doing to him.

"I'm not concerned about your family. I ain't here for them."

"Why are you here? I thought I told you to stay away from me."

"That's not going to happen, Iz. I can't leave you alone, not anymore."

"This changed nothin'! You're not even the father of this child. How could you stand up and make such a mockery of yourself. They're goin' to find out the truth. It's only a matter of time." I wasn't trying to threaten him, or bring him pain. I just wanted him to feel bad for adding to my stress.

"I don't care if they find out the truth. By that time it won't matter anyway."

I was intrigued. "Why is that?"

"Because you'll be in love with me."

His statement shocked me, especially coming out of his mouth. He was always so quiet, never cocky. "What did you just say?"

"I said you'll be in love with me." It was freaking me out that he was just standing over me, so I sat up and backed my ass further on my bed. He crouched down and leaned forward so our faces were even. "Once you admit it, there's no telling what we could be."

I used my feet to push him away. "You're foolin' yourself if you think that will happen."

"I know you feel somethin'."

"I know you're crazy. Please go home Rusty. I've had enough drama for one night." All I wanted to do was go to sleep, or at least try.

"I'll leave, but only if you let me say one more thing."

"Whatever. Say it and go." I crossed my arms and waited.

He pointed at me as he spoke. "You said something to me tonight that I can't shake off. I realize that I came onto you because of how you reminded me of my girls, but never since that very moment I felt those sweet lips on mine, have I ever compared you to them, or tried to replace them with you. This thing between us is real and it's new."

"Please leave." I could feel that burning in my throat again, and didn't want him seeing me emotional. If he stayed for another second I was going to beg him to be with me, and that couldn't happen.

"I'm telling you the truth."

"I don't care," I lied again. "Just go. I'm too pissed at you to ever consider hearing the words comin' out of your mouth."

He tossed his hands high above him. "Fine.

233

This is obviously hopeless."

I listened for him to exit out the back door before I let myself cry. My life was a mess, and I knew I had to get it figured out before my baby was born.

Chapter 23
Rusty

She'd shut me down again. You'd think I'd be used to it and stop trying, but no, I was always glutton for a punishment.

Halfway back to my trailer I saw headlights coming in my direction. Since I was trying to avoid the family at all costs I darted into the woods and crouched down. The last thing I needed was to be in some kind of brawl. I was a grown man with morals. Just because they all believed me to be a terrible person didn't mean it was real.

When I got back to my trailer I locked the door and just stood there with my hand on the knob. I leaned my head against it and closed my eyes. This was one of those times where I craved a drink. Even though I knew it wouldn't solve anything, it would at least numb the pain and frustration that I was feeling.

It took me a while to leave that spot and kick off my boots. All of my efforts to impress her family had failed. Not even my ridiculously expensive outfit was going to help my cause. Once I was down to my boxer shorts I headed for the bedroom. The night was ending, and I needed to calm down before I woke up and had to answer all of their burning questions and accusations.

I don't really know how long I'd been asleep, but when I peered at the clock I noticed it was nearly three in the morning. Something had woken me up, so I sat there, waiting to see if it was just a dream or maybe a critter underneath the trailer. Then I heard it again. A light knocking caused me to jump out of bed and cautiously make my way to the front door. Being that her family was out for blood, I grabbed my large flashlight and prepared to open the door. In just my underwear, I cracked the door, shaking and ready to attack.

Isabella stood there, her hands crossed over her chest. "Can you take a walk with me?"

"It's the middle of the night. Come inside."

The light of the moon was the only thing allowing me to see her. She looked down and then shook her head from side to side. "I can't come inside, because we both know what will happen if I do."

I have to admit that hearing her say that gave

me some comfort. It meant that no matter how mad she was at my actions, she still knew she'd want me. "I need to put on some pants. Can you at least step in here while I do that?"

Even though she was hesitant, I watched as she climbed the three steps and stood in the doorway. I headed back the bedroom, the whole time wondering if I was dreaming this whole thing. She'd obviously walked all the way to my place in the middle of the night. When I came back out she was sitting on the couch. I stood in front of her and reached out my hand. "It's warmer inside. Are you sure you want to walk?"

"I'm not sure about anything. That's why I'm here in the middle of the damn night. This is all so messed up. I don't know what in the hell I'm doin'." I kneeled down in front of her and placed my hand on her knees. "Don't."

"Don't what?"

"You can't touch me like that. You can't touch me at all." She stood up and pushed me to the side as she walked clear across the room. "This is the problem. I can't be around you and not want somethin' more. When you're around it messes with my head."

"I'm not following you, Iz."

She took several steps toward me. While peering into my eyes she began to explain. "This thing between us has to be over, Rusty. I can't keep fightin' this."

237

I reached forward, grabbing the elastic to her pajama pants. She moved closer with ease, and her breath was hot against my face as I attempted to change her mind. "I can't let you give up."

I watched her eyes close as I inched my lips to hers. My hand kept a firm hold on her pants, in fear that she'd try to pull away. Our first kiss was slow, and cautious. It wasn't until I felt her hands touching my upper arms that I finally let go and wrapped my hands on her waist.

Just as I was about to guide her back to my bedroom she pulled back. "No. I didn't come here for this."

I wiped my mouth before speaking. "Then what? Did you walk all this way to tell me to go to Hell? These mood swings of yours are making my head spin, Iz. It's like one second your right there with me and the next your somewhere else. I never know what to expect."

"Exactly!" She sat back down on the couch. "Don't you get it? You make me crazy. It's got to stop. All of this has to stop. That's why I want you to stay away from me. I need to make good decisions. Please, if you care about me at all, you'll let me do this."

I put my hands on my head unable to rationalize with her form of decision making. "This is ridiculous. I'm not some child you can send to the corner. I'm a grown man who wants to be with a grown woman. Why is that so hard for you to get? You say you're confused, but all I'm seeing is you fighting yourself. You and I both know there's something between us. Why can't you admit it? Why is it so hard for you to look me in the eyes and tell me how you feel?"

"You know why. I already told you. I'm not going to fill some void you have for your family. I don't care how good you'd treat me."

"Isabella, don't say that, especially when you know it ain't the truth."

"The truth is a joke." She began to sniffle like she was fighting tears. I pulled her to a standing position and forced her to look at me.

"My feelings have nothing to do with who you may or may not look like. I want you because you make me feel alive again. I think about you all of the time because I can't get your lips out of my head. I long to be with you because I'm falling in love with you." My next words were almost a whisper. "Why can't you believe that?"

She looked away and started crying. "Because I can't."

"You can't, or you refuse to? Is this even about me?"

She wouldn't answer.

"It's not about me at all." I let go of her arms and backed away. "It's about the father of your child, isn't it? After everything you've told me you still want to be with him?"

"It's not like that."

"How is it not like that? You either want to be with me, or you want to be with him. Don't tell me that you don't want your child to have a father, because one look at the bond you have with your own dad would prove that theory untrue."

I knew I was pushing the limits with her. If I knew anything I knew she was ready to break. It was never my intention to stress her out, but I certainly wasn't okay with her walking away from me when I knew I was the better choice.

"Rusty, please don't make me answer. Just let me go back to my house." Why was she avoiding it?

"So that's it? Does he know about the baby? Did you already call him, and that's why you're pissed at me? Did I ruin your plan to bring him back into the family?"

"Stop it," she pleaded.

"No. I need to know. Is that it? Is that why you can't let yourself fall in love with me?" Admittedly, saying that out loud brought up some feelings that I wasn't prepared to experience. I wanted this woman, more than I even knew. The idea of her pushing me away for someone else hurt. It was like an oozing cut that was going to get infected and eventually cause me to lose a part of myself. I focused on my breathing as I spoke. "Please answer me."

"Yes, okay? It's because of Tate. Are you happy now? Is this what you wanted, Rusty? Did you want me to come over tonight to hurt you? Does it make you feel better knowin' that I don't want to be with you?" Her words stabbed me in the heart, and for a few seconds I had to look away and clench my jaw to avoid showing her how her words were getting to me.

"No," I grabbed both of her arms and pulled her close to me. "I'm not happy, but I also know you're lying about something. There's no way that you don't feel what's between us. Look me in the eyes and tell me you don't want me. TELL ME DAMN IT!" I raised my voice and watched her jump. Her glossed over eyes looked petrified.

"I -." She tried to speak, but couldn't bring herself to do it.

I knew what I had to do, and I wasn't going to hold back this time. My lips smacked against hers, as my hand reached around and grabbed the back of her head. At first she tried to pull away from our kiss, but after only a few seconds she was being lifted in my arms and carried to my bed.

There was nothing slow and passionate about this encounter. Clothes were ripped off as I prepared to claim her, to take what I knew was going to be mine. She wasn't going to deny me what I already knew she wanted.

Her naked body welcomed me. I filled her with every bit of pent up emotion I had in me. She clung to my skin, digging those nails deep into the edges of my back. The harder she scratched, the more I got off on it. Our lips collided, vigorously meshing our tongues only to pull away and tease each other with them. Our pace never slowed, knocking the headboard of my bed loudly against the wall in the room. She reached back and held onto the top of it, allowing me to slam in and out of her. Her pussy, so wet, yet tight enough to make my dick feel smothered, fulfilled my lust for her. The second I felt those inner walls squeezing, I came hard, hovering over her while I gained some sense of stability. Finally, after opening my eyes to admit what we'd just done, I peered into hers, waiting for her to respond in some way. When she said nothing I leaned down and drug my lips overs hers. Her eyes closed again, and I watched as she sucked her bottom lip into her mouth and moaned. "I don't care what you say, Iz. I know exactly where you want to be."

Since I didn't feel like arguing, I fell to her side and held her close. We laid there naked, and together, falling asleep in each other's arms.

Chapter 24
Isabella

I woke up to a ray of sun coming in the bedroom window. It took me a second to realize that I wasn't in my own bed. Rusty's arm was stuck to my chest, and I took my time lifting it and moving it so that I could get up. I had every intention of being gone before he opened his eyes. It was better this way. No matter what he'd tried to get me to admit last night, it wasn't going to change anything. I knew what I had to do, and as much as I wished we could be something more, I knew it wasn't going to happen.

I'd given him one more night to say goodbye. Maybe I should have told him that's what it was, but some things were better left unsaid. That's why my plan was to get back to my house before he even noticed that I wasn't in his bed.

I made it to the edge of the bed when someone started beating on his bedroom window. It frightened me, causing me to jump and lose my balance. I fell back on the bed, putting my hand up to my heart. With the curtains closed I had no idea who was knocking, but I couldn't stand the thought of getting caught naked. Rusty reached over and I turned to look at him. He seemed tired, probably because we'd stayed up arguing, and then had sex. I was so stressed that sleeping wasn't happening anyway. "Who the hell is beating on the window?"

"I don't know. Help me find my pants." I scanned the room, but didn't spot them.

Rusty paid no attention to me being naked. He climbed out of bed and walked over to the window. The curtain opened and he shut it quickly. It was hard to not notice that he was standing in front of me without any clothes on. His morning erection was at full attention. He reached down and grabbed it, while heading for the bathroom.

I started to ask who was at the window when he made the announcement. "Your dad's outside. You should probably go let him in."

This was devastating. I'd made such progress with them only to be caught naked in Rusty's bed. "Are you jokin'?"

He had already started peeing when he answered. "Nope. He's out there pacing around. Take a look for yourself. I leaned over and opened the curtain enough to look out. His face was up against the glass. "I know you're in there. Let me in damn it."

I closed the curtain quickly and started rushing around the room in panic. The mirror on the bedroom door scared me when I saw my reflection out of the corner of my eye. Seeing my naked silhouette was also depressing. For a second I stood there looking at the bump that seemed to be growing every day. Rusty came in and headed for his dresser. "What are you doing? He's really outside, Iz."

"I just want to prolong gettin' reamed out for a couple minutes. I'm fat as shit. Look at my stomach."

He leaned over and nestled his head up to my neck, kissing me softly as he spoke. "You're pregnant and beautiful. There's a life inside of you. You're not fat."

"Ew, how can you say that? How can you want to be with me when I look like this? I'm just goin' to get fatter."

My dad beat on the window again. "I know you're in there, Isabella Mitchell."

Rusty dressed faster than me and headed out into the kitchen. I found him very brave to be able to invite my dad in when it was obvious that I'd spent the night. For a few seconds I felt like a teen again, who was about to be punished for months.

After I gave up on my pajama pants, and settled for a pair of his boxers, I threw on my bra and a t-shirt and walked into the living room. Rusty was making coffee, standing in the kitchen, while my dad sat in a chair near the front door.

I walked in and sat on the couch across from him, still contemplating what to say. "Hi, Dad."

"Your mom and I got up early to take you out to breakfast. When you weren't in your room, I figured I'd find you here. So," He scratch his head and looked toward Rusty, avoiding making eye contact with me. "did you want to go with us, Rusty?"

I looked over at the man I'd spent the night with. His hair was sticking up, and his t-shirt was on backwards. He'd gotten dressed so fast that he hadn't even noticed. My eyes were telling him to say 'no', so of course he said 'yes'.

"Great. I'm just going to wait over at your house until you both get dressed. Van's making a big breakfast for everyone, but I already told her we were doing our own thing. See you in a few, guys." My dad got up and left without looking at me one time. I couldn't believe how disappointed I felt with myself.

"Oh my God. My dad hates me."

"He does not. He's trying to be supportive. It's obvious that we're together, so he wants to get to know me. If that's what I have to do then..."

"We're not together, Rusty."

"I'm not doing this with you again. You say one thing when I know it's the opposite. You wouldn't have stayed with me if you didn't want to."

I was tired of fighting with him. "I'm tellin' my parents Tate is the father." It was the only way to get him to stop pushing me.

The room got quiet and Rusty sat down at the kitchen table, refusing to look my way. I suppose all men were stubborn like that.

"He's the baby's father. It's the right thing to do."

"Is it what you want though? Because the way you're acting is as if you're choosing to be with him. Is that it? That's what you want?"

I looked down at the old, warn, blue carpet. "It doesn't matter what I want. The baby comes before everything."

"Just answer the question, Iz."

I stood up and walked toward the chair where he sat. It was unnerving how much pull he had on my heart. I closed my eyes when I answered, because I knew I couldn't lie while looking in his direction. "I don't love you, Rusty. I'm sorry. You deserve to know the truth." While saying it, I lost control and started blubbering.

He turned around and looked at me with painstaking eyes. "Why are you crying then?"

"I need to leave. I'll tell my parents that you couldn't come."

Rusty grabbed my arm, preventing me from exiting the house. "I'm coming with you."

"You're kiddin'? I just told you that I don't love you, and you're..."

He didn't let me get the words out. His lips found mine and I was a puddle of angst in his hands. I didn't know whether to push him away, slap him, or throw my arms around him and beg him to take me back to bed.

I pulled away and put my hands up to keep him from coming forward. That pain in his eyes from before was back, and I knew it was because I'd hurt him. "You're shirt's on wrong. At least fix it before we go to my house."

There was no use in arguing. If Rusty wanted to go along with this charade for my parents it would at least give me time to figure out how I was going to tell Tate about the baby. Even a little time with Rusty was better than knowing he was on the same ranch as me and I couldn't be with him. How this all played out was still in the air. All I knew was that for the moment I was going to have to be content with Rusty at my side.

My parents insisted on driving their SUV to the restaurant. I sat in the back with my hands folded, waiting for them to start asking us questions from the front seat. I expected my father to be all over Rusty's business, but he said nothing to him, well not until we made it the establishment.

It was pretty obvious that he was collecting questions to ask while we traveled. At least he let us order breakfast before he started with third degree.

"How old are you, Rusty?"

"Thirty three," he answered and sipped his coffee, adding another sugar without taking his eyes off of my dad.

"Where are you from?"

He tasted his coffee again and seemed to be content with the amount of flavor it had. "Indiana. I lived in Maryland as a child."

"Are your parents living?" My mother asked.

"Yep."

"What do they do?" My dad was wiggling his leg under the table. I could see the water in my glass shaking and recognized it right away.

"My father is a veterinarian, or was. He's retired now." Rusty was being so calm, and I knew it was to prove to me that he could be the man I needed him to be.

"Have you ever been married."

He clenched his jaw, and looked away. I knew he didn't want to talk about his wife.

"Dad, seriously?"

"What? I just want to know if he's got another life out there somewhere. He could be a bigamist trying to look for his seventh sister-wife."

I put my hands over my face, completely embarrassed. "He's not a bigamist."

"Fine. When was your last relationship?"

The jaw was steady moving, but this time he placed his hands flat on the table and answered. "Two years ago."

"Who ended it?"

"Dad, please." I was begging.

"God did." Everyone at the table stopped

moving. My parents looked at each other, and while they were considering what to say next, I put my hand under the table and placed it on his thigh. I already knew his story, and he needed to know that he could get through this. "Can you excuse me for a minute. I'm just going to go wash my hands."

Rusty got up and walked toward the bathroom. I leaned across the table so I didn't have to say it too loud. "I told you to stop."

"How were we supposed to know? What happened?"

"Mom, I can't talk to you about it. He keeps that part of his life locked up. I'm real surprised he told you what he did. Uncle Colt and Noah have no idea. He's not a drifter, he's just a broken man with a lost soul. You can choose to believe me or not."

My mom put her hands up to her face. I could tell she was worried. My dad shook his head and looked at me. "How are we supposed to trust this guy when he has secrets?"

I nodded, and smiled when I saw Rusty coming back to the table. He scooted in beside me and I tucked my arm inside of his immediately. "Are you okay?"

He looked up at my parents when he answered me. "Yeah, I'm great."

Our food came shortly after that, giving my parents a reason to take a break. I ate quietly with my right hand, while keeping my left on his leg again. I think rusty surprised everyone when he insisted on paying for the meal. The ride home was quiet, and I was grateful. When we arrived back at the ranch he shook my dad's hand and thanked my mom before telling me that he had to go. I knew it was because he wanted to be alone, and a part of me hurt for him knowing why. I hated that he couldn't talk about them without losing it, and what made it worse was that now my parents were sure he had secrets.

At least they waited until he left to start talking about him. "I don't know, honey. He seems like he's got problems."

"Dad, please. I'm an adult. I think I can make my own decisions. Besides, we've got a party tonight, and I know you didn't come all the way here to meddle in my love life."

He pulled me into a hug. "Sorry. It's my job to worry. You can always come home with us if you need to. Just remember that."

I think that once Rusty was gone they loosened up. My mom made plans to come back to Kentucky when I went in for my first sonogram to see the sex of the baby, and we talked about what we could do to the spare room to get it ready for the little one. By the end of the day I think they were finally able to look at me and act normal. It was a step in the right direction.

Now all I had to do was convince the rest of the family, and then break the news that the one person they all hated in the world was really the father of my child.

Piece of cake!

Chapter 25
Rusty

I had to get away from them. In all of the times that I'd played it out in my head on the way there I'd never once thought about breaking down in front of them. They had every right to question me about my past, and yet I couldn't even open up for her. I wanted to be that guy that she could depend on, but I'd pretty much screwed it all up with my own insecurities.

Isabella didn't stop by for the rest of the afternoon, and with what happened the night before, I never even got a call from Noah telling me to come help out. I could accept that they all wanted to keep their distance from me, well all except Isabella. She had me so confused, and I had no idea what I was going to do about it.

It seemed like every day she had a reason that we shouldn't be together. She kept trying to convince me that there was nothing between us, but then she'd turn around and spend the night, or hold onto me when we were around her parents.

That night, when I knew their whole family was celebrating, I stayed locked away in my trailer, unable to be around any of them, most of all Isabella. I'd gone to breakfast with her, but the day had given me a ton of time to think about recent events. The truth was that if she wanted me she would tell me. I couldn't keep forcing myself on her if I expected her to figure out what she wanted on her own.

My mother used to tell me that if I loved something I needed to let it go to see if it would come back to me. This was what she meant, and I knew it was going to be difficult. Considering that I'd spent so much time thinking about her, especially since we'd been intimate, it was impossible to sit around knowing she was so close. All I wanted to do was head to the party and sweep her off her feet.

I could hear music playing in the distance, and honestly felt left out. A part of me longed to have a family again; to be a part of something that was unbreakable. The only problem with that was knowing what could happen when I opened my heart again. Isabella had already shot me down, so many times that I stopped counting. She'd told me to stay out of her life several times, leaving me to head back here and be miserable.

I didn't know how I was supposed to move forward, and let her go at the same time. While contemplating my options, someone knocked on my door. Excitement was soon turned to disappointment when I saw her dad standing there. "Do you mind if I come in?"

I opened the door and motioned for him to take a seat. His pockets were full of beers and he offered me one right away.

I put my hands up. "No thanks."

"More for me." I could tell he'd had a few from the way he said it. Just to be safe, I sat on the opposite side of the room.

"Is everything okay?"

"I came to talk to you about my daughter. She's asked me to leave your past alone, but you can understand how that concerns me." He took a few sips of his beer before continuing. "I think that in light of this situation between the two of you it would help everyone if we could spend more time together. Since we're leaving in the morning, I am here to invite you to come to North Carolina and see where my daughter grew up. We can spend some one on one time together, and start over without my relatives breathing down your back. I trust my daughter, Rusty, but she kept you a secret, and until I can figure out why I'm going to keep my guard up."

I sat there across from him with my elbows

propped on my knees. The man had every right to feel the way he did. I could have made things better by telling him the truth, but that wasn't an option for me, not until I could figure out how to handle myself without losing my shit in front of him.

"I'd be glad to accompany your daughter to North Carolina. I hope that it will put your mind at ease."

He stood up and I did the same. When he walked up closer to me I didn't know what to expect. He put his arm on my shoulder and looked down at the floor. "I'm still pissed you knocked up my daughter, but my wife says I've got to try. She wears the pants in our house, so I don't have a choice. If you know what's good for you, you'll learn how to accept that. Iz is exactly like her mother."

The distraught man turned and left without saying anything else.

For a while I sat back down and thought about what I wanted to do. On one hand I felt like I needed to let Isabella know that her father had come to me. On the other, I knew she needed space. My concern was that if I gave her that space it could all backfire on me, leaving me more alone than I'd ever been before.

It wasn't long until another knock came to my door. I half expected to open it and see her father back again, since he already looked as if he'd thrown back a few too many. I couldn't blame him.

This time when I opened the door I was met

with one of Isabella's brothers. He stepped inside before I ask him to. "Which one are you?"

He looked around the room, and then finally toward me. "Jax."

"So what's up? Your dad was just hear a bit ago. Were you looking for him?"

"Nah. My dad's got nothing to do with my visit."

I leaned against my arm chair, feeling a little uncomfortable about this kid being in my house. There was something strange about the way he was looking at me. "So what's up? Did your sister send you here?"

He smiled, as if I was way off. "Nope. I came here because something's been bugging me since last night. You see, me and Jake are real close to our sister. We know things that our parents don't."

"Just tell me why you're here. I'm not in the mood to decipher some hidden agenda of yours." He was annoying the shit out of me. I had enough to worry about than him standing there talking in code.

"That baby she's carrying, well I don't think it's yours. I haven't asked my sister, but I know for a fact that she spent the night with her ex a while back. I've been doing the math in my head for the last twenty-fours hours. She's never once mentioned you, dude. The whole family is asking her questions, and she refuses to talk about it."

All I could think about was the fact that he'd thrown his sister's secret out to me. What if I didn't know about her being with the ex? It was possible that she'd cheated on me, for all he knew. "You've got no right to come in here and make these kinds of accusations."

"That's where you're wrong. I'm not here to get to the bottom of some conspiracy. Some things are better left unsaid. I'm here because that baby is going to need a dad. So I'm going to ask you once. Are you just covering for my sister, or do you care about her?"

"I'm not covering for anyone."

"You didn't answer the question." He was plucking my nerves. What did this guy want from me?

"Just tell me why you're here."

"My sister has this problem with letting go of her ex. Yesterday she found out he'd tried to end his life, and I've got this feeling that she tried to contact him. I checked her phone last night and saw that she called North Carolina. I'm sure if I called the number, he'd answer. Now the way I see it you've got options. You can help me make sure she stays in Kentucky, or you can make sure that she's never going to want to be with that common asshole again."

"You seem to harbor some ill feelings toward this guy. She doesn't talk much about him. Can you tell me what's so bad?"

"He cheated on my sister for years. On one occasion she was assaulted because of him. God only knows what else he's done to her, aside from lowering her self esteem and causing her to want to leave her home in hopes of getting away from him."

The more he explained, the more I understood. In fact, it was all starting to make sense. "I appreciate that you want what's best for your sister. I wouldn't have stood up and taken responsibility if I didn't expect to step in. Your sister means a lot to me, and I intend to do whatever it takes to prove that to her, and to the rest of the family."

He stuck his hand out and did some kind of special handshake. I tried to go along with it, failing terribly. "I guess you're not a douche after all then."

"Thanks, I think."

He started to leave and stepped back inside. "Oh yeah. I forgot to tell you that if you hurt her, I'll do the same to you. It's not a threat. It's a promise."

"If I had a sister I'd do the same." I waved when he walked away and closed the door when he disappeared into the darkness.

It was odd to me that he'd stopped by while the party was going on, and I couldn't help but wonder what his sister was doing. Another thing that wouldn't leave my mind was the fact that she'd contacted her ex. It made sense why she'd tried to push me away.

Then it hit me like a ton of bricks. I had to convince her to be with me, because if I didn't I'd surely lose her forever. She'd move right back to her old life, without a second thought. I had to figure out a way to convince her to stay. She needed a reason to want to be with me. I had to prove to her that I'd be a good father to her child, no matter what I had to do.

Chapter 26
Isabella

I can't explain why it felt as if a huge weight had been lifted off of me. Even though my family only knew half of the truth, it was still enough to keep me from worrying so much.

While everyone around me talked about the upcoming nuptials, I sat at a table with my mother, quietly wishing that Rusty was around. Then I thought about Tate, and what he must have been thinking when he attempted to end his life. If he'd known I was pregnant would that have saved him? Was it worth me telling him at all? Could someone like him even be saved?

Suddenly realizing that my mind was in a clusterfuck of emotional turmoil, I decided to ask the advice of the one woman that had been through it all before. "Mom, if you had the chance to do it all over again, would you have told the sperm donor that I was his child?"

She was most definitely caught off guard. "Why on earth are you askin' me that? Do you regret tellin' Rusty that he's the father of your child? Is there somethin' you want to tell me about him?"

I immediately shook my head to reassure her she was way off base. "Of course not. He's a good man. I'm sure he'll be a great dad. This pregnancy just has me thinkin' about things. I just want to know if you regret tellin' him. I mean, you would have ended up with Dad anyway. It's a simple question."

"Honey, I don't know how to answer that. Your dad and I got together because of the shit that man put me through. Things could have ended up differently, and I'd never wish that. Our life is wonderful, and in some ways I'm glad that man didn't want anything to do with us. So no, I don't regret it. Although, I do sometimes regret the choice to sleep with him in the first place, but then I think about you and remember that even at the worst times somethin' beautiful can happen."

"I guess I understand. It's just hard knowing that he didn't want us. I don't want that for my baby."

"Of course you don't. Honey, all of those crazy thoughts you're havin' is normal. Your hormones are going crazy inside of your body. They're goin' to affect your decision makin'."

My mom and I both looked up when we saw Noah sitting down across from us. He folded his hands like he was waiting for his turn. My mom touched my arm. "We'll finish this later."

I leaned my chin on my fist and prepared to be reamed out, knowing he'd probably built up enough anger to fuel a locomotive. "Go ahead. Let me have it."

I could tell he was uneasy. "Bells, I just want you to be happy."

Though I'd always considered him predictable, this was definitely a new side of my cousin. "Come again?"

"You heard me. I mean, yeah, I'm pissed you snuck behind my back, but you didn't give me much choice. It's not like I can make the guy leave now. He's got responsibilities. I'm just worried that he's keepin' somethin' from all of us. I'm around him every day and never once has he talked about his past. Don't you think that's important?"

"I know him better than you, Noah. I can assure you that it's not what you think. He's a good man." My defending Rusty was only making it difficult to stand by my idea of telling Tate. No matter what I did, I was pulled toward the idea of staying in Kentucky and letting Rusty raise my child as his own. I'd never met a more sincere man, who given up so much. He was so honorable, and I wanted to think that him stepping up was his way of saying that he wanted to commit. The only thing holding me back was the idea of never knowing if he was going to compare me to someone else. I knew it seemed petty, but I needed to be loved for who I was, because I knew if I wasn't then my happiness wasn't real. In a sense it would be fake. I couldn't make a commitment with that on my conscience.

"If he's such good man than why ain't he here?"

I didn't have a good answer for that. Clearly he'd gotten upset earlier at breakfast. He'd stayed away from me all day. It didn't help that I'd pretty much told him we were nothing to each other right before that. "I'm sure he's tryin' to keep the peace for your benefit."

"My beef with Rusty wouldn't have ruined this party. I'm gettin' hitched to the most beautiful woman, my family is here, and my cousin is havin' a kid. We've got plenty of reasons to put our differences aside, don't you think?"

While Noah waited for my response, I thought about how hurt he must have been finding out that I'd lived in the same house with him and not been able to confide my secret. We were supposed to be best friends, yet I'd hid something so important. "I'm sorry I didn't tell you."

"I get it. It hurts, but I get it. Hell, I threatened your boyfriend so many times that I'm surprised you two didn't run off together. It's obvious he cares about you, or else he would have given up a long time ago. I'm just glad this baby isn't Tate's. I fuckin' hate that bastard. I wouldn't be sittin' here with you right now if he'd knocked you up. When you first made the announcement yesterday it's all I could think about. I was doin' the math in my head, trying to figure out when you were in North Carolina. Then Rusty stood up and put my mind at ease. Anyone is better than your ex."

I felt sick to my stomach. Hearing Noah saying that put new perspective on my rationalizing to tell Tate the truth. I couldn't lose Noah, and that's exactly what would happen if the truth came out. I stood up, causing alarm to my cousin's eyes. "I need to go."

"Where?"

"I need to see Rusty. He should be here with all of us."

He started to chuckle. "So you're finally goin' to admit that you're a couple?"

I shrugged. "Yeah, I think I am."

Since the family was so big, it was easy to sneak away without being noticed. I didn't know what I would say to him, and there was no excuse for my actions. I'd been a jerk to him so many times that I was having trouble counting. I was done fighting, and after I picked up my pace, I found myself almost running in the direction of his house. By the time I'd made it there I saw my brother walking out. What alarmed me was the way he looked at me as he approached.

"What are you doin' here?"

"I needed to talk to your boyfriend."

"About what?" I think I would have been okay if he'd threatened to hurt him if he hurt me, but something told me that wasn't the reason.

"I think you know what, sis."

"Please, Jax. Don't do this."

"Do what?" He took my chin and pulled it to look him in the eyes. "Tell everyone our secret?"

I couldn't fight the burning in my throat or the stream of tears pouring out of my eyes. "I don't have a secret," I lied.

"Yeah, maybe if you keep telling yourself that you'll start to believe it. You forget who picked you up that night, Bella. I did the math, and even though I know that guy in there cares for you, we both know he ain't the father."

I pulled away from his touch, refusing to look at him for another second. It wasn't the fact that Jax had figured out my secret. It was that he'd talked to Rusty about it. It was also the fact that he'd forever hold that secret over my head. I'd feel guilty every time I held my baby and knew that I was lying to him or her. More than ever I wished I could talk to my dad about it. I wanted to know how he felt when he'd decided that he'd be my only father. I needed his advice, yet knew I couldn't ask for it. "Please, Jax. Don't tell anyone."

"I'm not going to. Just be sure you can live

with yourself. It's one thing to not tell Tate, but one day that kid's going to find out the truth. What do you think that will do to Rusty? You can't let him fall in love with your kid if you're still thinking about running back to Tate. Have you even considered what this will do to Dad?"

Hearing Tate's name made my skin crawl. It was like he was demon I was trying to avoid. "Yes, I've thought about Dad. This is so messed up. What am I supposed to do? I didn't ask Rusty to take responsibility."

"You're not telling anyone the truth. He can only protect you for so long. I just don't want to see my niece or nephew resenting their parents because of a huge lie. Don't you remember what you and Dad went through?"

"Of course I remember. How could you even ask me that?"

"I just think you should have thought about all of this before letting that man make sacrifices for you."

I pointed at my brother. "Don't you dare play the perfect card with me, Jax. You've got no room to judge my actions."

He threw his arms in the air. "Whoa. Nobody said I was perfect. I'm just trying to look out for my sister. I don't want you getting hurt, Bella. Can't you see what this kind of secret could do?"

"Yes," I wiped more tears away. "I know what I'm riskin'."

He leaned over and kissed the top of my head. "You're my sister, my blood, and I love you. I know you regret that night, and I just don't want it to haunt you for the rest of your life."

I watched my brother walk away, while I tried my hardest to calm down. As much as I thought I'd made my mind up, I knew I was more confused than ever. Most importantly, I needed to know if Rusty would still want to help me if my family learned the truth.

I headed up the steps to his house prepared to find out.

Chapter 27

Rusty

This was the third time someone had knocked on my door, and I was starting to get annoyed. My issues with Isabella weren't anyone's business. Besides, she'd pretty much made it obvious that I was just some fuck buddy to her. It was more clear than ever after my talk with her brother.

I opened the door with a pissed off frown. My eyes adjusted, and I blinked twice to make sure that it was really her standing in front of me. Her makeup was running down her cheeks, and she was steadily sobbing. I grabbed her by the arm and pulled her inside, then pulled her to my chest to comfort her. "What's happened?"

"Don't make me talk about it. Please, Rusty. Just hold

me."

There was no place else I wanted to be.

Unlike her last visit, I didn't carry Isabella back to my room to make love. This time I picked her up and held her on the couch. She cried for along time, and then finally explained what had her so worked up.

I wasn't trying to be insensitive. It was obvious she was struggling with what she wanted to do. The fact that she'd come to me again only validated that she trusted me. I appreciated that, but at the same time also knew she didn't really have anyone else.

"Either way I go, someone gets hurt. Jax is right, Rusty. I've got to figure this out."

"You need to stop thinking about everyone else. They'll get over whatever has to happen. This decision is yours. If you want me I'm here, but if you want to be with your ex, than I think I deserve to know, because right now I kind of feel like there's things you aren't telling me."

"I just explained everything."

I shook my head and looked away from her. "Did you try to contact your ex-boyfriend? When your brothers told you about his accident did you attempt to call him?"

She looked down and sighed, appearing as if I'd caught her in a lie. I think before she answered I knew the truth. "Yes, I called him."

"Does he know?" I could feel the burn of tears accumulating in my eyes, but refused to let them fall in front of her. If she was going to choose him, than this had to end. I wouldn't be her consolation prize until her ex could come back in her life. If she thought she could come running to me to fix that problem she was very wrong.

"No. He doesn't know. He hung up on me. The guy hates me for ruinin' his life. I'm the last person he wants to talk to."

"So you were planning on telling him?"

She refused to look me in the eyes.

When she didn't answer, I yelled, "ANSWER ME. Were you going to tell him about the baby?"

"Yes." She started sobbing again, but this time I couldn't be her comfort. I was so distraught; so betrayed. Even though I didn't have any kind of hold over her, I wanted to believe that she was mine; that she wouldn't betray me after I'd stepped up and offered to help raise her child. Didn't she understand that I wanted to be with her? Did she not know how much being a father meant to me? This wasn't about my deceased wife, or even the child that I lost. This was about the life that I wanted us to have together. It was about being in love with her.

A few seconds is all it took for her to reached out for me. I pulled away and walked into the kitchen. Though I could see her, I knew I needed to be in another room. She sobbed more, while I stood there watching her, suffering from my own heartbreak. This wasn't how I saw things going.

Isabella didn't want me to be that baby's

father. She'd tried to tell me several times, but I kept pushing to be a part of her life. Her family would be leaving in a day, and at some point they'd find out that I was covering for her. I knew it wasn't my problem, but it didn't make it easier to take.

The fragile woman that I was crazy about was sitting on my couch crying, and I couldn't bring myself to be near her. I grabbed my shoes and started putting them on. "What are you doin'?"

"I'm walking you back to the party so you can be with your family."

"I came here to be with you, Rusty."

"For what? Did you want to play head games with me again? Did you want me to take you in my room and fuck you so you could forget about him? I'm not your damn punching bag, Isabella. This hurts too much."

"So you want me to leave?" Her question was obvious, so I guess she needed to hear me say the words.

"Yes. I need you to leave."

She went running out the door. I finished tying my shoes and ran after her. It wasn't hard to catch up, and to be honest I don't think she could run full speed if she wanted to. While stopped at a tree I caught up to her and stood there waiting for her to breathe normally. "I'm sorry I hurt you, Rusty. I swear I didn't mean it. None of this is about some hope of gettin' back with Tate. You have to believe me."

"Save it. The damage is done. Besides, this whole time you've been telling me that we couldn't be together. It's my fault for hanging on for so long. I get it. I'm older, with more baggage than anyone has to carry. You're young and beautiful, with your whole life ahead of you. I don't blame you for wanting more for yourself, but I can't say I'm okay with losing hope that one day we could be something more." I reached over and she let me touch her face. Her body began shaking when her arms wrapped around my back. I held her close to me as she bawled. It was practically impossible for me to be able to have her so close and picture watching her walking away. "This is killing me, Iz. Don't you know how much I want to be with you and this baby? Haven't I proven that?"

She lifted her head and nodded. "I want to be with you, too. That's what I came to tell you. It's not about Tate, or my family. I know you're the right choice. I just didn't want to string you along while I was tryin' to figure it all out."

I moved her hair off of her shoulders and kissed her forehead. "I don't care if we fight, as long as it's my bed you're sleeping in at night. Being without you is pure hell. I don't care what I've got to do to prove it. Just say you'll give me a chance. Say you're not running back to that guy. Please."

We were standing in the middle of the woods. The noises of the bugs kept it from being silent around us. In the distance the music still played, letting me know that nobody at the party would be able to hear us arguing. "How do I know you want me, and not just a reminder of the family you lost?"

"You're going to have to trust me, Iz. For now, all I can assure is that I'm not going anywhere. If you want me, I'm all in. I may have first been attracted to you because of my family, but the moment I met you that all changed. You don't remind me of what I lost, you show me what I have to look forward to. Can't you see that? Can't you understand that when I look at you I see my future?"

She put her hand up to her face and took a step back, as if she was in disbelief. I didn't know if I should keep talking or give her a minute to take it all in. I knew how stressful this all was on her. She was dealing with so much all at once. The anxiety was overwhelming even for me. "I wish you and everyone else could understand how difficult this is for me." I watched her face curl up as another bout of sobs came.

"I may not be able to feel exactly what you're feeling, but I certainly know what it's like to be completely lost. Let me be there for you. Who knows where this road's going to go, but we take the ride together. I may not have much to offer you right now, but I'll do whatever it takes."

"I can't ask you to make that kind of commitment. It's not fair. We've got a lot to learn about each other."

She had a point. "Fine. Let's give it a go. If you

decide that I'm not what you want than you can kick me to the curb." I ran my hands up her arms and pulled her close to me again. "But if you fall hopelessly in love with me I promise I'll be there waiting."

"I just don't want to hurt you, Rusty. You're a good man. You don't deserve to have some kind of built in family. I know you're tryin' to help me out and be kind, but it's not fair if I let you make this kind of commitment without promises."

I leaned in and kiss her slowly, playing her tongue against mine. Her lips trembled against mine, and I could feel her wet tears rubbing on my cheeks. Our emotional embrace signified what we both wanted. I knew it was going to be difficult, and we'd probably have more hard times ahead, but she needed me and I was going to be there.

When we both pulled away she stood there staring at me, with only the light of the moon giving us something to go on. "You're not goin' to give up, are you?"

I moved my head from side to side. "Nope."

"We have a sonogram next week. My mom's goin' to drive back to go with us. It's the one where we find out what I'm havin'."

"What we're having, you mean?"

She looked at me with shocked eyes and nodded. "Yes. If that's what you want."

"It is."

"Okay. We'll do it together."

"What about the ex, Iz? If we're doing this

together, I've got to ask about him."

"I told you already. He hung up on me."

"Are you going to call him back?" I had to ask, because it would break me if I wasn't in the loop. I either had to be all in, or I was going to have to walk away. I was never a jealous man, but that is something I couldn't compete with.

"No. I promise you. I'm not goin' to call him back. I'm ready, Rusty. I'm ready to admit that there's somethin' real between us. If that's really what you want."

I kissed her lightly again. "You know it is. How many ways do I have to make that clear?"

"Then it's settled. No more secrets. As far as the family is concerned that baby is and always has been mine."

"What about my brothers?" She had a point, but I knew they weren't a problem. After all, they obviously wanted her to be taken care of.

"They won't be a problem. I can assure you that they want what's best for you."

"Then I just have one more question for you." Her lips trailed over mine. As I ran my tongue over my own, I could taste the salty remnants of her tears. "Can I stay with you tonight?"

I held out one hand and waited for her to grab it. When she did I started walking us back to my place. Her family was too busy celebrating to notice what was going on with us. "I might not ever let you go."

Chapter 28
Isabella

After all of the stressing, things were finally settling for me. I had a child to think about, and their life was more important than anything else. As reluctant as my parents were about Rusty, they promised to give him a chance.

That's why waking up late for a Sunday breakfast was so alarming. I sat straight up in Rusty's bed and looked around the room. I could tell from how bright the sun was that it was past the time we were supposed to be at my great-aunt's house for Sunday pancakes. It was a tradition that has been going on since before I was born. When the family visited there was always Sunday breakfast.

I kicked off the covers, noticing the naked body lying next to me. He was so handsome, and seemed peaceful. Instead of alarming him, I rolled over and ran my fingers through the tiny patch of hair on his chest. He found my hand and opened his eyes. "You okay?"

"Yeah, but we're late for breakfast."

"Oh shit." He rolled off the bed and started rustling around for his clothes. "How late are we?"

I located my phone and checked the time. "Forty minutes."

"Damn. Get some clothes on. I don't want them to have more reasons to hate me."

"You know, if you told everyone the truth they wouldn't hate you at all. Besides, I don't even think it's that. They're just skeptical about people they let in. Don't take it too personal. My family can be a bit over-protective."

He walked over and handed me my clothes. "Maybe you need protecting."

"What I need is to change my clothes."

We hurried out of the trailer and made our way to my place. It was easier to get around on the golf cart, and in this case I was glad we had it. As fast as I could, I showered, washing everything except for my hair, changed, and put on fresh makeup, while Rusty paced around my house. When I came out I could tell he was freaking. We rushed over to the main house, noticing that my brothers were standing outside with Christian. I approached them with caution, knowing that they probably had something up their sleeves. "Is everyone here?"

"Everyone but you. Dad was in there telling everyone Rusty cut you up into pieces. I think they called the police a few minutes ago," Jax announced, while Jake laughed.

I flipped him the middle finger. "Screw you guys. Rusty's already on edge." Christian was on her phone off to the side. She hung up and walked toward us. "I just got home myself. Don't listen to them. They think they're funny."

"Just got home?" It was shocking to hear that she'd just gotten home. I knew for a fact that she was at the party.

"I went out afterwards. There was another party I needed to be at. Anyway, I've already heard shit from my dad this mornin'. He thinks he's a preacher or somethin'."

When I turned to look at Rusty I could tell he was worried. He wanted to make his presence known, and as the minutes went by it was bothering him more. "I'll let everyone know you're here."

I grabbed his hand and started pulling him toward the front door. It opened before I could reach the handle. My dad stood there with a link of sausage in between his lips. He spoke without removing it. "I was just coming to get you two. Breakfast is ready." He froze in place, sucking the sausage in and out obnoxiously. I looked to Rusty and saw him shaking his head, and just began to giggle.

With my hand, I grabbed the meat out of my dad's mouth and started to walk past him. "Grow up, dad. Don't you know it's immature to play with your food?"

He stole the link back and took a bite. "Nobody takes my meat without asking."

My mom came to my rescue. "Tyler Mitchell, it's way too early for that kind of talk. Get in here and make your plate." She lead my dad into the kitchen with us following. In the large kitchen was most of my family. Outside in the pool yard I could see my uncle Colt with his youngest daughter, Addison. They were sitting at one of the tables with plates in front of them. For the most part we'd all retreat out there to eat so we could spread out. It let me know that I'd either missed eating with everyone, or that we'd arrived just in time. Thankfully it was the latter. My great-aunt hugged me right before handing me a plate. "Hi, sweet girl. I haven't gotten a chance to congratulate you yet. If you need anything you know we're here for you. Me and your grandmother are going to spoil that little one."

I found my grandmother over by the coffee pot and suddenly realized that I'd left Rusty alone with everyone.

For the most part he knew everyone in the room. My grandmother and grandpa John, my mother's parents, were around every weekend. John would always help my uncle Colt with projects, and we'd throw lots of barbeques in the summer, which the ranch help were always invited to.

Our eyes met and he winked, letting me know he was all right. I motioned with my head for him to follow my lead. My great-aunt greeted him, hugged him, and handed him a plate.

After grabbing bacon, and a couple links, we headed out to the pool yard, followed by my parents. Uncle Colt was too busy giving his daughter a hard time to notice that we'd even sat down at another table. Rusty gave me a look, and I understood that it was because she was getting reamed out over something she'd done with my brothers. I caught a few words of the conversation. Bad influences was the one that stood out the most.

I couldn't be mad. My brothers were trouble makers. They thought that everything in life was a joke, and you weren't living unless you were getting into trouble somehow. Who could blame them when our father acted like a kid most of the time?

I smiled when I looked over at Rusty. It was nice to know he was there with me.

Then Noah came and sat at our table, followed by Shalan. He gave us both a once over, and focused on his plate of food.

Shalan broke the awkwardness. "Good morning, you two."

"Morning," Rusty said as he chewed. He swallowed before continuing. "Did you just get here?"

"No. We were upstairs. Apparently Addison snuck out with your brothers last night. God only knows where they all went, because none of them are talkin', but I'm sure it was to one of her friend's parties. She told my parents that she was staying at Gram's house. Apparently they partied somewhere, because she threw up all over the bedroom she slept in. We were up there tryin' to get it cleaned up."

I looked over at Addison getting yelled at and knew exactly where they'd partied it up. "I bet they were at my house."

"Your house?" Noah asked.

"She stayed with me last night," Rusty announced proudly. I don't think he said it to rub it in Noah's face. It was more to make it a point that we were definitely together. I think he felt that if he kept reminding my cousin he'd finally get over the hostility he was feeling for Rusty lying to him.

"I didn't notice nothin' out of place at the house when I went to change my clothes, but I bet they were there. My brothers might be assholes, but they don't drink and drive, and they certainly wouldn't have put her in danger."

"She's under age," Noah said loudly.

"Babe, calm down. Your father has it handled," Shalan did her best to settle Noah. Once he got a hair up his ass he was exactly like his father. It was pretty comical when I thought about all of the times he'd said he didn't want to turn out like him.

282

When he started eating, instead of bitching, she turned her attention to me. "I hear you have a sonogram coming up. That's so exciting! Do you want to know what you're having?"

"Yeah, I think I might," I said.

"You don't want it to be a surprise?" Rusty asked.

"You two haven't discussed this yet? Ain't this a big decision?" Noah was onto us.

"We just can't decide, that's all. I hate secrets, and I don't like not knowin' if it's a boy or girl. I want to have the name ready, and be able to decorate the room."

"In other words, she wants pink or blue," Rusty teased. "I think we all know the color she'd like it to be."

Noah shook his head and started chuckling as he spoke. "Yeah. She's a girl through and through."

I threw a piece of meat at him. "Shut up! I hunt. I four-wheel. Just because I like lookin' pretty don't mean I can't hang with you men."

They both agreed to give me a look and change the subject.

Ignoring them, I turned my attention back to Shalan. "I was thinkin' that maybe since everyone knows, you'd want to help me to decorate the room, once we find out the sex of course."

"You know I will. It's so exciting. I can't believe you were able to hold it in for so long, especially from me. You know I would have had your back." Shalan ignored the dirty look she got from my cousin.

"The truth is, I didn't want you to have a secret from Noah. I didn't want anyone having to be burdened with my secret. Rusty was the first person to know, and together we decided to wait until I was far enough along. I wanted the whole family to be around, so that I didn't have to explain it a million times."

"So what happens now that the secret's out? I'm thinking y'all will live in your house, and not the trailer?" Noah's question caught me off guard. It was my fault for not thinking that far ahead. Technically, Rusty and I had just become a couple. We'd hooked up several times, but I'd always fought my feelings because of my situation.

"I'm going to move into her house," Rusty reached for my leg under the table. I stuck my hand down and placed it on top of his. When I looked his way he formed a small smile at the corner of his lips.

"I'm not rushin' you, but Seth's been bunking in the office for a few weeks. It would be nice to offer the trailer to him, if that's all right. I know your job requires me to house you."

Rusty motioned with his hands. "It's not a problem. I know where I belong."

He stared deeply into my eyes when he said it and I couldn't help but feel chills all over my body. This thing between us was really happening, and I was going to have to accept that it was a good thing. I'd worried for a long time, and finally it was all starting to settle. I had a boyfriend that wanted to take care of us, and a family that was accepting it.

I was able to finally breathe.

Chapter 29
Rusty

Things settled down once everyone left and went home. I think at first I was reluctant to move some of my things over to Isabella's house, considering she'd been so indecisive for such a long time. It was nice to be able to get off work and head straight to her place to see her, and even better to be welcomed by her beautiful smile.

Since she worked off the ranch, I decided that if I was home first I'd make the meals. She'd come home and put her feet up, allowing me to pamper her. I think I was going above and beyond just to prove to her that it was what I wanted. Now that I was taking on the father title, I needed to get used to taken care of a family again.

Sometimes it reminded me of my daughter

and wife, but not the way that Isabella would assume. I couldn't help miss them, and I knew they'd be on my mind every day for the rest of my life. Still, I'd been offered a second chance at a good life again, and this time I needed to make things right.

With her mother coming back into town for the sonogram in just a few short days, I decided that I needed to have all of my things moved over and put away. Isabella insisted on helping me get things organized. The baby was going to be here soon, and there was still a bunch to get done.

Even after making the commitment to be the child's father, I was still nervous about it all. My love for Isabella had blinded a lot of my decision making, because I'd been so desperate to be with her. Now I was faced with what every new couple had to endure. I had to learn to live with someone again, after a long period of being alone. I think even when I tried to walk on eggshells, at times I was still annoying to her. To make matters worse, I felt as if the harder I tried the more I'd fail.

Isabella's sonogram was scheduled for that following Monday. Her mother came back to Kentucky on Sunday afternoon, along with her father, which neither of us expected. Thankfully, by that time all of my stuff was neatly stored in her house. Because we'd been so busy with everything else, we hadn't had time to reflect on our new relationship, which in turn left us with little to talk about when we were around her parents.

I think to lighten to mood, and get us both out of the house, that Sunday he took me out to get a bite to eat. Sitting there with the father of the woman that I was in love with reminded me of being young and going through the motions of asking for Simone's hand in marriage. I was so nervous that day, and swore her father was going to tell me to take a hike. It got me wondering where he was now, and if they'd ever been able to forgive me for skipping out on all of them.

Isabella's dad kept to small talk until we'd been sitting in the tavern for a while. He'd ordered a beer, and watched as I requested a tea instead. I couldn't blame him for wanting to know why I didn't drink. "What's your story, Rusty? I suppose I should have asked this sooner, but we're here now and it's been bothering me. I need to know that something from your past isn't going to ruin my daughter's happiness. You see, she's too trusting when it comes to men. Her last boyfriend was a piece of shit. You understand how I'd want her to be with someone that's going to treat her right; someone who is who he says he is."

I nodded, knowing that I had to tell him about my past. I was ready to take that leap with his daughter. "You're right. You need to know the truth, and I'm willing to tell you, if you give me your word that you won't tell Colt. My job is my business and I don't want people giving me any kind of special treatment."

"You do realize you shovel shit for a living?"

I nudged my head upwards. "I'm not a stable boy."

He took another sip of beer and laughed to himself. "Sorry, I was getting you confused with one of my wife's porno novels. She's always reading shit about Indians and cowboys."

I smiled, feeling like he was trying to lighten the mood. "My story probably isn't as interesting as you may think. I do have a past that I'm running from."

"Do I need to call the family lawyer? Are you in some kind of trouble?"

"No," I immediately reassured him. "I'm not a criminal."

He placed his hands on the table and smiled, but it wasn't because he was happy. It was more like he was holding in his anger, waiting for me to get to the point.

"I had a wife and daughter. Simone and Sydney. They were my life, my reason for living, until one day my daughter got sick. We took her to the hospital, but she didn't make it past dinner." I took a few deep breaths, noticing his facial expression had changed. I knew he was feeling my pain, and I appreciated that he was giving me time to control my emotions. "Bacterial meningitis is what they told us had killed her. They don't know how she got it, and once she was gone it wouldn't have helped us anyway."

"I heard many marriages end when couple lose a child. Is that what happened?"

I sat there trying to come to grips with why Simone would take her life. We could have gotten through it together. We wouldn't have been one of those failed marriages. "I wouldn't know how things could have turned out. My wife took her own life shortly after my daughter's death. In fact, they're buried together it was so close. I reckon she couldn't live another minute without our little girl."

"I'm real sorry to hear about your family, Rusty. Man, that's just terrible. I can't imagine having to go through something like that." His brow furrowed, and I did my best not to make eye contact. I was supposed to be someone who was strong; someone that could protect his daughter. Instead I was crumbling in front of her father, showing him how weak I really was.

"Our families did their best to console me, but I couldn't handle it. I left my house, my job, and everyone I ever knew to be alone, because I couldn't go another day with someone asking me if I was going to be okay."

I looked down at the condensation forming on my glass of tea. I watched it drip down, leaving a trail as it moved. It reminded me of the tears that I'd shed for my girls, and how I'd never be able to fully get over them.

"I'm guessing my daughter knows all of this?"
I nodded. "She does."

"Can I ask what you did for a living? You're obviously good with horses. Did you live on a farm?"

"My dad was a veterinarian, as was I. We had a practice in our little town."

He chuckled. "You're telling me that you're a god damn vet and you'd rather shovel shit?"

"Well, I don't shovel shi-."

"You know what I mean," he corrected.

I shrugged. "I get to be around animals, and a family that reminds me how good life could be again. It's not so bad. It also came with a house, so that was a plus."

He seemed to study me for a couple moments. I had no idea what he could be thinking. He could be thinking I was damaged goods, and that I had no right to be with his daughter. He could be thinking of a way to send me packing. I just didn't know.

"Do you love my daughter, Rusty?" His question was legitimate. Of course he'd want to know how I felt about his daughter. After all, she was the reason we were here.

"Yes. I do. I love her very much." Admitting that out loud made my heart beat faster. It was a word we'd never talked about. Still, I knew how I felt. There was no question about it.

He reached his hand across the table. When I shook it he started talking again. "You have my blessing, but just know that if you hurt her in anyway, I'm going to hurt you. That means if you fuck her in the ass, I'm going to fuck you in the ass. Understand?"

I raised my brow and looked at him as if he were crazy. "Come again?"

He laughed to himself and wiped his face, as if he was tired. "That sounded pretty gay didn't it? Shit. You know what I meant, right?"

I laughed and shook my head. "I sure do hope you don't want to fuck me in my ass, sir."

"It's not sir. Ty's fine. Definitely don't ever call me dad. I don't give a shit if you do marry my daughter someday. I'm not having someone your age calling me dad. I draw the line there."

He waved the waitress for another beer. I sipped at my tea and watched her bring him his drink. "When I first lost my girls I drank too much. I said things to my father, and got myself into situations that I wasn't proud of. Once I got my shit together I promised I'd never drink again."

"My daughter might drive you to drink. She's a spitfire, who sometimes makes it her life mission to annoy the hell out of people. She thinks she's always right, and you can't tell her anything and expect that she'll follow directions. Trust me, I'm married to her twin. I just agree and call it a day. It's not worth the effort."

"I hear ya on that. You're daughter can be difficult. She's pretty fickle. It's hard to handle, but I'm getting the hang of it."

He pointed his beer in my direction. "I think we're going to get along just fine, Rusty. Your secret is safe with me. If you want to tell the family, it's up to you. I'm sure when the time is right you'll be able to talk about it more."

Lunch with Isabella's father had given me hope that everything was finally going to be okay. I had his blessing, and knew that he'd support my relationship with his daughter. I hated that we were lying about the paternity of the baby, but completely understood why she didn't want anyone knowing the truth. The only thing I was still worried about was her changing her mind. The indecisive woman that had my heart could change her mind at any time, and the longer we were together, the harder it would be to handle.

I had to pray that I was the right guy in her eyes, because hope was all I had left.

Chapter 30
Isabella

I feel like I'd waited forever to see my baby for the first time. Due to my crappy insurance, my first sonogram wasn't until I was twenty weeks along. I'd literally waited months for this day to come.

With the company of my parents and Rusty, we watched the screen for the first sign of life.

And there it was, curled up comfortably waiting to be attended to. The tool maneuvered over my belly, only stopping when the technician was plugging in data. Then came the moment we were all waiting for. I'd heard it's heartbeat each month after my first appointment. As exciting as it was, nothing could compare to seeing my real baby on that screen, with ten fingers and ten toes.

"Did you want to know the sex?"

I gave her a nod and watched as she focused in on one area.

"It's a girl. Congratulations."

In that moment my heart skipped a couple beats. Growing inside of me was a beautiful little girl, who I knew was going to be absolutely perfect. My parents, who stood behind Rusty held each other and kept watching, but as my eyes scanned the room I saw something I never expected.

Rusty had tears in his eyes. In that instant all of my excitement was put to the side when I realized what he was going through. It's when it finally occurred to me that he needed her as much as I needed him.

At times my feelings for Rusty were still confusing, albeit this wasn't one of those times. In this moment I felt more connected to him than I'd ever been before. I could see both pain and excitement. I could feel his love radiating through me as our fingers intertwined. This beautiful man had found his hope again, and it meant everything to him.

Our relationship hadn't started out good. We bickered more than we appreciated. There were times when I truly thought he was a criminal, a creepy stalker, preying on the right moment to cause harm to me. I felt bad for that now, knowing the real man under that tough façade. He couldn't hide himself from me anymore. That man I thought I knew was just a distant memory. The man who was peering deeply into my eyes was beautiful. He may have been broken, but I could see life shining in those grey eyes.

For both my parent's sake, and my own, I smiled at him, while squeezing his hand tighter. "We're havin' a little girl, Rusty."

He nodded and used his free hand to wipe his eyes. "I know, Iz."

As soon as he said my name I looked at my father. He'd been the only person in my life to call me that, and I feared how it would make him feel. Instead of sensing hurt, I saw happiness. He was smiling from ear to ear, winking at me, letting me know that I'd done good.

It was the happiest moment of my life. I couldn't remember ever feeling so complete, so loved. All of those months feeling like the world was out to get me had suddenly gone away. They no longer mattered, because I'd finally realized what I'd gained.

Stability.

Companionship.

Faith.

They were all things that I just assumed were a lost cause for me. Now I'd been presented with this miracle, and I was finally able to grasp just what it meant for my future.

I'd fought so hard to deny my feelings for Rusty, on account of my own selfish reasons. In some ways I'd used him, and I didn't know how I could have been so inconsiderate. It was obvious that he was crazy about me, and I had a choice to make. I could be with him, raise my child with him, and be happy, or I could dwell on the past.

It was unfortunate that Tate was in a bad way. When I'd sent that late night message to his ex I didn't know it would make him want to end his life. All I wanted was for him to learn a much needed lesson. He couldn't string on two women and make promises that he couldn't keep. Though I felt guilty, his actions had gotten him where he was.

The truth was that I didn't want him being a part of my child's life. I didn't want to have to see and deal with him. We lived in two different states, and clearly I wasn't about to give up what I had in Kentucky; a good job, and man who wanted to be with only me. I just couldn't justify that telling him would benefit anyone.

The technician printed out the pictures and caught my attention when she handed them to me. In return, I put them in Rusty's hands. "This is our daughter."

They were just four words, and probably not the four he was waiting to hear, but I watched that grown man smile with such compassion in that moment. Maybe he was always meant to come into my life to teach me what real devotion felt like. At the end of the day my mind was made up. Rusty was my future, and nothing was ever going to change that.

In the weeks that followed, Rusty and I grew as a couple. We spent our free time learning everything about each other; our flaws, our dreams, and mostly our desires. Each day I fell in love with him a little more, and when I thought there was nothing left to feel he'd surprise me and show me that it was never ending. I'd been blessed, truly, and looked forward to the journey of being a family.

At the six month mark of being pregnant we sat down and had a heart to heart about his family. It was too hard for me to watch him with my own family and not wonder about his parents, and all of the people that he'd shut out so long ago. With the baby's due date getting closer, it was important for me to reach out to him, in case he wanted to include them in our future.

We sat on the couch, so close that our bodies were touching. His focus was on the television, while mine was on the amount of food that I'd consumed at dinner. I held onto my growing bump while addressing my concerns. "Can I ask you somethin' without you gettin' mad?"

He looked away from the show and smiled, having no idea what I was about to say. "Sure. What's up?"

"Are you happy?" I needed to start out slow and work my way to the point.

He seemed confused that I'd asked something so ridiculous. We were clearly happy. "You know the answer to that. I've got everything I want sitting on this couch with me."

"Not everything." I paused to prepare myself.

"If you're happy, why haven't you gotten back in contact with your parents? I mean, if we're goin' to raise this little one together, don't you think they should be a part of it too? I just feel like if we're going to make this kind of commitment than all parties should be involved. Whether you're adopting her or not, she's still going to be your daughter. I want you to treat her like she's your flesh and blood." I think it was hard for me to imagine different when I'd been raised by a man that refused to admit he wasn't my sperm donor. I think in his mind he was the one and only dad, no matter what any kind of test could prove. I needed Rusty to be that committed, because at the end of the day, he was going to be her only daddy.

Rusty sighed, but never let his eyes move from mine. "It's been bothering me for a while. I reckon it's easier to ignore them than to face them. It's not that I don't want them knowing about you, and about the baby. It's just that I don't know how to approach it. I left my dad in such a bad way. Honestly, I don't know if he'd even want to see me."

"He's your father. Of course he wants to see you."

"You're not going to let this go, are you? You're going to keep on me until I break down and go to see him?"

I nodded. "I'll go with you. We can do it together."

Rusty reached over and touched my cheek

with the back of his hand. "I know you will. If it means that much to you, I'll reach out to my parents, but I can't make you any promises where they're concerned."

"I just want you to try. It's important to me."

"If it's important to you, than it's also important to me. We're a team, remember?"

Though it was getting difficult to do, I sat up on the couch, bringing my legs overtop of his lap. I faced him wrapping my arms around his neck. He immediately touched my back with both hands, holding me there on top of him. His smile let me know that he wasn't irritated with my request. "How did I get so lucky to find a man like you?"

"I found you, remember?"

I reached forward, pressing my lips against his. When I pulled them away his eyes were still closed. "I love you, Rusty Tillman."

I could tell from the way those same eyes shot open that he was shocked I'd finally said it. "I was wondering if you were ever going to say that to me. It's okay if you didn't. I would have stuck by my decision no matter what, but it's sure good to hear. Honestly, Iz, it feels good to be loved again. You don't know how long I've waited to feel this way again, especially when, for the longest time, I thought it couldn't happen."

I lifted my hand up and touched his cheek, running my palms over the coarse hairs that were growing in. "It is happenin'. You and me, we're better

301

together."

Rusty rocked us forward, lifting me in his arms while he stood. He held me tight as he started carrying me back to our bedroom. Once inside, he sat me down on the mattress and then joined me. "I think this calls for a celebration, don't you?"

I nodded and accepted his next kiss. "I think we have a lot to celebrate."

Chapter 31
Rusty

It wasn't just the idea of calling my parents. It was a matter of admitting I was in the wrong. I'd run away from my problems, leaving everyone else to have to deal with my mess. Losing my wife and daughter hadn't just destroyed me. I watched my own mother break down more times than I cared to admit, and each time it had broken me a little more. The idea of seeing them made all of those ill feelings come rushing back, and I wasn't sure if I was willing to give up what I had at the moment to rehash something I never wanted to go back to.

But she'd asked me.

She knew what I needed to do, even if I wasn't willing to admit it myself.

Isabella had made good points, leaving me

with no choice than to reach out to them.

I waited until the next morning to call them, considering that it was already too late to get into any kind of detail. Even as I dialed their home telephone number, inside I was dying.

Then she answered.

I knew my mother's voice. It was something that one doesn't forget. Even her one-word greeting sent shivers through my spine. This was the woman that I'd abandoned in her time of need. We should have grieved together, but I'd left and given her more reasons to suffer. I'd been a coward, and it was time to make amends, or at least do my best to try.

"Hello?"

I took a deep breath and responded. "Hi, Mom."

In all of my thirty three years I'd never been so nervous to hear my mother's reply. This wasn't like getting into trouble as a kid. I'd made an adult decision, and I was responsible for the consequences. If my parents wanted nothing to do with me it was my own fault.

"Russell? Is that you?"

"Yeah, it's me." I think she just needed to hear me confirm it.

"Oh my heavens, son. We've been so worried about you. Please tell me you're okay? Every time the phone rings I pray that it's you. We didn't know what to think. You just left without a single word. You didn't even leave a note, or tell the clinic. For a while we thought the worst. Then your dad hired an investigator, who confirmed that you were alive and all right."

"I am. I wasn't for a long time, though. I couldn't take it. I couldn't wake up every day in that house and see all of those reminders. I couldn't even drive to the store and not think of things they liked to buy. Everywhere I turned was a memory. I was miserable. I hope you know that's why I had to leave. Mom, I was so messed up over the girls. I couldn't be around anyone. It hurt way too much." The burning was lingering in my throat from explaining something so horrifying for me.

I could hear that she'd already started sobbing. "I know. It hurt us too. You weren't the only one to lose them. You leaving destroyed your father."

"I know. I'm so sorry. Is Dad there? I'd like to talk to him. I want to explain it myself. He needs to hear my apology."

"Rusty, your father's not doing well. He's been in and out of the hospital. He had a stroke a couple of months ago and it paralyzed his left side. He's doing better, but I can tell a big difference."

Guilty couldn't even begin to explain how I felt hearing the news of my father's health. I sat there silently trying to come to grips with the fact that I could have missed the opportunity to say goodbye to someone else in my life. It grabbed at my heart, and tore me up. "How bad is it?"

"He spends most of his time in a recliner. The nurse comes once a week to get him up moving around. I try to do it myself, but he's so stubborn. He complains all the time, but that lets me know he's still with us. That man will complain up until the Lord takes him." She was quiet for a moment. "Where are you, Russell? Are you calling because you want to come home? After all this time, I think it would do us all some good to see each other."

I watched Isabella come into the room and sit down across from me. She must have sensed the pain in my eyes, because she reached across the table and grabbed my hand. It wasn't much, but it gave me strength. "I'm in Kentucky. I've been here for two years, working on a ranch."

"And you're okay?"

"Actually, I'm better than okay. Mom, I met somebody. She's helped me through a lot. We've been together for a little while now, and we're expecting a baby."

The line seemed like it had disconnected. I sat there, staring across the table, praying that my mother hadn't keeled over and passed out.

"Mom, are you still there?"

"Ye..yes. I'm still here. Give me a second to sit down, son." I could hear her scuffling around before she got back on the line. "Please tell me you're going to come home and let us meet this person that's helped you. It would mean everything to me. I've worried about you so much. For the longest time I wondered if something terrible had happened to you. I can't tell you how good it is to hear the voice of my son again."

I didn't even hesitate. "We can come this weekend."

"We're not living in the same place, Russell."

"Oh. Well, if you don't have room we can get a room nearby,"

"I think before you make that decision you need to know something. When you left we understood your reasoning, but you have to keep in mind that it was hard for us too. Your father worked so hard to be able to leave you with a good life. The practice was supposed to be your future. He went back to work, up until his stroke. He hired another vet to rent the space and manage the clientele, but we get a percentage of the profits. The business is still in our name."

"Dad came out of retirement for me? He didn't have to do that. I knew what leaving meant for my occupation."

"He did it because he knew you were broken. We hoped that one day you'd come home and want to live again."

It was hard to imagine that my dad worked until his body started to give out on him. I'd put that added stress on him. I'd been the reason that he was so bad off. "Jesus, I'm so sorry. You must think I'm a coward. He probably can't stand me."

"I think that we all have our own ways of dealing with pain. You did what you needed to do, and so did your father. He was holding onto hope."

"I still feel terrible."

"Rusty, he didn't just come out of retirement for you. We sold the old house and purchased yours when it went up for auction last year. We couldn't lose the one thing in this town that reminded us of you and the girls. Plus, you'd done so much work to the place. We didn't want you to not have a home to come back to."

It was too much to bear. I sat the phone down on the table and turned it on speaker as I wept, right in front of my girlfriend. She got out of the chair and rushed to my side, holding me, and offering me comfort.

"Russell, are you there, son?"

"Yeah," I sniffled. "I'm still here."

"It's up to you if you want to stay in the house. We didn't change much. The pictures are still out and everything. I know it's a lot to take in."

I didn't know how I was going to walk into that house and see the walls filled with memories of them. "We'll be there Friday around dinner time. Don't do anything special for us."

"We love you, son. I just want you to know that. Your dad and I aren't going to live forever. You're our only child, so we wanted to leave you with something you'd treasure, instead of our old place. I hope you understand."

I nodded, even though she couldn't see me. "I love you too. We'll see you in a few days."

"I'll prepare us a nice dinner. I can't wait to tell your father. See you then."

When we hung up I covered my face with my hands and sat there at the table finally losing control over my emotions. This trip home wasn't just to see my parents, it was to see if I was ready to move forward. I couldn't tell Isabella about my concerns. She didn't need to know that I obviously still had demons to deal with. It wasn't like they could come between us.

I hoped.

Isabella let me calm down before asking me to explain what had happened. She was so patient with me, only reminding me more of how far we'd come as a couple. I know we were working for the common goal of being a family, but our hearts were also in the same place, which helped.

Though difficult, I was able to tell her about my dad's health, and the ultimate sacrifice they'd made in hopes that I'd come home one day. Her pregnancy hormones kicked into full gear as I explained that part. We spent the rest of the morning comforting each other.

What brought us out of our depressing mood was feeling our little girl kicking. She'd been doing it for a couple months, but each day they were getting more prominent. I loved feeling her little body moving around, reminding me that she would be with us soon enough. I think my conversation with my mom didn't give her enough time to take in the fact that I'd announced I was going to be a father again. She'd see soon enough, and the tears we shed today wouldn't compare.

The bottom line was that I knew I couldn't move forward until I left the past behind. In order to do that I had to face it. With Isabella by my side I was going to do it, because her love was my reason for wanting to live again in the first place.

Chapter 32
Rusty

Isabella took off on Friday so we could get an early start on our drive to Indiana. The last time we'd taken this journey it had been for a different reason. She says she never would have went through with an abortion, but I'd like to think that I made sure of it. It was also the first time that we'd made love.

Passing by the hotel that it happened in brought back all of the memories of that night. She turned to look at me, full of smiles. "I know what you're thinkin', Rusty."

I nodded. "You're damn right I'm thinking it." I was trying to keep my mind off of what was about to happen when I pulled up at my old house that I shared with my wife and daughter. "The moment I went between those legs you knew you wanted more."

She giggled and pulled her legs up on the seat. "Don't flatter yourself."

I ran one hand over her smooth skin. "I don't have to. You know it's the truth. Do I need to remind you what you sound like when my tongue hits that little clit of yours?"

It was turning me on talking about it. When I looked over she was blushing. A sudden jolt from my dick reminded me how great it was to wake up naked next to her each morning. "Behave, or I'll pull this truck over and take you right in the back of it, pregnant belly and all."

She crossed her arms. "Stop it. You wouldn't do that."

I pulled over the vehicle, just to be funny. Her arm started flailing as she began freaking out.

"Rusty, stop. Oh my god, I am not gettin' naked out in public. Have you seen my body?"

I looked her up and down, while still chuckling to myself. "Yeah. I see it everyday. Your ass has really filled out by the way. When you bend over I feel like getting some of that every time."

She lightly slapped my arm. "Cut it out. You're not funny, mister. Get back to drivin'. My legs hurt, and I've got to pee."

"You really know how to kill the mood, babe."

She took her fingernails and ran them over my jeans, right between my legs. "Don't worry. I know how to start it back up again."

It was a shame that we'd started pulling on the road to my old house. I tensed up immediately, realizing that in a matter of minutes I wouldn't be smiling. It took everything in me to squeeze her hand and pretend to smile.

She knew what was wrong when I put the truck in park and looked at the white house with the wrap around front porch. I remember painting the shutters blue, and almost falling off the ladder on the last one. In the living room windows hung the curtains that Simone had sewn herself. I took a few deep breaths and stared at the steering wheel.

Isabella put her hand on my back. "You okay?"

"I'm not sure yet."

"I'm sorry for askin' you to do this, Rusty. Do you want to go home?"

I turned to face her. "I do, but I need to do this, for you and for our future. We can't move forward until we deal with the past."

She leaned over and kissed me on the cheek. "Just remember that you're not alone. I'm here for you, and I'm not going anywhere. I promise."

We stepped out of the truck and I carried our bags up to the front porch. Isabella stood by my side as I opened the door. It was so difficult walking in and recognizing the smell of being home. I focused on the hardwood flooring, instead of the furniture and pictures that I knew were hanging. "Mom. It's me."

She looked the same as she did the day I left. Wearing an apron, she stepped out of the kitchen

313

opening and approached us. Her arms opened and I leaned down to hug her, and felt a rush of warmth hitting my eyes. The tears were easy to choke back and hide, especially considering what happened next. "My son. I missed you so much. You look so healthy."

I heard my mother gasp, and pulled away frantically to figure out what was wrong. I followed her eyes to see what had her so worked up. Then I saw what she saw.

Isabella.

Except that's not who she saw at all.

My mother stared at her like she was seeing a ghost. I hadn't even noticed the transformation until this very moment. In her pregnancy she'd gained weight in her face, making her almost a twin to my deceased wife, Simone.

If there were ever a time when I didn't want them compared to each other it was now. I put my arm around my girlfriend and pulled her close to me, knowing that she was fully aware of what was going on. She looked to me with worried eyes. "Mom, this is Isabella Mitchell. Isabella, this is my mom, Janice Tillman."

My mother didn't move. "Nice to meet you."

Iz, smiled, but couldn't bring herself to say anything. As the seconds passed without a single sound, I knew I was going to have to separate them to be able to calm my mother. "The bathroom is right down the hall on the left. The light is on a dimmer so make sure you turn it to the right for brightness."

I watched her walk away before speaking to my mother. "I know what you're going to say."

"Son, is this some kind of sick joke?"

"Mom," I had to calm her down before Isabella came back into the room. "Please, it's not at all what you think."

"The similarities are uncanny."

I brought her over to the couch and sat her down, noticing that on the end table was a picture of me with my girls. Sydney looked to be around two, and I immediately felt the room start to spin. I sat down in the seat beside her and took a few short breaths. "Listen to me. You can't say stuff like that in front of her."

She shook her head and looked up at me. "I thought you were better, son. I thought you'd finally been able to move on, but it's clear that you haven't. Why else would you pick a woman that looks just like the wife you lost?"

It was too late for me to hush my mom. I turned my head to see my girlfriend standing behind the couch with a hurt look on her face.

I stood up and rushed toward her, ignoring the fact that we'd just walked in the door. She didn't argue as I pulled her along up the stairs. She stopped me halfway and stared at a picture that hung on the wall. It was Simone when she was pregnant. She was holding her stomach and looking down at it.

Isabella put her hand over her mouth. "Oh my

god. This can't be happenin'."

"Come on. Just don't look." I tried to get her to budge, but she just stood there looking at the rest of them. Feeling defeated, I sat down on the top step and gave up. This had all been a terrible idea, and the fact that I hadn't considered this outcome was exactly why I had no business coming here at all. "Please, Iz. Let's just get a hotel room instead."

She shook her head and pointed down the stairs, while she spoke in a low voice. "Your own mother can't even look at me, Rusty. How am I supposed to feel?"

"I don't know." I really didn't know what to say. "I never should have let you talk me into coming here," I whispered. "How was I supposed to know that my mother would have a whole house as a shrine to them? You think this is easy for me? This is the reason I left this life. I couldn't stand to be here and see all of this."

"Look at me and tell me that I'm not a constant reminder of her." She pointed to my wife's picture.

"You're not. I swear. You may resemble each other, but to me you're different. You know that. We've talked about this, babe." I was trying my hardest to settle her down.

"Babe? Don't you dare babe me. That's probably what you called her, isn't it?"

I put my head down. Nothing I did was right,

and I was making it worse as it all played out.

"Iz, I love you. We're having a baby. This has nothing to do with my wife. She's dead and she's never coming back. The life I have with you, our life, it's perfect. Don't let this change your mind. You only look so much like her right now because you're pregnant."

"So you're admittin' it? Every mornin' you wake up next to me and it's like bein' with her again, right?" She started walking back down the stairs. I ran after her, desperate to get her out of the house and away from my confused mother. When she turned the corner and stood in front of mother, I stopped dead in my tracks. "Mrs. Tillman, I'm real sorry that I've given you such a shock. I can assure you that the thought never crossed my mind. If it's alright with you I'm just goin' to go to the hotel and call it a night. I'll let you catch up with your son for a while alone."

She was leaving me?

"Iz, please hold up," I said as she headed for the front door. She never turned around until she'd reached the truck. Her hands were shaking, and there were tears running down her cheeks. She could hardly get out the words in between her sobs.

"This was what I've been afraid of this whole time. I asked you so many times why you were with me, Rusty. You assured me that it wasn't because we looked alike. You even told me that it wasn't much at all. Those pictures inside of that house don't lie. I felt like I was looking at myself in another life." She

317

opened the truck door more and started to climb in it. I grabbed her shirt preventing her from moving and she jerked out of my reach. "Don't touch me right now. I'm so humiliated. You brought me all the way here to be treated like a replacement. How could you do this to me?"

"I swear to god that this isn't what you think. I want to be with you because I love you. This isn't about Simone, or the fact that you have the same color hair and eyes. I don't love you for your looks, Iz. I love you for what's inside."

"My baby? Is that it? You want a kid so bad that you picked the first one available?"

"No! God no! Why would you even say that?" I was shaking, losing control of myself as my foot continued to drive into my mouth with each comment. "Please don't go."

"This truck belongs to the ranch, so I have every right to take it home. You obviously need to work things out with your family, and I need to get out of here. I can't go inside of that house anymore. There's even a picture in the bathroom, Rusty. How fuckin' creepy is that?"

In my defense they were pictures of us in the bathtub. At the time I'd fought with Simone about hanging them, stating that they were inappropriate. "Please don't leave me. I need you."

"You need to leave me alone. I've got to get away from you. I need to think."

"About what?" I worried.

"About everything. This is messin' with my head. All of this is just crazy. That woman looked at me like I was a ghost. Are you goin' to deny that?"

"Please, just promise me that you won't leave. I love you so much. I came here for you, for us. I swear that's all this is. All that's left of my girls is what's in that cemetery we went to the first time we came here. I know that. You aren't some shrine to me. I promise." I grabbed her hand, clinging to hope that she'd reassure me. "Can I have a kiss goodbye? Will you at least call me when you get to the hotel?"

She leaned forward, but did not initiate the kiss, nor did she comment on calling me.

After I ran in and grabbed her bag, I watched as she pulled away in the truck. For some reason I had this sick feeling that something terrible was about to happen.

Chapter 33
Isabella

I couldn't take another minute in that house. Everywhere I looked were reminders of his dead wife, not to mention it was as if we were long lost sisters. The resemblance wasn't just something his mother had noticed, I too was caught off guard by how uncanny it was. By the time I'd made it inside of that bathroom all I wanted to do was figure out a way to escape. I couldn't handle seeing that woman looking at me as if she'd seen a ghost.

Now, I could tell the difference in overreacting, and being in shock. That woman was in complete and utter shock. I knew without a doubt that being in her presence wasn't healthy for either of us.

Whether Rusty knew what was happening, or even if he didn't, he hadn't warned me just how much of his family remained in that house. I had no idea what I was walking into. Leaving was my only option.

I know I was supposed to go straight to the hotel, and call him once I was settled, but I was too angry; to angry with him, and with myself. I'd been so naive to think that we could build a future when neither of us was over our past. I'd made one compulsive decision after another, and was left heartbroken and absolutely distraught.

Rusty called my phone until I finally answered.

"I can't talk to you right now, Rusty. I honestly don't even know what to say."

"Just come pick me up. I don't want to be here without you."

"That's too bad. I left the state hours ago." I really hadn't I'd been driving around in circles until I came to the cemetery that he'd taken me to. Little did he know I was probably less than a mile away.

"You what?" I knew he was going to freak out. "Iz, I know you're upset, but that's no reason to go home. We need to work this out."

"Why didn't you tell me? How could you not warn me about your mother?"

"Iz, I haven't been home in over two years. How was I to know she'd go to such extremes? Just tell me where you are. I'm sure my bike is here in the garage, since pretty much my whole house is exactly the way I left it. You know, you're not the only one here that's creeped out. You think I want to come here and see all of Sydney's things still sitting in her room exactly how she left them? Do you honestly think that is easy for me? Or how about the fact that my mother took me on a tour of my own house, down to the details of how Simone used to organize our junk drawer?"

I opened my mouth to speak, but suddenly understood it from his angle. This wasn't just difficult for me. It was killing him. "This wasn't what I had in mind when I asked you to make amends."

"I know, babe. Trust me, I know. I think I'd forgotten just how crazy my mother could be. Listen, my dad is still sleeping, and it would mean a lot to me if you would just tell me where you are. I'll come to you. Please, Iz. I need you."

Sensing the desperation in his voice, I sighed and decided that we were better together, instead of apart. "I'm at the cemetery. Don't ask how I ended up here, but that's where I am."

"Give me a few minutes. I'll be there. Please don't go anywhere."

"I won't."

I think I was crying even before I hung up. While I sat down on the stone bench in front of the girl's graves, I thought about the love they had for each other, and wondered if I'd ever be able to have that kind of love from Rusty. All I knew was that I was totally in love with him, and insanely jealous. The worst part was that I knew I'd never be able to compete with them. Rusty would always love them, and I would never want him not to. It was a problem that I was going to have to learn to live with if I wanted to be happy in my life.

This trip hadn't just opened my eyes to my feelings and issues with Rusty; it had made me once again think about Tate. I wanted to do the right thing, and not have to go through the hurdles that my parents did with me. It was as if I could either have Rusty, or tell Tate. Rusty wasn't exactly giving me that ultimatum, but I knew him enough to know he wouldn't do well with sharing. This to him was a second chance at having a family. It only made sense that he'd want us to always be together, and not have to deal with visitation.

I think if my biological father would have been a normal human being I'd have a different opinion. I feel like he'd never had a right to know me. Because of that experience, I was more okay with the idea of never telling Tate.

While fighting with myself about my own matters of the heart, Rusty rolled up on a bicycle. He had this old ball cap on backwards, and appeared to look half his age. I wanted to giggle, but it wasn't the time and place. Before he was close enough to hear, I looked down at the two side by side graves. "If you're out there somewhere watchin', please help me make the right decision. I love this man, more than I ever thought I could."

Rusty walked up and put his hands in his

pockets. He looked down at the headstones, seemingly wanting me to speak first.

"I'm sorry for runnin' out on you. I know I overreacted, I just couldn't take another second in that house."

"Yeah, I get it. She didn't mean to freak you out. I think I probably should have warned her."

I didn't want to talk about his mother. "Did you get to see your dad at all?"

He shrugged. "Mom wants us to come back for dinner. Before you say no, she's assured me that she'll be on her best behavior. I've let her know we won't be staying the night either way. You may not believe this, but I don't want to be there with that stuff, and it's not because it brings up old feelings. Iz, don't you get it? What I feel for you is nothing like I felt for them. It's new, and it's different. They may have been my life for a long time, but you're my future. I don't want you to try to replace them, but it's not a competition either."

I ran my hands over my face as I spoke. "What if I can't get past that though? It's selfish and you may hate me for it, but what if I'm not okay with you lovin' someone else. Even though I know she's gone, it's still difficult for me."

He looked away and the finally back at me. "Look, I didn't agree to come here to fight with you. I'm trying so hard to be the man you want me to be. Can you please stop making it so hard? Have I not proved to you time and again that I love you?"

"Yes, but it's not enough for me."

"Well then we've reached a conundrum," he noted.

I stood up and pointed to the two markers. "For the last couple years you've been hidin' from your past. As much as I want to think that it's easy to come here and let things go, I know it's not. I think it would be best if you stayed for a while to figure out what's next for you. Clearly you've got a ton to deal with."

"My life is in Kentucky with you. Where is this coming from?"

"Russell Tillman belongs here in Indiana, runnin' an animal clinic. He doesn't have to shovel shit and deal with my family any longer. Don't you get that? You don't have to hide anymore."

He sat down next to me and looked out into the distance. "I get what you're saying, but you're missing the most important thing. My life is in Kentucky with you."

"You're not obligated to stay with me because you promised to be the father to my child. That's what I'm tellin' you. Rusty, I can't expect you to commit to a life raisin' another man's child. We should be goin' out on dates and doin' what new couples do, instead of movin' in together and plannin' a family." I couldn't believe those words were coming out of my mouth. It had to be the adrenaline, causing me to have the strength to say what was on my mind. I didn't want

Rusty feeling like he settled. I wanted to be together because he loved me, and then fell in love with my daughter.

Again, it all went back to me not knowing if he'd chose to be with me because I gave him back some kind of stability. I wondered if his feelings for me were only there because he was desperate to feel something again, after so long.

It was as if each time I felt content, something would happen to make me question it all. With a growing baby inside of me, I had to make a decision to protect her. I had to do what was best.

He reached over and put his hand on my knee, waiting for our eyes to meet before he spoke. "In some ways I agree with you, but in others you're very off base. The bottom line is that I can't keep trying to reassure you of something you're never going to be able to accept. I could tell you that I love you every second of every day, but I don't see it ever being good enough. I get that our relationship is unconventional, but it's real. Can't you see that?" His eyes were so filled with pain, albeit they couldn't change the way I felt.

"I think you need to stay here, Rusty. Get things handled. Help your parents. When you get all of that taken care of, we'll see where we're at," I was almost losing it as I spoke. As soon as the sentence was done I began to sob. My body trembled and I felt him putting his arms around me.

We sat there for the longest time in silence,

both of us not knowing what to say to change each other's minds. I knew he didn't want me to go, but it was the right decision. I wanted him to know without a doubt what he wanted before the baby was born.

Chapter 34
Isabella

We couldn't move forward until we dealt with the past. Rusty had been brave going back home and facing his buried fears. I watched him suffer through so many emotions, and felt the pain of his insecurities. In order for him to love himself again he had to be able to accept that he couldn't change what happened to his girls. They were gone, and he had to keep living. He couldn't hide from his old life and pretend that it never happened. These were his demons, and until he figured them out there wouldn't be a future for us.

After a very long and emotional discussion we came to an agreement that I'd catch a flight to spend my weekend with my parents, and Rusty would pick me up on the way home. It wasn't exactly how I wanted to spend my weekend, but it sure as hell beat being freaked out for another two days.

On the bright side of things my parents were excited to see me. My mom planned a whole day trip so that we could shop for the baby's room. I'd talked about a pink room for a long time, but ended up going with a soft yellow. While in town we were going to get me registered for baby supplies, and with my mom's help I'd be able to get everything that I actually needed, instead of picking the things that seemed utterly adorable.

Obviously, my parents required an explanation of why I'd flown in from Indiana, without my boyfriend. I could tell from the look on my dad's face that he wasn't going to let me go more than five minutes without explaining. After he put my bag in the back, he climbed into the driver's seat and turned to face me. "What happened, Iz? Do I need to kick some ass?"

I rolled my eyes. "No, Dad. It's not like that."

He reached over and tugged on my ponytail as he spoke. "Did my little girl get her feelings hurt?"

I swatted his hand away from my hair. "Stop. He's in Indiana dealin' with his family. It's complicated, but I couldn't stand bein' there."

"Uncomplicate it."

"Fine, but I'm only tellin' you because you're my dad and I trust that you won't make a big deal out of it. Apparently I'm a dead ringer for Rusty's ex. I about gave his mother a heart attack. To make matters worse his parents bought his old house and made it a shrine. It's creepy as shit. I had to get away from all of it, and I even feel bad that I left Rusty there. It was quite obvious that he didn't even want to be there."

"Hold on. Are you telling me that you look exactly like his dead wife?"

"We could be sisters."

My dad seemed to be as shocked as I was when I first discovered it. "I'm probably not supposed to say how weird that is."

I put up my hand. "Seriously, Dad. I love the man, but it still gets to me."

"Honey, are you sure that he's not trying to replace what he lost? It seems to me like that could be happening. I just don't want you getting yourself involved with a man long-term that's in it for those reasons."

I knew by telling him it would open a can of worms that I wasn't in the mood to discuss. Still, I knew I had to defend my relationship, even if sometimes I felt the same way. "At first, before I would give him the time of day, yes. He was most definitely obsessed with me because I reminded him of her. I felt like he was stalking me. Come to find out, it was because I resembled Simone so much. When we started bein' friends all of that changed. He saw me for who I am, and not who she was. Trust me, Dad, I would have never given him the time of day otherwise."

"If that's the case then just appease me with this. How many times has he called you Simone?"

I didn't have to think about it, because the answer was obvious. "Never."

"There's your answer. If Rusty had some hidden complex about you becoming his ex wife, he would have slipped by now."

He was absolutely right. Maybe it took my dad giving me the advice to realize it. I think a part of me would always wonder if the little things I did reminded him of her, but for the most part that could happen in a relationship. We're all human, and we share the same tendencies. It was only natural for me to say or do something that would remind him of his old life.

I just needed to learn that we we're going to make our own memories. "He's a good man, Dad. I promise."

"You know," he paused to pull out onto the main highway. "Your mom is so excited to take you shopping tomorrow. I think she might be a little too excited about being a grandmother. She had me up in the damn attic last week digging around for your old stuff."

"Did you find anything good?"

"I found your rocking horse I made you. There was a crib up there, and a changing table. Most of your clothes went to your cousins, but your mom saved some of the special things."

"Is the crib in good condition?"

"It is, but we were thinking we could get a new one for your house, and keep the old one here, for when you come to stay with us, which we hope is more often. I've got a feeling your mom isn't going to want to be away from that baby for long periods of time." I couldn't help notice that my dad wasn't talking about his excitement. It could only mean one thing.

"Dad, are you mad at me for gettin' knocked up?"

He peeked at me before turning his attention back to the road. "I'm not going to lie and say that thinking about my daughter with a man doesn't disturb me. You're always going to be my little girl, Iz. Nothing can change that. As far as being mad at you, well that's not the case. I think it's more of a personal fight with myself. You see, I always pictured having grandkids, but never before I had white hair and balls that sagged down to my knees. Since none of that has happened yet, it's freaking me out."

"Dad, really? I don't want to hear about your testicles." Leave it to him to make a joke out of something serious.

"You're my daughter. Anything that comes from you is also a part of me. You're a reflection of me and your mother. I know you'll be a good mom, and I'll be very proud of you." This was yet another reason why I'd never felt adopted by my dad. He believed with his whole heart that I was his child. It only personified the relationship that we had. It also reminded me that Rusty could be the man that I wanted him to be.

"Thanks. That means a lot to me." It did too. Of all the people in my life it had been my father that I looked up to the most. Making him proud had always been a reward.

Pulling up at our farm was always an exciting feeling. It would always be my home, no matter how old I'd gotten.

After a nice dinner I retreated to my room to get some much needed rest. Before tucking myself in, I pulled out my phone to call Rusty. Since we'd been living together I'd convinced him to get one. It hadn't even been twenty-four hours and I was already missing him.

How is it going? – I

I miss you something fierce. Spent some time with my dad today. It was good to see him after so long. My mom says she's sorry again. It's going to be hard sleeping without you tonight. – R

I just got into bed. Dreading waking up without you next to me. I miss you too. Going to register for the baby in the morning. – I

I love you, Isabella, not because you look like someone else, or because you're carrying a baby in that beautiful body of yours. I love you because every second with you makes me happy. I hope you know that. – R

I love you too. I'll call you tomorrow. – I

It was easier to be able to sleep alone knowing that he was thinking about me. Questioning the way he felt was silly, especially when I knew in my heart that his feelings were genuine. When I closed my eyes I thought about my little girl, and how she'd want for nothing. It certainly made me feel content.

Chapter 35
Isabella

My mom woke me bright and early to get started on a day of shopping. She fed me pancakes before we were off on our girl's day. Being with her, alone, was so special to me. It wasn't that I minded having my brothers, because I didn't. It was just that sometimes I wanted her all to myself.

My mom parked the car and we headed into the huge baby store. Because I basically needed everything, we decided to separate with the scanners to cover more ground. My mom was going to handle all of the necessities, since she knew about them more than I did. My job was to pick out décor, and bigger items like strollers and swings.

I made my way to the aisle with all of the car seats and started looking at the features of each one.

When I approached the third one, a gentleman was squatting in front of it appearing to have been checking out the wheel mechanism. After noticing that this model converted for when the child outgrew it, I wanted to find out more about it. I bent over, trying to read the tag without being in this particular guy's way.

That's when I saw him.

My eyes did a double take and I took a few steps backward. "Tate?" I couldn't believe that it was him. Did he know I was pregnant? Had my brother's told someone, who had in turn told him? My life was flashing in front of my eyes as I stood there contemplating what I was going to say to him. Still, I couldn't figure out why he'd even be in this kind of store, unless he was somehow making an attempt to win me over, by showering me and my baby with expensive gifts.

"Bella? Holy shit. What are you doing here?"

"I could ask you the same thing."

I watched as his eyes scanned my belly. "Holy shit. You're pregnant?"

He didn't know. Confusion hit me all at once as I tried to figure out why he'd be in this store if he'd not learned about my pregnancy. "Obviously."

I waited for him to do the math, but he didn't even seem interested. "Well, it's good to see you. I know I was shitty to you on the phone when you called. Everything was a mess for a while."

"So it's better?" I wanted to know.

He nodded and smiled. "Yeah. Actually, it it's great. For a while I thought that giving up was my only option, but something happened, and now it's all how it is supposed to be. What you did to me was wrong, but it made me see what I'd been doing. I treated you and Jenn badly, and neither of you deserved to be lied to."

"I'm glad you feel that way." The baby started to kick, causing me to hold onto my belly. Just as I was about to say something I saw Jenn heading in our direction.

Then it hit me like a ton of bricks. I wasn't the only one carrying a child. Tate's child. She placed her hand on her bump and walked toward us, before realizing who I was. To say that she was in shock would have been an understatement, especially when she noticed my appearance. "Tate, honey, I was looking everywhere for you."

The first thing after noticing her pregnancy was the huge diamond that she had on her hand. With one quick glance I noticed the band on his left finger.

"So you guys got married? That's great." I wasn't lying. It was good that Tate had a life now. His life would no longer be something I felt guilty about.

"I thought you moved away, Bella." I could see in her eyes that she was assuming Tate was lying again.

"I did. I live in Kentucky with my boyfriend." Tate's eyes were on me, as if I'd kicked him where the sun didn't shine.

"How far along are you?" Her question made me freeze. We could all do the math in our heads, especially with her pregnancy due date probably being so close to mine. This was my opportunity. The decision had to be made.

"I'm just five months along. How about you?"

She looked at Tate before answering. "We're seven months along, right baby?"

Tate gave her a worried smile. "Yeah. Seven months now."

"Well, for all that it's worth, I'm glad you to are so happy. Congrats on the baby and the marriage."

I turned to get the hell away from both of them, felling as if the room had suddenly begun to spin. If I didn't find some fresh air and a seat I knew I'd be waking up on the ground. I no sooner found the rocker section and sat down when I saw Jenn approaching me. Tate was nowhere near her and I had no idea what was about to happen.

"Bella, can I talk to you?"

I nodded, even though I was freaking out. "Sure."

"Listen, I know you hate me, and that you probably think I had it out for you. I honestly didn't know about you for a long time. When you sent me that video it killed me, but I dumped him. I couldn't trust him anymore." She looked down at her belly. "Then I found out I was pregnant. I thought about having an abortion, but my heart wouldn't let me. I've loved Tate since we were kids, so my decision wasn't hard to make. We got married before telling my parents, so that they couldn't try to talk me out of it."

"Why are you tellin' me all of this? I have nothin' to do with Tate."

"I need you to be honest with me, Bella. When I came around that corner and saw you in your condition one thought crossed my mind. I may be way out of line, but I need to know if that baby is Tate's. I know you slept together, so just tell me. Please." She started to break down in front of me, as if my being there was destroying her happiness. It was at that exact moment when I realized that I wasn't ever willing to destroy their happiness, mostly because I wanted the same for myself. "This baby isn't Tate's, Jenn. It's my boyfriend, Rusty's."

She smiled through her tears and nodded. "That's really good to know."

My mom came out of nowhere with her hands full of items. "You okay, Bella?"

I stood and walked toward my mother, waving to Jenn as we left the aisle. The moment we were away from her, I grabbed the stuff in my mom's hands and sat it down, then pulled her out of the store as quickly as I was able to move.

"Bella, what is the matter with you? Is it the baby?"

I fell into my mom's arms, clinging to her as I started to collapse. The rush of emotions overwhelmed me, sending me into a uncontrolled crying fit.

We stood there in the middle of the parking lot until I could calm down enough to explain. "The baby is fine, Mom." We climbed into the car and I wiped my tears with a napkin. "There's somethin' I need to tell you. You're probably never goin' to forgive me."

"The baby is Tate's, isn't she?"

I nodded and looked at my mother. "How do you know that?"

"Mother's intuition."

"No, really. How did you know?" I was going to kill Jake and Jax if they'd told her.

"There's a couple of reasons. The first is that I knew you went to see him when you came to visit last time. Then at the party you asked me about Tucker. You've never asked me about him, Bella. It was a dead giveaway."

"He can't find out, Mom. He can't ever find out."

"Bella, are you with Rusty, or is he just coverin' for you?"

"We're together. We're in love, and he wants to raise her as his own. Please don't tell Daddy. He'll never forgive me. Nobody will." I continued to be over-emotional, realizing that this could destroy the relationship I had with my family.

"This decision is yours to make."

"That female in the store was Tate's wife. She's pregnant and they went and got married. Don't you see? He's already got a baby on the way. He's got a second chance at a future with her, and I have a new life that doesn't include him. This secret needs to be buried. My baby is goin' to be Rusty's. He's goin' to raise her as his own."

"Honey, that is all so easy to say now, but what happens if the two of you don't work out? What happens if your child needs medical attention and they require the father's information?"

"I will cross that bridge if it ever happens. Mom, I want my daughter to have a good life. Rusty's already lost one child. Even if something happened between us, he'd never give up another child. That's why I know it's the right decision. If Tate gets to have a second chance at happiness, why can't Rusty?"

My mom reached over and placed her hand over mine. "Oh, Bella, he can. You both can." We hugged each other for a few minutes, both crying at this point. My mother just wanted me to be happy, and even though I thought I was before, I knew this time it was going to happen. "Who else knows about this?"

"Jake and Jax. That's all."

"This secret stays between our immediate family. You don't need to share it with anyone else."

"What about Daddy?"

"I'll explain it to him. There's no need for you to get this upset again. It's not healthy for the baby.

He'll be fine, Bella. Your father loves you no matter what."

"I really am sorry, Mom. I thought I loved him."

She wiped the tears away from my face as I spoke, like she'd done whenever I cried as a child. "Until you fell in love for real, right?"

"Yes. Is that how you felt with Dad?"

"Yeah, sweetie. It's how I felt with your father. When I fell in love with him I knew the difference right away. It made me hate Tucker even more, because he'd been such a waste of my time. I'm just thankful that I had you. If that man did one good thing in his short life, it was giving me you. You're perfect in every way, honey. Your daughter is goin' to be lucky to have a mom like you."

My mom drove us home early that day. She took my dad into their bedroom and gave him the news, while I sat in the kitchen freaking out. I heard the door open and turned to see him smiling at me. He walked right over to the table and sat down beside me. "No more secrets, kiddo. Life is too short to do it all alone."

"I didn't want you to be disappointed in me." That burn was forming in my throat again. "I want you to always be proud of me."

He cupped my face with his hands. "Isabella Mitchell, I am proud of you. We all make mistakes. You know that."

"So you don't hate me?"

"Of course not. I don't hate Rusty either. In fact, I'm kinda liking him even more now. It takes a real man to step up and take responsibility for a child that isn't his. I mean, guys like that should be considered superheroes, or maybe even Greek Gods."

My mom and I started to laugh. "Dad, really?"

He put his hands up. "What? I'm just saying, we're pretty freaking cool. They always say that women marry their fathers. I thought it was meant to be incestuous, until now. I mean, what was the chance that you'd go out and find a younger version of me?"

I shoved his playfully. "Dad. You're ridiculous. I'll be sure to tell Rusty how you feel."

"I'll tell him myself. He's a good man, Iz. He's got problems, but so does everyone. All that matters is if he makes you happy."

"He does."

"Then go be happy. Stop coming here unannounced. It's bad for my health."

With my dad's sense of humor in full effect, I knew that I'd finally found peace. Tate was married, with a child on the way. I wasn't keeping him from anything that he didn't already have with his wife. If anything, I was protecting him from a truth he didn't want to know about.

Then there was Rusty.

He claimed that I'd given him his life back, but in reality he'd taught me that love went beyond what I'd always assumed. He was going to be a good father, and a partner.

All I had to do now was figure out how to combine his old life with our new one. I didn't care what I had to do. I'd make it happen, for our future.

Chapter 36
Rusty

After one night, I was already on my way out of Indiana. It was going to take me a long time, but I was determined to get to Isabella. She'd left me so that I could take care of things that I'd left unsettled, but the truth was that there was nothing more important in my life than being with her. I couldn't afford to lose her over something from my past. My mother was going to have to learn to accept what she couldn't change. The resemblance was only skin deep. What was inside of Isabella was nothing like

347

any woman I'd ever met. She was heard-headed, always had to be right, caring, loyal, and above all the woman that I wanted to spend my future with.

It took me eleven and a half hours to get to North Carolina, and another hour after I'd called Noah and got the address of the farm. Beat, and ready to honestly sleep for another twelve hours, I pulled into the driveway and parked where I saw her parents SUV. She'd told me which house was hers on the farm, and I'd seen a ton of pictures, so I knew which house to walk up to. I knocked twice before one of the twins came to the door. He saw me and leaned on it. "Which one am I?"

"Is this a trick question? I've been driving for twelve hours, man. Can't you give me a break?"

He opened the door and let me all the way inside. "Bella, there's some dude here to see you."

"Jax?" I guessed.

He chuckled. "Close, but nope, I'm Jake."

"Quit messing with him, Jax," Tyler Mitchell yelled as he walked into the room. He stuck out his hand. "Rusty. Did you just come all the way from

Indiana?"

"Yes." I was a little upset with myself for not asking their permission to visit their daughter. She's clearly been upset when he picked her up from the airport, and here I was beating down the door to get to her. I was lucky this guy didn't jack me up and force me to be on my way.

"So you heard that her mother and I know the truth?"

I was stunned. Had she been so upset that she'd gotten to her parent's farm and told them the truth? Did they know I wasn't the father? "About what?"

I heard her voice before I knew she'd entered the room. "Everything."

I put my hands in my pockets and clenched my jaw, trying to remain calm when I felt like the whole world was about to come crumbling down again. I'd driven so far to see her, to prove to her that my love was unconditional. After one fight she'd turned around and told them the truth. I didn't understand how all of my efforts had turned to shit. "Why?"

She walked toward me, breaking the distance

between us. When her arms wrapped around my waist I felt confused. Clearly her parents knew that I'd lied. They lose all respect for me, and probably help her come to some kind of agreement with her ex. Was this hug her way of saying she was sorry? Was this going to lead to her telling me we were through?

"I saw Tate today, Rusty." The mere mention of his name made my heart wrench. This was the one person who could singlehandedly ruin my life. He could rip her away from me without a single consideration for what I was willing to do for her.

I cut her off. "Where? Why? I thought we talked about this." It didn't matter that her dad was standing there with us. I needed to know what had happened. I was determined to find out if I'd caused this. Was I the reason that she'd run to North Carolina and told everyone the truth?

"How about we go talk about this outside?"

This wasn't going to be good.

She grabbed my hand and pulled me outside, where we walked further to a large red barn. Inside it was finished off, for entertainment purposes. She sat down on a couch and I plopped down beside her. "I still can't believe you came all of the way here. Did somethin' bad happen in Indiana?"

"No." I was antsy. "Everything is fine. Iz, I just came all this way to be with you. You're scaring the shit out of me. What's going on? Did you tell Tate about the baby to spite me?"

"Absolutely not. I didn't tell Tate nothin'. We ran into each other in a store. It wasn't difficult for him to assume I was pregnant. I look like one of the cattle in the pastures. In fact, if I dressed in black and white you wouldn't even be able to tell us apart."

"Don't say that. You're beautiful."

"I don't feel beautiful."

My heart couldn't take much more. I silently prayed that this was all a nightmare; that I wasn't about to lose two people that I loved for the second time in my life. "I promise that you are. So then what happened?" I couldn't let her change the subject, not when our future was riding on what had transpired.

She shrugged and looked down. I felt like she was trying to find the words to break my heart with as little pain as possible. She didn't know I was already breaking apart inside.

"Then his wife walked up to us."

My eyes shot up to meet hers. "His wife? I'm confused."

"Let me help you out with that," she offered. "Tate isn't the depressed soul he was a couple of months ago. It seems that he and Jenn have gotten back together. The main reason being that she's pregnant with his child."

In a matter of seconds everything had changed. "He's having two children at the same time?"

She shook her head. "No, Rusty. He's having one child." She grabbed my hand and put it on her belly. "This little girl is yours."

I can't say that hearing that didn't get me choked up. I wanted nothing more than to be a father to the child she was carrying. I'd made it my life's mission to make it work. Just when I thought that all hope was lost, she was sitting across from me reassuring me that it was really going to happen. "So, he doesn't know?"

Iz shook her head. "No. I lied about my due date so he couldn't even inquire. Tate has a wife and a child on the way. Finding out the truth would just ruin his life again. Jenn would never be able to look past it. Besides, our daughter deserves to grow up in a stable environment, with two parents that love each other. Don't you think?"

I ran my fingers through her wavy blonde hair. "Yeah. I do."

"My parents know the truth now, Rusty. They've promised not to tell the rest of the family."

"Are they pissed at me?"

"No. contrary to what you might have thought, my dad now considers you his hero. It's no secret that he's not my biological father, but he'd never admit that to anyone else. The moment I told him what you were willin' to do for us, he was sold on you bein' a part of my life."

I pulled her against my chest and held her there as I spoke. "I was afraid I'd lost you. I can't imagine spending a single day without you, Iz. That's why I had to drive out here to find you. Indiana holds my past, and I get that you wanted me to have some kind of closure, but the truth is that I let go of it a long time ago, before you and I were even a thought. I explained to my parents that my future was in Kentucky, and I was staying there. While driving here I thought about what was best for our daughter. I'm going to see about getting back into the medical field. I'm sure there's plenty of livestock that needs to be attended to. The Mitchell ranch alone pays the current vet a ton of money each year. I think if I got my license current, I'd be able to offer your family a more cost efficient plan than they're paying. Maybe we could even open an animal hospital locally. With your business degree and my medical expertise, we could have our own family business. It's going to take some time to see it all through, but don't you think it will -."

She cut me off before I could finish. Her lips pressed against mine, and I was lost in the moment. Not only had I not lost Isabella, but I'd somehow gained the respect of her father. It was a win-win situation for both of us.

We sat there on that couch for the longest time.

Her parents were waiting when we headed back to the house. The look on their faces let me know immediately that they approved of me stepping up. Her dad approached me first. He held out his hand. "I may have a man crush on your right now."

"I'm going to pretend that's not as weird as it sounds," we both laughed as we shook. "I appreciate the gesture all the same. For a second I thought she was kicking me to the curb."

"We wouldn't have let her do that." He patted me on the back. "We'd just kick her to the curb and adopt you." He winked at his daughter when he said it.

From that moment I knew that everything was going to work out.

That night after everyone else was asleep, Isabella snuck us out to the old barn. Instead of taking us into the party area, she lead us back to a private quarters. A small cot was folded up on one side, and a couch was on the other. She pushed me backwards until I was forced to sit down on the sofa. She then climbed on top of me and leaned in to kiss me. Her belly pressed on my chest, but it didn't offend me. I knew that inside of her was something beautiful; something that was going to change our lives forever. Our fingers intertwined on both hands. The peaceful quiet of being in the closed barn reminded me that we were totally alone. She rocked her body back and forth, letting me know what she wanted from me. I pulled away from her lips, letting mine linger there still so close. "I love you."

"I know, Rusty. I'm going to thank God every day for bringin' you into my life."

"I should be the one thanking him. Just when I was ready to give up I found you."

"Are you goin' to make love to me, or sit here givin' me more reasons to be crazy bout you?" She pulled her hands away from mine and ran them up my chest. "I'll accept both, but prefer to have you naked."

I picked her up and laid her down on the couch, so that I was hovering over her body. My hand coursed over her belly as I leaned down to kiss it gently. "My girl," I whispered. Then I stood up and lifted my shirt over my head. "I think I'm going to do both, Iz." I began removing my jeans. "I'm going to give you reasons to want me, while I'm making sweet love to you."

From the smile on her face I could tell that had been the correct answer.

There was no telling what our future had in store for us, but I'd been given a second chance, and I was going to live every day like it was a treasure.

Epilogue – 1 Year Later
Isabella

"Jax, please don't break that mirror. We drove all the way to Indiana to get it. I'd hate to see it damaged after we got it all the way here." My brother steadied his hold and helped me get it into our mimi and poppy's front door. I still couldn't believe that we were moving into the original farmhouse in North Carolina.

A lot had changed in the past year. Aside from planning the biggest wedding that my family was ever going to see, for my cousin Noah, and his fiancée Shalan, Rusty had started practicing medicine again. We were content in Kentucky until my parents offered us an opportunity that we couldn't refuse. My grandparents were getting older, and barely used the upstairs of their house, except for storage. With a little work, my dad and uncle Conner had remodeled the entire second floor, giving us plenty of space to move in. For the most part my grandparents used four rooms that were located downstairs. My mom and dad had started making all the meals when my mimi had fallen asleep one night and almost burned down the house.

When my parents asked us to move back it wasn't just so that I could babysit my grandparents. It was so they could all see our daughter Sarah more.

Sarah Mitchell Tillman was born on a cold winter's night, during a full moon. The airports were closed, and it was impossible to drive from North Carolina to Kentucky. After they'd missed her first six days of life, my mom and dad were determined to be around for everything else that happened in her first eighteen years of life.

Aside from being amazingly supportive to me,

my dad had given Rusty back something he's been working hard to get. He had the front of a part of our property commercially zoned. In six months he and my uncle had gotten all of the permits, and started the construction of a state of the art Veterinary hospital.

The Tillman/Mitchell Medical Hospital was opening it's doors in two weeks, and we hadn't even finished moving from Kentucky yet.

We'd spent the past week in Indiana, introducing Sarah to Rusty's parents. All it took was one glance and they were both in love. For the first time I felt like they were finally able to look past my appearance and see that I loved their son, and he felt the same about us.

We returned from the trip with his late daughter Sydney's bedroom suite. I was reluctant at first, but could see how much it meant to Rusty to give it to Sarah. We also brought pictures to keep in her room of her sister that was up in heaven keeping her safe.

It was funny how things that would have once bothered me no longer did. Rusty hadn't just proven to me that his love was real. He'd become close with my parents. He and my father hit it off early on, and even my brothers came around. Now, I had to fight with them to be alone with my boyfriend.

Speaking of my dad...

I turned to see him holding my daughter, then throwing her high into the air. My little nine month old was full of giggles, making me smile immediately. He wasn't just happy to have me back home. The fact that he could spoil her every day had made both of my parents the happiest that I'd seen them in years. Not to mention the fact that they always wanted to babysit.

Just as I was watching the two of them bonding, I noticed Noah coming down the dirt road pulling the last of our things on a long trailer. Shalan waved before climbing out of the passenger seat and making her way over to where my dad and Sarah were. I met her halfway and hugged her, before heading in the direction of my cousin. "It took you long enough."

"Shalan had to pee five times. I told her not to bring that jug of tea with us. I'm surprised she ain't jigglin' around." I hugged my cousin mid-sentence.

"Thanks for doin' this, Noah. I know you're probably happy I'm gone, aren't ya?"

He gave me a grumpy face. "Now, come on. You know I loved bein' able to see my favorite cousin every day. It was only a matter of time before you came home to your daddy and momma. I just hope my sister doesn't think she's movin' into that house now that it's vacant."

"Good luck with that. I think Christian needs some freedom, if you ask me."

Noah lightly shoved me. He wasn't good with hearing that his little sisters were growing up. Lord help him when they get serious with a guy.

"Mommy, somebody pooped her pants." My father pretended to maker her fly as he handed her to me.

"What's wrong, Dad? Can't you change her?"

"My years of changing shitty diapers are over."

Rusty walked up and held out his hands. "I'll take her. Go grab all the bags out of the back. Me and this little princess will meet you upstairs." Sarah leaned toward him, going right to her daddy. I couldn't get over how much she looked like me. We were thankful that it wasn't the other way around, not that it would matter.

Tate's life had taken him in a different direction. His parents sold their property and moved to Florida, where they were originally from. My mom said that after his baby was born that him and Jenn followed them. Our secret was going to stay buried. Tate had his family, and I had mine.

I turned my attention back to Rusty and Sarah. He kissed her on the forehead before lurching back to kiss me. "Don't forget that little picture under the seat of the truck. I want to hang that tonight with the rest of them."

I watched him walk in the house before smiling to my father. He made a sound and pretended to be cracking a whip. "You've got that man by the balls, honey. I'm so proud."

"You're terrible. I'm goin' inside with my family. You should get on over there with yours."

"My family is dwindling. Pretty soon your

brothers will move out too."

I shook my head and laughed when he pretended to cry. "Dad, this family is growin'. Don't worry about Jake and Jax. They'll live with you forever if you let them."

I saw fear in my dad's eyes before he turned to walk away. It was funny seeing him getting older, but rewarding to watch him loving all over his granddaughter. Why I ever thought that my family wouldn't support me was beyond me. They obviously would move Heaven for me if they could.

I found Rusty inside with Noah and Shalan. The guys were putting the twin-sized bed together, while Shalan changed Sarah's diaper. "How'd you get conned into this?"

"I offered. I'm going to need to practice if we're going to start trying right after the wedding." I was delighted to hear that my cousin, Noah, was ready to start a family. He was so in love, and I knew he'd be great at it. "Sorry you had to postpone the weddin'."

"Did you honestly want to wear the dress I picked out at nine months pregnant?" She asked.

"No way!"

"It's not a big deal. We've had more time to make it perfect. Pretty soon I'll be Mrs. Noah Mitchell."

I smiled, knowing that pretty soon I'd be saying the same thing. Rusty and I were waiting until everything settled down to tell my parents that we'd been talking about marriage. We didn't need to hurry, but I wanted to have the same name as my daughter when she was old enough to understand. It wasn't like I was worried about Rusty going anywhere. He had two reasons to stick around now, and a new business venture starting that he was thrilled about.

Later that night, after my cousin and Shalan had gone over to my parent's house to sleep, Rusty and I laid in bed holding each other. He stared up at the ceiling, while I watched him. I still couldn't get over how handsome he was to me, or the fact that a year ago we'd been so lost.

"Are you watching me? It's a little creepy."

"Creepy is how you were when we first met," I teased. My naked leg looped over his as I lifted my body. "I can look at you if I want to."

He reached his hand between my legs and started petting my pussy. "You know, I'm really good with cats."

It took me a second to get his joke. I slapped him lightly. I knew right away where he'd gotten the idea from. "Oh my gosh. Did my father put you up to that?"

He chuckled against my naked chest. "No. He asked if I was good with cats. I just figured I'd let you know that I was. Would you like me to demonstrate my talents?"

I bit down on my lip and nodded, smiling from ear to ear. I already knew how good he was with my cat, the one he was sliding down to give special attention to.

My eyes closed as soon as I felt his tongue touching me there. I dug my nails into the new sheets, feeling him licking me top to bottom. "If the animal hospital fails, you could always make how-to videos on this," I cackled.

He groaned, ignoring my comment and focusing on one thing.

Making me happy.

Isabella Mitchell

THE END OF BOOK 2
LOOK FOR BOOK 3, Christian, IN November
2014

Jennifer Foor

You can follow Jennifer Foor - www.jenniferfoor.com
Or Facebook – www.facebook.com/jenniferfoorauthor
Twitter - @jennyfoor
authorjenniferfoor@gmail.com

www.ingramcontent.com/pod-product-compliance
Lightning Source LLC
Chambersburg PA
CBHW070733180626
46818CB00007B/2824